More Praise for Edna Buchanan

"A supremely expert yarn-spinner."

—Los Angeles Times Book Review

"Buchanan knows her crime scene: the cops, journalists, perps and witnesses; the hairpin drive of high-speed deduction . . . nobody beats her for sass and realism."

—People

"Few writers can touch Buchanan."

—Chicago Tribune

"If you like crime, you'll love Buchanan."

—Tampa Tribune

"Get Buchanan on the trail of a story and the writing, as well as the action, simply sizzles with power, passion, and pizzazz."

—Cleveland Plain Dealer

"The Queen of Crime."

—Los Angeles Daily News

And Acclaim for *THE CORPSE HAD A FAMILIAR FACE*

"Joseph Wambaugh beware: Buchanan has written a page-turner. . . . *The Corpse Had a Familiar Face* straps you in the front seat for what is essentially a high-speed car chase through sin city. . . . Buchanan covers the kinky, the weird, and the weirder. . . . An education on the reality of the streets, and a reminder of what makes a great newspaper reporter."

—Washington Journalism Review

"Extraordinarily readable. [Written with] passion, humor, and caring."

—*Chicago Sun-Times*

"Honest. . . . Brave reporting."

—*The New York Times*

"Bizarre and memorable."

—*People*

"Lively. . . . Witty. . . . Choice anecdotes about the sordid things human beings, or at least Miamians, do to one another."

—*USA Today*

"She's tough. She's funny. . . . Buchanan has a genuine, unquenchable passion for raking muck, and Miami has risen to the challenge."

—*Playboy*

"[Buchanan is] a superb reporter and writer. . . . A fascinating book."

—*Pittsburgh Post-Gazette*

"Buchanan crackles, even cackles, with irony. Her life and writing are colorfully woven with twines of grit, street smarts, determination [and] compassion."

—*The Philadelphia Inquirer*

"An informative, highly entertaining book that tells a great deal not only about police and news reporting, but also about Miami. Her style is absolutely delightful."

—*Houston Chronicle*

ALSO BY EDNA BUCHANAN

EDNA BUCHANAN

Shadows

POCKET BOOKS

New York   London   Toronto   Sydney

POCKET BOOKS, a division of Simon & Schuster, Inc.
1230 Avenue of the Americas, New York, NY 10020

This book is a work of fiction. Names, characters, places, and incidents are products of the author's imagination or are used fictitiously. Any resemblance to actual events or locales or persons, living or dead, is entirely coincidental.

ISBN-13: 978-0-7434-7664-5
ISBN-10:   0-7434-7664-6

This Pocket Books paperback edition May 2006

10 9 8 7 6 5 4 3 2 1

POCKET and colophon are registered trademarks of Simon & Schuster, Inc.

Cover design by Ray Lundgren

Manufactured in the United States of America

For information regarding special discounts for bulk purchases, please contact Simon & Schuster Special Sales at 1-800-456-6798 or business@simonandschuster.com.

For Mitchell Ivers, an editor you *can* trust.

Fate is the gunman all gunmen fear.

—DON MARQUIS

PROLOGUE

MIAMI—AUGUST 25, 1961

What began with love and surrender now ends in death and guilt. My blood thunders through my veins and I quake with rage as I think of him. Only one of us will survive this night.

The full moon burns a bright hole in a hot, black summer sky. I hide amid wild orchids, poincianas, and tangled passion vines, overwhelmed by the smells of ripe earth, the windswept water, and my own fear. The superheated atmosphere smothers me in its damp, deathlike embrace, the sweet scent of night-blooming jasmine a poignant reminder of other nights like this. I am dizzy and close my eyes as the planet picks up speed. This night was meant for urgent kisses and breathless promises, not sudden death.

The gun weighs heavy and my hands tremble. But what's left to fear? I'm already damned to hell. People would agree with what I am about to do if they only knew the truth. But nobody will listen, and if they did, who would believe me?

My thigh muscles burn from crouching here beneath the gumbo limbo trees. Mosquitoes feast on my sweat-slick skin. I can endure the pain but not the waiting. Yearning to rest my feverish brow against the cool metal of the gun's long barrel, I fight the urge, knowing where it might lead. How easy it would be to surrender to the gun. It whispers a promise in the dark, an end to all this in one great fiery explosion of light. Who would care? Not the man for whom I wait. Finding me dead would convince him that he was right about me.

My shallow sigh is lost in the vast darkness. Night sounds close in around me: the croaks and mating calls of frogs and toads, a nightingale's lonely song. Foxes yelp nearby. I swear I can hear harsh breathing, the sounds of lovemaking in the dark. Is that a memory, my imagination, or the pulse-beat of this sultry night? I despair as the mosquitoes swarm louder and louder around my face.

How long can I wait? Where is he? Will he ever come? The other one was easier. Was it all for nothing? My frustration level reaches the danger zone.

No more. No more waiting. I'll leave it to heaven. God, if He exists, decides who dies tonight. I swear to my only witnesses, the fast-moving moon and the clouds racing like pirate ships across its face, that I will count down from one hundred—if I finish and he has not arrived, it ends here for me. Forever.

It's in God's hands now.

Whispering numbers like a prayer, I count down the final moments of a life. Mine or his.

Ninety-seven, ninety-six . . .

Destiny awaits. The world grows still, as though the planet has paused to watch. This place has always had an appetite, a fatal enthusiasm for sudden death.

Seventy-four . . .

I place the gun barrel in my mouth and run my tongue around the muzzle's rim in anticipation. The oily metal tastes like blood.

Will he will find his own fate waiting—or my corpse?

Sixty-five . . .

The life I was meant to lead fast-forwards through my mind, unfurling like a memory, alive with color, light, and passion, a future I will never have.

Sixty-one . . .

Outrage overtakes my despair as time ebbs away. He had no right. I take the gun from my mouth and spit out the taste of smoky metal as though on his grave.

I lick my parched lips and my stomach churns. When did I eat last? Not since early yesterday but I still gag. His belly is probably full, his mind at ease, sated by excellent food and better liquor.

Fifty-five . . .

None of his prestige and power, or friends in high places, can deflect a shotgun blast. My resolve is fueled by my need for revenge.

Fifty-one . . .

I will do it. I gaze at the big, rambling house and imagine its secrets. Music, dance, and laughter live inside those walls. The power to change laughter into tears is mine tonight.

Forty-six . . .

Whose tears? Only God knows.

I grasp the gun tightly.

Forty-three . . .

No fear.

Thirty-nine . . .

A car. I hear it! At last! As my time runs out. Thank you, Jesus. Please let it be him.

Thirty-four . . .

I creep forward, inching through the dense foliage, my cheeks wet.

Twenty-nine . . .

He laughed. He'll soon know I was someone to fear. Am I? Can I take him down? Will I escape? Assailed by doubts, limbs suddenly weak, I almost fall back into the bushes. This is so different from the other. The gun slips on sweaty skin as I brace it against my cheek and shoulder and raise it into firing position.

Headlights sweep around the curve as the big Buick rolls toward the house. He is alone. Music playing. Skeeter Davis singing "The End of the World" on his car radio.

I can do this.

Nineteen . . .

I stop counting and hold my breath. My temples throb but my hands are steady. I *can* do this.

I grit my teeth and focus as the car's headlights bounce crazily off the broad gray limbs of the banyan trees.

Damn. To my left, light spills out of the house into the darkness like secrets from a confessional. Someone has swooped aside the filmy curtains at a front window. Fear cramps my heart. Someone inside is watching. They must have heard the car, too. Please, God. Don't let them come out.

Something else! Nightbirds cut short their hymns as a shadowy creature crashes through the crotons on the far side of the house. I see and hear it simultaneously. Something big. Moving swiftly, close to the ground. I am not alone. My eyes strain against the dark. What . . . ? Is that a wild animal or my inflamed imagination?

My throat closes as the hunched shadow scrambles through the thick ficus hedge. Branches move and snap. It is real. What *is* it? No time left. Whatever it is, I can't let it stop me. Not now.

The headlights suddenly go dark. The driver cuts the engine. All is silent. My heartbeat accelerates.

He is alone. I watch him roll up his window, crunch open the door, and ease out. His athletic frame unfolds gracefully for a man of his size and power.

Larger than life, moments from death, he reaches inside for his jacket, then slams the car door.

I know what I must do. Ignore the monstrous shadow breathing hard in raspy gasps behind the ficus on the far side of the driveway. Pray that no one steps out of the house. "Don't come out," I warn in a long, low whisper. It's too crowded out here now. The evening star emerges like an omen, a beacon in a clearing sky, as I level the gun.

Keys jingle in his hand as he locks the big Buick.

Unsuspecting, almost jaunty, not a care in the world. He pauses for a deep breath. He smells the jasmine, too. Let it be the last scent he inhales except for the smell of his own blood.

He walks toward the house, his stride long-legged and comfortable, then stops, startled. He sees it, too. The thing that is hiding, crouched in the far hedge. Distracted, he stares. Nothing distracts me. I rise from the bushes, level the gun, close one eye, take aim, and ever so slowly, like a caress, I begin to squeeze the trigger.

"Hey! What are you do—" he shouts at the shadow as my gun roars in a fiery explosion of sound and light. The recoil slams my shoulder and hurls me off balance. My ears ring. I blink, through distorted vision, and see him stumble.

He reels, one arm extended like a Saturday-night drunk trying to steady himself. Bewildered, he sees me for the first time, then lurches unsteadily toward the house, calling, "Diana! Diana!"

Beyond him, a high, inhuman howl pierces the dark. A wild thrashing and scrambling ices my spine. I try to stay focused.

Still on his feet, my target staggers toward the lights of the house. No! Propelled by panic and rage, I rack another shell into the chamber and rush him. No time to take aim. I close the distance between us, thrust the barrel toward him, and squeeze the trigger again. The music from inside the house stops. Or am I deaf from the blast?

No. The front door bursts open, screams shred the

soft blanket of night. Shouts. Footsteps, confusion. More cries in the dark. I flee for my life, adrenaline unleashing the speed of wings. Something savage runs as well. The creature from the shadows rounds the back of the house. It's coming after me! My heart races. My shoulder aches. I barely breathe, pounding blindly through thick brush that rips and tears at my clothes. Too late, too afraid to look back, its hot breath at my heels. Oh, God, what have I unleashed?

CHAPTER 1

MIAMI—TODAY

People applauded when Craig Burch walked into the office. His face reddened. He wanted no attention, no fuss. He wanted his first day back to be like any other day on the job. But that didn't happen.

Two of his detectives sprang to their feet. Pete Nazario, usually quiet and introspective, moved in for a bear hug, then hesitated.

"It's okay," Burch said, and hugged back.

He exchanged a high five with Stone, who grinned like he'd won the lottery. Other homicide detectives pumped his hand.

"Looking good!"

"Attaboy!"

A sea of smiles and good humor, except for Emma, Lieutenant K. C. Riley's tiny, middle-aged secretary, who blubbered uncontrollably into a flowered handkerchief. She removed her spectacles, wiped her eyes, and blew her nose loudly. "Thank God you're back." She hiccuped.

Where is Riley? Burch wondered. Joe Corso, his temporary replacement, was missing in action as well. He scanned the sprawling homicide office and spotted their heads together in the lieutenant's glass-enclosed office, the door closed. What's that all about? he wondered. Corso, who had seniority, had been appointed acting sergeant in Burch's absence.

The two emerged to join the welcome.

"So ya finally got off your lazy ass and came back to work!" Corso trailed behind the lieutenant's welcoming smile.

"Yeah, had to make sure somebody was doing some detecting around here."

Burch had made certain, despite his impatience, that before he returned he looked suntanned, robust, and fit, as though back from a vacation, not life-threatening gunshot wounds. He wore a new jacket, shirt, and shoes, and had had his hair cut a week earlier.

No dead-man-walking look for him. Cops rush to donate blood, money, and vacation time to a fellow officer in need. You can take that to the bank. But reappear limping and scarred, with a hospital pallor, and the camaraderie pales as well. Survivors can read it in their eyes. Nobody on the job needs a daily reminder that there but for the grace of God . . .

Hailed from all directions, Burch made the obligatory rounds, to briefly shoot the breeze.

"You won't believe the one I caught today, Craig," homicide detective Ron Diaz said. "Guy shot a dozen times—by his own kids."

"Not those little rugrats out there?" Burch had seen them in the hall on the way in. A curly-haired thumb-sucker with wide, frightened eyes. She and a sturdy boy about seven clung to a plump middle-aged woman with a half-closed, swollen, and purpling left eye. They huddled on a hard wooden bench.

"That's them. The two little ankle biters."

"Holy crap! He at the morgue yet?"

"Hell, no. He's at Jackson, in the ER. Doing okay."

"Where'd he get hit?"

"Both legs, groin, chest, face, arms. You name it, they shot it. Guy looked like Swiss cheese."

"What'd they use? Old ammo with no punch?"

"Nah! Get this. He picks a fight with 'is old lady, lands a right cross to 'er eye. They're in a shoving match when she starts screaming, 'Shoot 'im! Shoot 'im! Shoot 'im!' to the kids.

"Unlike mine, *her* kids listen. They open up on Dad with the trusty Red Ryder BB guns he got 'em for Christmas. Keep shooting even after he falls down the front steps and cuts his head trying to get away. Damn good shots; guy should be proud.

"Moral a this one is: Be careful what you give 'em for Christmas. Don't buy 'em nothing they can use against you.

"Pisses me off, 'cause now I gotta figure out who to charge and with what. An ASA said I could charge the kids with agg battery, a felony. They're five and eight. I could bust Dad for spousal abuse instead. Or lock Mom up for neglect, child abuse, and contributing to their deliquency. I'm leaning toward the last one at the moment."

"A little harsh with that shiner she's sporting."

"Yeah. Ain't it a beaut." Diaz shrugged. "But the ASA says it's a crime to encourage kids to break the law. Or I could just bust both parents for spousal abuse on each other and let a judge sort it out. . . ."

Burch sighed. "Some people shouldn't have kids."

"Tell me about it."

An attractive long-haired woman sat at a detective's desk, waiting to give a statement, her expression forlorn.

"What's her story?" Burch asked.

With her silky, low-cut blouse, dangly earrings, billowy skirt, and high heels, she looked dressed to go dancing, except for her tear-streaked makeup—and handcuffs.

"Yeah, all dressed up with no place to go. Domestic. Long history. Husband lies to 'er, cheats on 'er, beats on 'er. Separated for a while, but he claims he changed, turned over a whole new leaf. Talks 'er into letting him move back in. Promises to take 'er out on the town to celebrate last night. At seven, she's ready and waiting. She's still waitin', sittin' out front, when he finally gets home this morning, drunk as a skunk, lipstick on 'is shirt. Poor bastard hops outta 'is car with a big grin. 'Qué pasa, baby.'"

"'Qué pasa, my ass!' she says, and shoots him between the eyes. DRT, dead right there."

"My wife would call that justifiable," Burch said.

Another weepy suspect inside a small interview room wore open-toed stiletto heels, a miniskirt, and a bad case of five o'clock shadow.

"You don't wanna know about that one," Diaz said.

"Rivers's case. Fatal shooting up on the Boulevard. The victim was dumped out of a pickup on Seventy-ninth Street. He was wearing a red dress. Some kind of transsexual turf war up there in hooker heaven.

"So how ya doing, Burch?" The detective eyed the taller sergeant speculatively. "Heard it was touch and go for a while."

"They exaggerated. I'm good."

We all have a case number waiting for us, Burch thought. His hadn't come up yet. Life was good. He sighed as he returned to the Cold Case Squad's corner. Home at last.

Two hundred and thirty rumpled pounds occupied his space. Corso was slumped in Burch's chair, one big foot up on his desk.

"You mind?" Burch gripped the chair back.

"Sure. Sure." Corso took his time vacating the seat. "Force a habit. Made sense ta use your desk when you were laid up. More convenient."

Sure, Burch thought. He and Corso, a transplanted New Yorker, had worked patrol at the same time years ago. Time had mellowed Corso some, but edgy and unpredictable, he could still be a loose cannon. If Burch had had his way, Corso wouldn't be on his team, but the man knew how to win favors from friends in high places. After a stint as a city commissioner's driver/bodyguard, he returned recommended for a coveted homicide slot. After a brief, but lucky, run of cases, he'd applied for the Cold Case Squad. The regular hours appealed to him, too.

"Time for the Monday-morning case meeting," Burch announced.

Stone and Nazario exchanged glances.

"Oh, yeah," Corso said nonchalantly. "I changed that to Wednesdays."

"So today," Burch said mildly, "it's changed back."

Hell, he was only gone a few weeks. What was Corso's big rush to change things?

"Stone, what's the status on your case?"

The husky black detective, the youngest on the squad at twenty-six, shook his head. "*Nada.* We decided to wait for you to come back." Stone avoided Corso's eyes.

"Okay," Burch said, sensing an unpleasant undercurrent in the air between them. "We take a hard run at it. Now. Give it top priority."

"So, what was it like?" Corso said. "When that SOB shot you, when you hit the deck and thought you'd bought the farm, what were you thinking?"

"What we all think," Burch said quietly. "That the worst thing is that you might not die. You don't want your family to have to spoon-feed you the rest of your life. I was lucky." He glanced at Nazario. "I had good backup."

"Damn straight," Stone said.

"It makes you appreciate what matters most."

"Exactly right." Corso nodded wisely. "Me, too. Been there, ya know." He stared at the other detectives. "Didn't know I got shot, did ya? On the job, like Craig." He exposed his left forearm. "See that scar? Right there. That's where the bullet hit me."

The detectives squinted at his hairy arm and saw nothing.

"Right there." Annoyed, he pointed, and looked to Burch for confirmation.

"Yeah, right." Burch's eyes rolled. "Won't ever forget that. Started over the price of a lime. Haitian guy in a Cuban market claims he's overcharged seven cents.

"The owner tells 'im get the hell out, we don't need your business. The Haitian guy refuses to go without his groceries. The argument escalates into a scuffle and the store security guard shoots the customer. Before air rescue can even evacuate the victim, angry Haitians are milling around outside. There was already bad blood between them and the owner.

"We're shorthanded. It's hot, Saturday afternoon, and all of a sudden, we've got a riot situation on our hands.

"We tell the owner to close up for the day. He gives us an argument. Rocks and bottles start to fly. We have just three, four cops out there. No riot gear. It's locked up back at the station. Nobody knows who has the key. This whole situation came outta nowhere. People start smashing the store windows, knocking down displays, snatching merchandise.

"Corso here draws his gun."

"Right, we were overrun." Corso shrugged.

"Somebody punches his arm," Burch said, "his gun flies outta his hand, up into the air, crashes to the curb, discharges—and shoots him in the goddamn forearm. I'm thinking, Oh, shit. He manages to retrieve his gun, thank God."

"Shoulda seen my arm," Corso said proudly. "Blood like a waterfall, flying everywhere."

Burch nodded. "It worked, believe it or not. Broke up the whole damn riot. Everybody ran. Know why? They figured this crazy cop means business. He's so mad, he already shot himself, he'll shoot us next. Scared the hell outta all the would-be looters.

"I don't recommend it if you guys ever find your-selves in the same situation," Burch said. "But it worked."

"Yeah," Corso said. "They ran like hell."

"Came out smelling like a rose," Burch said. "Don't ask me how, but he always does. Even got his name on the plaque in the lobby, 'Heroes Wounded in the Line of Duty.'"

Nazario and Stone struggled to keep straight faces.

"So what's the joke?" their lieutenant interrupted.

"Just war stories." Burch shrugged.

"In my office, Burch," Riley said.

She still looked too thin, he thought. The gun on her hip, a standard Glock, looked bigger and badder because she was so slim. She settled in her creaky leather chair, her blond shoulder-length hair backlit by Miami's radiant morning light. It cascaded through the window behind her, glinting off the hand-grenade-shaped paper-weight on her desk.

He took a seat, eyes roving across the books—*Why They Kill, Sexual Homicide: Patterns and Motives, Inside the Criminal Mind, The Handbook of Forensic Sexology, When Bad Things Happen to Good People*—lining the shelves. He felt like a stranger seeing them for the first time yet comforted by the familiar titles. The framed photo of her and the late Major Kendall McDonald, carefree and laughing aboard a fishing boat, had been relocated to a less conspicuous spot, he noted, moved down a shelf or two. Maybe that was a good sign. Maybe she was healing, recovering at last from the loss.

"Glad you're back, Sarge. Sure you're ready?"

She always got right to the point; he liked that about her.

"Absolutamundo. In better shape than I was in the academy. Pumping iron, working out, swimming. Couldn't be better."

"You talk to the shrink?"

"Had a session, only because it's SOP. Said I don't need to come back unless I have a problem, which I won't." He shrugged. "Said I had a great support system."

Being back home with my family is the best medicine, he thought.

"Connie and the kids have been great. Couldn't ask for more. Did a lotta work around the house. Fixed up the patio. Drove the family upstate, did some canoeing on the Peace River. Spent a lotta time together."

"Connie okay about you coming back to work?"

He shifted in his chair. "A few boo-hoos from her and the girls this morning. Only natural. You know how girls are. Connie knew me before I put on a badge, she knew what she was getting into. She's taking some kind of course now, some kinda interior design, I think. It'll keep her busy. Craig Jr. kept a stiff upper lip. He's thirteen now. A cool kid."

"Takes after his old man," Riley said. "Okay, if you're sure you're up for it."

"Absolutely. The docs give me a clean bill of health."

Her look remained questioning.

"What?" he asked, nettled. "Is Corso so attached to my desk that he wants it permanently?"

"Sure, he's willing." She looked amused. "But far as I know, he has yet to pass the sergeant's test."

"Thank God for small favors."

He lumbered back out into the squad room, where a stranger was distracting his detectives.

Though petite, she had a larger-than-life presence. Attitude, he thought. She wore shades and crinkly white cotton under a blue linen suit, had tanned bare legs in high-heeled sandals. She knew how to dress for a Miami summer. Masses of curly light-brown hair had been captured by tortoiseshell combs and piled up on the back of her head. Late twenties, early thirties.

The plastic card issued at the front desk and clipped to her blouse identified her as a visitor.

"I want to report a crime." Her voice was low-pitched and earthy. Her name, she said, was Kiki Courtelis.

"This is Homicide," Burch said. "I think you're on the wrong floor."

"No." The word was brisk, her tone assertive. "You're the Cold Case Squad. I read about you in the Sunday *News* magazine months ago. I have the article right here. Someplace." She fumbled in her bulging soft-sided briefcase, then withdrew a manila folder. She replaced the shades with little gold-rimmed granny glasses.

"See?" She displayed the clipping. "It even has your pictures."

"That's us," Nazario said agreeably.

Was this broad about to cop to an old homicide? Burch wondered. He brightened. Maybe she bludgeoned a bad boyfriend with a baseball bat or blew away a cheating spouse. Walk-in confessions are rare but occur often enough to keep hope alive. Like lightning, they do happen from time to time. He smiled expectantly.

She returned his smile with a grateful expression that lit up her brown eyes.

Yes! She found Jesus, he thought, and wants to confess. Feels the need to come clean, unburden herself of secrets, and face the music. His eyes roved the room discreetly. No lawyer in sight. She hadn't brought one with her. A good sign.

Nazario invited her to sit down. She crossed her ankles, daintily tucked them beneath the chair, and stood her briefcase on the floor beside her.

She might be copping to a still-unreported homicide, Burch thought. A missing person whose body remains undiscovered. Catching Stone's eye, he recognized the same hopeful gaze. Both were thinking dirty.

Her attitude was cool, her brown eyes honest. She didn't look the type. But do they ever? He thought of Betty Newsome, the wholesome-looking Miami housewife who, with the help of her apple-cheeked fourteen-year-old daughter, dismembered her husband, the girl's father, in their garage. With faces that could be on Ivory Snow boxes, they might have been mother and daughter of the year, except for the black plastic garbage bags they left in Dumpsters all over Miami. Piecing that body back together at the morgue had been a chore. He wondered wistfully where mother and daughter were now. Damn shame they'd been freed on a technicality. Thank God it wasn't his case.

"What kind of crime?" he inquired, voice friendly.

"Where did it happen?" Nazario asked.

"The crime scene is in your jurisdiction, if that's what you're asking. I can show you," she offered.

Will we need a backhoe? Burch wondered, thinking ahead. He knew where to rent one.

Even Corso, checking out the woman's legs from his desk across the aisle, had perked up.

"Actually," she said somberly, "it hasn't happened yet. But it will if you don't stop them."

Burch averted his eyes and stared past her. So often, he thought with a sigh, the deranged don't look disturbed. Off their medication, they are not readily apparent until they begin to talk to garbage cans and bark like dogs.

"You need to step in. Now," she said urgently, pausing to scrutinize each face in turn. "We have no time left."

Corso smirked.

"You," she said, her voice growing louder, "are our last hope."

She could have walked in here yesterday, two weeks or a month ago, Burch thought. Why now? Why me? Does anybody screen visitors at the front desk anymore or do they just wave them through the metal detectors and send them here?

"What sort of crime we talking about?" Stone gnawed his lower lip.

"Murder," she said succinctly. "Miami's most famous

unsolved murder. Bulldozers are poised to level the scene of the crime. Isn't tampering with a murder scene and destroying evidence a criminal matter? Doesn't it compound the felony?"

"What case?" Burch said, dubious.

"The shotgun murder of Pierce Nolan. The most notorious unsolved homicide in the entire state. As well known as the Chillingsworth case in Palm Beach and the Von Maxcy murder in Central Florida. They were solved, ours wasn't. Nolan was a former mayor, the son of a prominent and colorful pioneer family. If you let them bulldoze the Shadows, his murder will never be solved. Isn't it vital to preserve a crime scene?"

"Why don't I know about it?" Stone asked, puzzled.

"You weren't born yet," Burch said. "None of us were. I've heard stories. It happened way back. He was a popular one-term mayor in the fifties, then bowed out of politics to spend more time with his family."

"Shot down outside his own front door, at the Shadows," Kiki Courtelis said, "the historic house built by his father, the notorious rumrunner Captain Cliff Nolan, back in the twenties, during Prohibition. The night of August twenty-fifth, 1961, a killer ambushed Pierce Nolan as he arrived home from a Miami civic association meeting."

Kiki Courtelis had done her homework.

"How do you know so much about it?" Stone asked, arms crossed.

"I'm a Miami native. My family's been here forever. I heard a lot about the case growing up. My thesis was on Miami history and I'm on the board of the Historic

Preservation Society. The Shadows, on three waterfront acres, was somehow overlooked and never placed on the registry of historic houses, which would have protected it. It stayed in the Nolan family, but they haven't occupied it since shortly after the murder. Recently, before anyone realized what was happening, out-of-state family members sold the property to a high-rise developer. The new owner had the house declared unsafe, and despite our protests, the city has issued him a permit for demolition. We've done all we can to save it, but they intend to bulldoze it later this week." Her look was pleading. "You can stop them."

"I sympathize," Burch said. "I'm no fan of what developers have done to this town, either. But we investigate cold cases, not ancient history."

"But," she protested, "in this article written by that reporter . . ." She reopened her carefully labeled file folder. "Right here." She indicated a paragraph highlighted in yellow and read aloud: " 'There is no statute of limitations on first-degree murder,' said Sergeant Craig Burch." She peered meaningfully over her glasses at him. " 'No homicide case is too old, too cold to pursue.' Aren't those your words, Sergeant?"

"Yes, ma'am. But—"

"What makes you think the case could be solved now?" Nazario asked.

"As the story says, 'New high-tech forensics undreamed of when the crime occurred can now be applied to old, cold cases.' "

"Don't believe everything ya read in the newspaper," Corso said.

She paused for a beat or two, then asked politely, "May I speak to your lieutenant?"

"She ain't gonna tell ya anything different," Corso warned.

"You're clever and creative," Stone said, "but you can't use us to fight your battle. We have other cases that might really be solved."

"A brief stay of execution is all we ask. We're seeking legal support from the National Heritage Trust, an injunction to block the developer, but that takes time and we have none. Once the house is gone, it's gone forever."

"Sorry, we've got a meeting." Burch checked his watch. "Wish we could have helped. Good luck."

"I'd like to speak to Lieutenant Riley," she said, making no move to leave.

"Somebody mention my name?"

Burch sighed. Timing, again.

Kiki Courtelis's eyes lit up as she scrutinized the lieutenant's face.

"You're one of the Allapattah Rileys. I can see that. I thought you were."

K. C. Riley did a double take and cut her eyes at Burch. "Well, yeah, way back. My—"

"Grandmother," Courtelis finished. "Of course. Our families were close."

"Excuse me?"

"Wasn't her name Margarite?"

K. C. Riley did another double take.

"Here." Courtelis fumbled in the briefcase again.

What the hell is she about to pull outta there now? Burch wondered.

Courtelis came up with an old sepia-toned photo, an eight-by-ten, a dozen women wearing big hats, seated around a wooden table in the shade of a huge banyan tree.

"The Lemon City Garden Club, 1934." She handed the photograph to Riley, who studied it for a moment, frowning.

"That's Memaw!" Riley's jaw dropped. "I've never seen this picture before. Where did you get it?"

"See the woman on her right?" Courtelis asked. "That's Lilly Pinder, my grandmother. They were best friends."

Oh shit, Burch thought.

"I'm Kiki Courtelis. I would have recognized you anywhere. You have the Riley jaw and your grand-mother's eyes."

Riley gazed fondly at the photo. "She was a tough lady. Came from a little town in Georgia. Was a teacher at eighteen when the Miami school superintendent wrote to offer her twice her Georgia salary. She boarded the train to Miami the day after the 1926 hurricane.

"They had to stop dozens of times along the way to clear trees, debris, and dead cows off the tracks. When she stepped off the train, it was into water above her knees. She waded to a Miami boardinghouse carrying her little bag. The owner said, 'Grab a broom and start sweeping.' She helped sweep out the storm water and started to teach the next day.

"Her first classroom was outdoors under a stand of palm trees. She propped a blackboard up against a tree and taught the alphabet and numbers to three dozen children.

"She met my grandfather at a dance. The night he proposed, they drove over to the Congregational Church in Miami Beach."

Kiki Courtelis nodded. "The city's first place of worship, built in 1920. Carl Fisher donated the land. That old mission-style church is still on Lincoln Road, beautifully restored."

Riley nodded. "That's the one. She told me about how they found the Reverend Elijah King at work in his study. He married them in the little chapel that night. They were married for fifty-two years.

"Memaw become an elementary-school principal and then a school board member. Stayed sharp as a tack till the day she died. Did you ever meet her?"

"Sure, she taught my Sunday school class when I was little. I remember how sad she was when your uncle was killed in Vietnam."

"Do you have time for a cup of coffee, Ms. Courtelis?"

"Sure, Katherine. Please call me Kiki."

The two women went off to the coffee room chatting animatedly.

"Who'da thought Riley even *had* a grandmother?" Corso said.

This can't be good, Burch thought.

The women returned a short time later, laughing and talking.

"I've explained to Ms. Courtelis," Riley told them, "that we can't officially intervene in a legal demolition, but since the scene is about to be lost, you can go out there, shoot photos and video, do some diagrams, and see if you find anything that might have been missed. There's a good possibility since, according to Kiki, the place hasn't been occupied since the shooting. It's smart to augment the file, in the event anything ever comes up. Take a metal detector. See what you find."

Riley arranged for Kiki to join the investigators at the Shadows the next day and then Kiki receded like a wave gliding back out to sea.

"She just sold you a used car," Burch told Riley.

"Do it anyway." Riley shrugged. "Why not? It's an open case."

"The shooter is doing the big dirt sleep or drooling in his soup at some nursing home by now."

"But how good would it look if we closed it? It might even persuade the chief to keep this unit in next year's budget."

• • •

"It'll take less than a day," Burch reassured his detectives. "No muss, no fuss."

"I have a bad feeling about it." Nazario shook his head.

"Did your built-in shit detector kick in?" Stone asked. "Did little Kiki lie to us?"

Nazario's talent, inadmissible in court but priceless to a detective, was that he could unfailingly sense a lie when he heard one.

"She didn't lie. It's more what she didn't say."

CHAPTER 2

The man had thrown his right arm across the woman at the last moment, as though trying to protect her. Her left palm was extended as though in supplication, a plea for mercy not granted. Her open eyes reflected her terror. His were orbless blood-filled craters.

The crime scene photographs were the most devastating he had ever seen. Sam Stone stared at them for a long time.

He barely recognized his mother. That was the way he'd felt the last time he'd seen his parents. They had looked like strangers then, too, lying side by side in matching caskets. His mother had always been warm, animated, and laughing. The hair of the cold-looking stranger occupying her casket was arranged in a stiff, elaborate style she had never worn in real life, and the new dress she wore was one he had never seen. The Bible in her hands was small and white, not the big, well-worn family Bible his mother always read at home. He reacted with relief. This was all a mistake. These people were strangers. He had tugged at his grandmother's arm.

"That's not them, Gran. Where's Momma? Where's my daddy?"

Women wept. His great-aunt Marva lifted him up, held him over the casket, and insisted he kiss his mother good-bye. Eight years old and obedient, he complied, surprised at how soft the cheek of this mannequin-like stranger felt against his lips. He never forgot it.

Stone felt numb, as he had then.

He had never seen the case file before. Thoughts of it had consumed him for years. Afire to examine it, he had forced himself to stay patient, to wait for the right time. He might have only one chance. He had to learn all he could first, then prove himself on the street. Then he applied again and again for assignment to the Cold Case Squad. When he finally succeeded out of sheer persistence, talent, and creativity, he had to learn all he could again, earn the respect of his teammates, then persuade them to take on the case.

He confided in no one. His fellow detectives were taken aback when a reporter wrote a story and, against his wishes, prematurely revealed the secret tragedy in his past. Sergeant Burch immediately suggested taking on the old case. Then Burch was shot and Stone himself put the investigation on hold until his return. He wanted everything done right, by only the best. Now, at last, it was time.

Eyes wet, his lips dry, Stone studied each eight-by-ten photo. Both victims wore their plain gold wedding bands. He recognized the familiar white apron, the white shirt and red-checkered scarf his father always wore on the job. The scarf was to stop the sweat as he worked the fire, barbecuing juicy ribs, pork chops, chicken, and shrimp. He paused at one photo, staring at the puffy white baker's hat, blood-spattered and askew.

His mother had always teased his father about it, calling it his "cupcake hat." But Sam Stone Sr. insisted they maintain a consistent professional image at their tiny takeout restaurant.

He barbecued, she waited on customers and prepared the salads. They worked hard. Side by side, thirteen hours a day, seven days a week.

He had complained once and his mother had explained to him that all their hard work was to insure the future. It would not be forever, she promised. She was right.

He swallowed hard.

"Hey," he whispered to the people in the pictures. "It's me. Sam. Your son. Momma, I grew up. I have so much to tell you. I'm a policeman now, a detective. Wish you coulda been here. I did good in school, Momma, like you always wanted. Did real good in the academy. The police academy.

"Solved a big FBI case a few months ago. Was even on TV. In the newspapers. Wish you coulda seen it. I did good. Gran is fine. I'm taking care of her now, like she took care of me. She misses you, too.

"You're gonna like my friends, the detectives I work with. They're good. We'll find out who did this. I promise. Talk to me, Daddy. Momma? What happened? Talk to me, please. Who did this to you?"

He wanted to put his head down on his desk and cry like a baby. Like the day in third grade when the other kids teased him, called him an orphan, and he suddenly realized it was true; he would never see them again. His mother and father were never coming home.

He blinked back tears, squared his jaw, took out his small black notebook, and began to match the crime scene diagrams to the pictures. He sighed at the quality of the photos. Primitive by today's standards, relics from a time when police technicians only used .35 millimeter cameras. Today's digital cameras often provide sharper, clearer pictures with better detail. Photographers can instantly review their shots and shoot them again if dissatisfied.

Back then no one knew how good the photos were until they were processed. Anything missed was lost forever.

He noted that a step stool had been overturned and a wooden knife block knocked off a work table. No knives appeared to be missing. The bullet-scarred menu was still legible on a wall behind the counter.

A heavy cast-iron pot steamed on the stove. Potatoes, boiling for the next day's salad. In a flood of sensory images, he remembered the smell of meat smoke and the rib racks sizzling in their own juice as they turned golden brown.

A grainy shot of the street outside revealed a wet, rain-slick sidewalk, eddying swirls of water, and the small Overtown storefront with the sign STONE'S BARBECUE. He hadn't seen that since the murders. The place had never reopened.

This look was preliminary, only the beginning. He didn't want to see the photos for the first time in front of other people, even his fellow detectives.

He paged through the reports, searching for names,

appalled at times at the skimpiness of the follow-up. Where were the transcripts of witnesses' statements? The evidence inventories? There had to be more than this.

He did find the one name he wanted most—a man he had thought about for years. He printed it in his notebook, underlined it twice, then locked the case file in his desk.

Sam Stone, named for his father, walked out of Miami Police Headquarters into the late-summer dusk a different person, he thought, than the one who had walked in that morning.

The afternoon heat still rose off the pavement. Though somber, he was full of hope about the task ahead. He loved this season and its spectacular sky still bright with deepening hues of pink, blue, and gold until nearly nine P.M. By contrast, winter's early darkness had always reminded him of death.

He drove to the tiny shotgun cottage where he grew up in Overtown. He found her in the kitchen, as usual. At the sink, a dish towel in her hand.

"Here's my girl!"

"I thought I heard your car, Sonny." Her head barely reached his shoulder, her gray hair brushed his chin, and she felt more frail than ever inside his hug. She weighed less than a hundred pounds.

"Hungry, Sonny? I'll fix you a plate."

"I was hoping to take my best girl out to dinner. We can drive down to Shorty's. Or someplace nice over on the Beach."

"I had a bite at four o'clock. And don't you be trying

to spend your money on me. You have better things to do with it."

"Nope. I don't, Gran. We need to celebrate." He felt exuberant. "I've got good news."

Her eyes lit up, then darted expectantly to the door. "Where is she? Why didn't you bring her in here?"

"Why is matchmaking always on your mind? This is something more important."

"Must be. Haven't seen you so worked up since that big football game you won in high school."

"The team won, Gran, not me. Shoulda called you earlier, but I wasn't sure. I'll take you to dinner Friday. We'll go early."

"That's when you should be taking your girl out, not me. Now, what is it? What's the big news?"

"Sit down," he said, drawing her into the small living room, "and I'll tell you."

She insisted on fixing them each a glass of iced tea first. His sweet, the way he liked it.

Impatient, he sat in the old armchair where she used to read to him. His parents smiled from a silver-framed photograph on a shelf. That was how he had always remembered them. Would it ever be the same after what he'd seen today? His own picture stood near theirs. Age five, posed in front of a vintage television set, wearing a little navy blue suit, saddle shoes, and an uncertain expression. In another, he stood tall in uniform, Gran pinning on his badge at the academy graduation.

He focused on his parents' faces. They'd hoped so hard, looked forward to so much. At last he was in a position to make it right—as right as anyone could ever make it.

She insisted he taste his tea to be sure it was sweet enough, then sat herself down on the little wicker settee facing him. She sipped from her glass and smiled.

"Okay, Sonny. Tell me now."

"It's really good, Gran. You're gonna be so happy."

She leaned forward, face alight with anticipation. "Stop your teasing and just spit it out."

"We're gonna do it, Gran." His voice was tight with excitement. "We, me, the Cold Case Squad, we're gonna investigate Momma and Daddy's murder."

Her lips parted but she didn't speak.

He gestured toward his parents' photo. "It's gonna be hard, but we're gonna find the SOBs who did it and send them to jail, or to death row. That's where they belong."

"You watch your mouth, boy." She tried to stand but dropped her glass, splashing the contents onto her skirt. The tumbler fell to the floor, scattering ice cubes as it rolled across the carpet.

"Now look at what you went and made me do!" She seemed near tears.

"Sorry. Sit still, Gran. Sit still. I'll get it."

"You'll cut yourself!"

"No, I won't."

He scooped cubes back into the broken glass, took it to the kitchen, and returned with a fistful of paper towels. He placed several on her lap, then blotted the carpet and wiped the floor with the others. Unlike her to fuss about a broken glass, but only natural that she'd be startled.

He disposed of the wet towels and returned. She scrubbed vigorously at her wet skirt. He couldn't see her face.

"Realize what this means, Gran?" He paced the small room, fueled by pent-up energy.

"Officially, on paper, I can't be lead investigator. But it will be me, I'll be the catalyst."

She rose abruptly, wavered for a moment, unsteady on her feet, then left the room.

"Gran?" Frowning, he followed her into the kitchen. "We need to talk about everything you remember from that night. Your take on it all. Everything you heard and thought. All the details. Stuff we never really talked about."

She picked up a sponge and began to wipe the stainless-steel sink he had installed for her last spring.

"You and me. We'll work on it together."

"No point digging up old ghosts," she muttered, scrubbing harder. The sink gleamed, already clean.

"I do that every day, Gran." He grinned. "It's my job. We've always wanted justice—"

"Not me," she snapped.

He stared in disbelief. "Gran, we're talking about your son, and my mom. Your children. You always said Momma was like a daughter to you."

Focused on some invisible blemish on the sink, she refused to meet his eyes.

He crouched in front of her, took her hand. "What is it? What's wrong? I need you to help me."

Her eyes flooded and he saw something in them, something he had never seen before.

"No." Her voice was firm. "The people who did it are still out there. Still evil. The world changes, but they never do, Sonny."

"That's why we have to find them. You're my link to that night, Gran. I was too little to absorb much. 'Member how we used to read the Sherlock Holmes mysteries together? You always picked up on the clues first, knew the answers right away. We can go over everything together."

She said nothing.

"Want me to stay in my old room tonight?"

She shook her head, mouth tight.

"I know it's sudden, but think about it. I need you."

"I need you, too, Sonny." Her voice sounded thin, about to break.

He stepped out into the darkening night. Shifting storm clouds swirled and spit lightning across the horizon. The deluge began, pelting him as he sprinted to his car. Rain depressed him. It always had. Violent, wind-driven sheets of torrential rain slammed into the windshield. He had never felt so alone. So bleak.

His grandmother had raised him. They never kept secrets from each other. He had always believed that. But he was wrong. She knows something, he thought, bewildered. Something she won't tell me; something she never told anyone.

CHAPTER 3

Burch left the Blazer in the driveway.

The front door stood open. Every window in the house was open as well. Unusual for summer. The ceiling-fan blades were motionless, the silence deafening. No radio, music, or TV. The cat ran to greet him, rubbing his face on Burch's shoe. Sprawled on his bed in a corner, the big dog opened one eye but otherwise ignored him. White candles flickered in the foyer. Damn. Power outages had been all too frequent since the last hurricane.

"Connie?"

His wife emerged from the kitchen.

"Hi, babe." He loosened his tie. "How long has it been out this time?"

She flashed the brilliant smile that knocked him out the first time he ever saw her, in high school, then clapped her hands.

"Okay, kid. Can the applause. So I got quite a reception this morning. Who told you?"

She clapped again, then spun around, tossing her shiny dark hair, hands high above her head.

It reminded him of her cheerleader days.

"Con? Whatcha doing?"

"Clearing our space," she sang out. "Drawing in positive energy."

He took off his gun, removed the clip, and placed the unloaded weapon in the lockbox on the closet's top shelf, as usual. "The hell you doing?" He squinted at her.

"Visualizing a pure white light," she said. "Driving out the negative and filling the house with loving energy."

•　•　•

"Fung who?" Nazario wrinkled his brow the next morning at the office.

"Feng Shui. It's Asian, all about the flow of energy, or something," Burch said uncertainly. "The power wasn't out. Connie was clearing our space. That's what they call it. You turn everything off, open all the doors and windows so the bad energy can escape. Clapping chases it out." He shrugged.

"Bottom line is to eliminate negative energy from your environment. Hey, makes her happy, I'm all for it. Helluva lot better than other things she might be up to, as we all know."

"She wants to eliminate negative energy," Corso said, "she should just kick your ass ta the curb."

"Yeah, and we want to eliminate it up here, we could just kick your ass back down to Patrol." Burch dropped a dusty box onto Corso's desk. "Here, dive into this."

It was one of half a dozen boxes delivered from the warehouse, the Pierce Nolan file. "Everybody grab one and pitch in," Burch said. "We're looking for crime scene diagrams, photos, news stories, and original reports."

"Look who's here! Hey, dawg," Corso greeted Stone, who ignored him.

"Where you been?" Burch said.

"Bad night. Sorry," Stone said. "Couldn't sleep. Didn't drop off until five A.M., then I overslept."

"Called your crib, no answer," Corso said.

"What's all this?" Stone asked.

"This," Corso said, digging into a musty box, "is the Nolan file, believe it or not. Thanks to the lieutenant's new best friend, that little house hugger. Lookit all this. Somebody worked the hell out of it."

He opened an old manila envelope. "Bingo! Got ya the scene photos."

"Jeez, long time since I saw 'em in black-and-white," Burch said. "The shooter used double-ought buckshot. The first blast took off part of Nolan's elbow and his arm, according to the reports. He was still on his feet when the kill shot, fired at close range, took him out."

Corso whistled through his teeth. "Somebody sure didn't like him. What was he into?"

"The follow-ups all state that the victim's character was never in question. Nolan was an Eagle Scout, an athlete, World War II hero, a family man—and an honest politician."

"Ha! Ain't no such animal," Corso said. "Not in Miami, anyway."

"The original investigators dug deep into his background and came up dry. Nolan was pushed to run for senator, according to news clips in that box on my desk. Said he had no plans to get back into politics until his kids were grown.

"A thousand people at his funeral, including the governor," Burch said. "Never came up with a motive. That's what made it tough. Usually, the more money the victim has, the more suspects.

"We have to meet that Kiki gal and the property owner at the site at eleven. Stone, call your buddies in Forensics, see if we can get some talent down there. We need a metal detector, a photographer, a video camera, whatever."

Stone reacted, his look exasperated.

"This is nothing but a minor diversion," Burch assured him. "The lieutenant's hot on it. The sooner we do it, the sooner we get it out of the way."

"I pulled my case file yesterday," Stone protested.

"Good. Tomorrow we go through it, brainstorm, and see what we come up with." Burch checked his watch. "Maybe even today, if we can wrap this in a hurry."

"Count me in," Corso said. "Don't mind hanging with that Kiki babe. She's got something going on."

"Uh-oh," Nazario said sotto voce. "Speak of the devil. Is that who I think it is in the lieutenant's office?"

"Holy crap, what's she doing here now?" Burch asked.

"Where's her pith helmet?" Corso said. "She takin' a safari?"

Kiki Courtelis gave them a breezy Miss America wave. She wore a gauzy white cotton shirt with sleeves that buttoned at the wrist, khaki trousers with a series of sturdy, zippered pockets in the side seams, and leather boots. The detectives eyed her bulging, ever-present briefcase suspiciously as she and the lieutenant joined them.

"Mind if I hitch a ride with you guys?" Kiki said sweetly.

The lieutenant nodded.

"Sure," Burch said.

"I can be your navigator," Kiki offered. "The Shadows isn't easy to find—and my car's in the shop."

"We could probably manage to locate the crime scene on our own," Corso said. "That's why they call us detectives."

• • •

Even with Kiki Courtelis's help, it was nearly noon before they found the Shadows's hidden gravel driveway. Masked by an overgrowth of dense foliage it was nearly invisible. They had passed it twice. Maidenhair ferns sprouted from fissures in stone gateposts covered by tangled vines and towering bougainvillea that cascaded like a brilliant crimson waterfall across the gravel drive. A wrought-iron gate, rusted off its hinges, had been all but devoured by the relentless semitropical vegetation that had totally enveloped it.

"This climate eats up everything sooner or later," Burch said.

"Mostly sooner," Corso muttered. He and Nazario sat in the backseat of the unmarked Chrysler with Kiki

Courtelis. "I keep trying to place your perfume," Corso told her. "What is that scent you're wearin'?"

"Mosquito repellent," she said, amused. "We'll need it. I've got extra."

"We're okay," Burch said.

"Suit yourself," she said, entertaining them with a brief history of the house while they waited for the developer. "There was nothing else here when Captain Cliff Nolan built this place in the twenties. He had reason to want seclusion. Captain Nolan was a rumrunner, a smuggler. This site, on a limestone ridge with access to the water, was perfect. He brought workers from Jamaica to quarry the oolite out of the ground to build the house and the gateposts.

"Many of the local pioneers used that type of limestone. It comes out of the ground pure white, soft enough to cut with saws. After exposure to the air, it hardens, darkens, and you can see all the little seashells and fossils in it. Those houses are rare now, one reason it should be preserved.

"Another is that it's a historic site. Captain Cliff was an adventurer, one of South Florida's most notorious and colorful pioneers. A marksman, a deep-sea captain, a born risk taker. He smuggled illegal booze in from the islands during Prohibition, ran it all the way up the coast as far as Rumson, New Jersey.

"On his last run, the feds and local police up there were waiting to intercept his boat, the *Sea Wolf*. When Nolan refused to surrender, they opened fire. He dumped the booze over the side and shot back. Two lawmen were killed in a wild, running gun battle. A dozen

boats chased the *Sea Wolf* all the way down the coast.
Nolan knew every inlet, had friends at every pit stop
along the way. He managed to elude capture and make it
back here. Shortly after that, under pressure, I guess, the
local sheriff raided the Shadows.

"A posse surrounded the house, armed to the teeth
and ready for a fight. Captain Cliff had sworn that it was
his castle and he'd never let them onto his property.

"But he wasn't home. Must have been tipped off.
There were all kinds of characters here then. Al Capone
wintered in Miami Beach. The locals loved Scarface. The
law didn't. Captain Cliff was considered a local hero, a
Robin Hood type.

"Miami was pretty wild then."

"Nothing's changed," Corso said.

"The sheriff and his men confiscated five hundred
bottles of illegal liquor from the Shadows that day. A
photograph of the deputies with the contraband was
published in the *Miami Metropolis*, the local paper. I've
seen that picture in the archives at the South Florida
Historical Museum. But Nolan was never arrested or
tried."

"Where the hell's the developer?" Burch scowled at
his watch. "Maybe he's waiting up at the house." He
maneuvered the unmarked around the remnants of the
old gate, fallen palm fronds, and wind-blown branches.
"What eventually happened to Captain Nolan? He meet
a bad end?"

"No one is certain," Kiki said. "The Nolan family
plot is in the old Miami cemetery, but his name isn't
there. There was a story that he and the *Sea Wolf* were

lost in a storm off the coast of Cuba. His son, Pierce, your murder victim, was still a small boy. He was raised at the Shadows. Went to Miami High, played football, worked hard, was successful, and built a reputation as straight and civic minded as his father was notorious. He raised his own family here. Three daughters, Spring, Summer, and Brooke, and a son, Sky, the youngest.

"He and his wife, Diana, opened the Shadows up to the community with chamber music recitals and parties, made it into a showplace. He served a term as mayor, was well liked and respected. People said he was a man with no enemies."

Despite the sun, high in the sky, it was as dark as a tunnel as the unmarked crunched slowly along the winding gravel driveway beneath a tangled canopy of black olive, ficus, and royal poinciana trees in brilliant bloom.

A raucous flock of bright green-and-yellow parakeets suddenly swooped out of the trees, shrieking angrily at the intruders.

"Lookit 'em. Hundreds of 'em," Corso said.

"Monk parakeets," Nazario said. "Smart as hell. Can learn to talk if you capture them young enough. Hand raised, they're great pets. They'll eat mangoes, seeds, and nuts right outta your hand. But ones who grow up in the wild like these aren't people friendly. They bite and scratch."

Kiki nodded. "Their predators are raccoons, foxes, pet cats—and us."

"How is that cat you took home from the Beach?" Nazario asked Burch.

"Terrific. Was worried at first 'cause the only thing Max, our big, dopey sheepdog, barks at is cats. But he's so dense, didn't even notice there was a cat in the house for three days. Can't see a thing with all that hair hanging in his face. I always knew that dog had no natural animal instincts.

"On the fourth day, he wanders into the kitchen for a drink, and yikes! A cat's drinking out of his dish! He puts on the brakes, does a double take. The cat keeps drinking, watching 'im out the corner of one eye. They say people worshiped cats a couple a thousand years ago. This one musta never forgot it. The dog's jaw drops, he backs up, then goes berserk, barking like hell, trying to catch him, crashing into walls and furniture."

"So what happened?" Nazario said.

Burch shrugged. "Forty-eight hours later, he's totally intimidated. You open the door to let him in, and if the cat's anywhere in sight, Max'll circle the entire house to avoid walking past him. Takes no chances. Won't go within six feet of him. Doesn't trust him, thinks cats are too unpredictable."

"Like women," Corso said.

The birds' shrill, earsplitting screeches escalated.

"They build multi-room, multi-family nests, like condos," Kiki said wistfully. "Generation after generation use the same nests. They'll be homeless when these trees are bulldozed."

"Yeah, if they could talk," Nazario said, "you know what words they'd be using."

The birds screamed louder.

Corso shifted uneasily in his seat, scanned the

sky, and scowled. "It's like that damn Hitchcock movie.

"Hey! We're getting the message!" he shouted at the noisy protesters.

The car bounced around a final rutted curve and the Shadows stood before them.

No one spoke. The car's occupants held their breath. The angled rays of the high summer sun and dappled reflections off the water slanted between the trees behind the house. The effect was one of a dark energy emanating from inside, as though its cracked and broken windows were illuminated from within.

The wide front door hung open, a seductive invitation to a dark interior veiled by dust motes that glittered in the spectral greenish glow of light filtered through chlorophyll.

"Dios mío," Nazario murmured under his breath.

"This is it," Kiki whispered.

In its abandonment, the Shadows had become half-hidden, dwarfed by the lush and verdant, wild and overgrown subtropical forest around it. Nature had become part of the house. They were as one.

Creeping vines and the winding, intrusive roots of a walking banyan tree had crept over the hanging wraparound porch. A strangler fig tree had attached itself to a copper rain gutter, then climbed up to traverse the tin roof. Native lignum vitae and ficus trees towered over the Shadows, which was surrounded by stands of palm trees: sabal, royal, Keys thatch, and areca.

The jasmine had run amok and yellow-and-black long-winged butterflies fluttered among the intricate purple flowers on passion vines that had swallowed the porch railings.

"Look at those vines," Kiki Courtelis whispered. "The early Spanish thought that the Passiflora's three-part stigma represented the nails used in the Crucifixion and that the five stamens signified Christ's wounds."

"The developer ain't here yet," Corso said. "Or he gave up on us and left while we were still trying to find this godforsaken place."

Ripe mangoes lay everywhere, rotting on the ground, unharvested and forgotten.

"Lookit that," Corso complained, climbing out of the car. "I got a mango tree I can't get the first piece a fruit outta. Pruned it, mulched it, sprayed it. Spent a fortune on fertilizer. Wound up with one lousy mango that never got ripe. One! Damn thing musta cost me a hundred bucks. Nobody's touched these trees for years, and lookit that, a bumper crop all over the ground."

He picked one up. Round, firm, and fragrant, the color of a summer sunset.

"Ya know, somebody tol' me that when a tree doesn't produce, you should take a baseball bat to it. Just beat the living crap out of it and it'll get scared into producing fruit. Ya know, it feels threatened, that it's gonna die, and starts to deliver."

"Good idea. Maybe I could try it on detectives who don't produce," Burch said mildly.

"Where's Edelman?" Stone frowned. "He should have been here already."

"We have permission. We can start without 'im." Burch stepped carefully around the wicked spines and red flowers of a crown of thorns. Like drops of blood, they crowded the stepping stones from the driveway to the front stoop.

"Listen," Kiki Courtelis said.

They heard the rumbling of a big engine and wide tires on the gravel drive.

Is that what the killer heard that night as he waited in ambush? Burch's eyes roved the property, then met Stone's. He knew he and the young detective wondered the same thing. Where was the gunman concealed? He sighed as Stone shook his head. The untended foliage was so wild and overgrown, it was impossible to tell. Hell, it had been more than forty years.

Stone took the Rolatape, a digital tape measure on wheels, out of the car trunk, along with his own camera and a sketch pad.

The approaching vehicle swept around the final curve into view. An SUV, a silver Lincoln Navigator.

"That's him," Kiki Courtelis murmured in disgust, "the worst pirate to plunder South Florida since the sixteenth century."

Jay Edelman, toned, tanned, and well-manicured, was in no hurry. Cell phone to his ear, he was in excellent shape for a man in his fifties. His shades were expensive, his silk shirt sea-foam green, his pale trousers linen, and his shiny loafers Ferragamo.

"Gentlemen." He snapped the cell phone shut. "And the ubiquitous Ms. Kiki Courtelis. Why am I not surprised? She's everywhere, protesting my permits at City Hall, presenting petitions at public gatherings, a very busy girl.

"Don't tell me she's the reason you're here?" He turned to the detectives.

"Routine," Burch said, introducing himself and the others. "The homicide here was high-profile, so we decided to update our records while it's still possible."

"Help yourselves, Detectives. Isn't it a fabulous piece of property?" He stood in front of the Shadows, basking in his pride of ownership. "Look around. What do you see? A jungle. A raw, overgrown, underdeveloped piece of land. You know what I see? One hundred and thirty thousand feet of luxury waterfront condo living. Two hundred and fifty-two units. Just four apartments to a floor, the smallest, three thousand square feet under air, the largest, forty-two hundred square feet. Ten-foot ceilings, twenty-five hundred feet of twelve-foot-wide wraparound balconies with summer kitchens outside."

"The price tags?" Burch asked.

"Apartments will range from two-point-five to five million." He shrugged. "Each owner will have a private two-car enclosed parking space in the main garage and each will spend an average extra million dollars on upgrades and interiors."

"What are you calling it?" Nazario asked.

The latest trend for new luxury condos rising all over Miami was one-word names: Onyx, Everglades, Apogee, Continuum . . .

The developer's face lit up. "We considered Utopia, Elysium, or Paradisio, but after Ms. Kiki Courtelis was kind enough to bring it to everyone's attention, we opted to keep the historic name—Shadows. Part of the sales pitch, it has a certain appeal, a theme.

"A tile mural will dominate one wall of the lobby: the famous rumrunner, what's 'is name? The old captain at the helm of his trusty boat crashing through a stormy sea." He chortled.

"The residents' private lounge will be called the Rumrunner." His smile widened. "I even offered Ms. Courtelis a consulting job with our interior designer. The offer is still open."

He winked at Kiki, who turned her back.

Edelman's cell phone rang and he wandered off for a brief conversation, then returned, checking his expensive gold watch.

"How did you happen to acquire the house?" Burch asked.

"Saw it from my company's chopper, out scouting waterfront properties. Had my eye on it for a long time." He rubbed his palms together. "One of the last undeveloped parcels on the bay, in the same family since the twenties, believe it or not. Took some time to track down the out-of-state owner. Once she heard our offer, she was happy to unload it."

"If you don't mind me asking . . . ?" Burch said.

"Forty million." The developer smiled.

"Jesus," Stone said.

Nazario gave a long, low whistle.

"People unfamiliar with the local market are always shocked at how much waterfront property values have escalated. I'm sure it was a windfall for the widow. Old what's-his-name, the captain, probably paid twenty bucks an acre back in his day. Let's just say the owner was thrilled. So am I. In this area, it's a bargain.

"Look, you don't need me for this," Edelman said. His heavy onyx ring gleamed dark in the light filtering through the trees. "Be careful if you go inside. The place could fall down around your ears."

"No way, Edelman," Kiki sputtered. "This house weathered hurricanes before you were born. It wouldn't look bad if you hadn't deliberately exposed it to the elements so it would deteriorate."

"Not me," he said smoothly. He shook his head. "It must have been the homeless. You know how they break into vacant buildings, take over, and do irreparable damage." He took a last eager look around. "We're about to break ground," he said, "on the most exciting project in South Florida."

Kiki was fuming. "He set the house up for demolition," she said as Edelman's SUV disappeared around the big curve of the winding driveway. "He did the same thing to an irreplaceable Art Deco hotel in South Beach's historic district," she raged, loud enough for Stone to hear. He was taking notes, measuring the distance from the front porch to the driveway.

"He made a deal with the city to construct a high-rise tower on the Beach. The condition was that he preserve and restore the historic three-story hotel already on the property. He agreed, then broke out the windows, removed the doors, and exposed the old building to rodents, insects, wind, rain, and salt spray. Then he convinced the city it was unsafe, impossible to save or restore. The city condemned it, knocked it down, and gave him permission to increase the size of his project. That's his MO, how he skirts the law. He should be in jail.

"We can try to get on the agenda for the next city commission meeting," she said, focusing on Burch. "You and your detectives could testify that the Shadows should be preserved."

"Oh, no you don't," Burch said. "You're not dragging us into that one."

"Can't they move the house to a city park or some other location?" Stone looked up from his notes. "I've heard of that being done."

"How?" Nazario demanded. "You'd have to take the trees with it. No way to separate them now."

"Yeah," Corso said. "It would be like doctors trying to separate those Siamese twins."

"Conjoined." Stone grimaced.

"Whadaya talking about?" Corso said. "Where I come from they're Siamese."

"That's politically incorrect," Burch said.

"Hell with that," Corso grumbled. "They pussified the whole damn department with that politically correct crap."

Stone sighed.

"The house might survive a move," Kiki said hopefully.

Corso scratched his neck, then his elbow, and began swatting mosquitoes and no-see-ums, tiny, nearly invisible insects whose nasty stings create angry red welts.

"You still got that mosquito repellent?" he asked.

Kiki dug the can out of her briefcase.

He sprayed himself from his bald spot down to his ankles, then passed the can to the others.

Stone and Nazario flagged the spot where Pierce

Nolan bled to death in the arms of his wife and daughters, according to the notes and diagrams in the case file.

"There's so much mystery here," Kiki Courtelis said, watching them wistfully. "Lots more than just an old murder case. You know, the Devil's Punch Bowl is on private property right near here."

"I've heard of it," Stone said. "Never saw it."

"Me, too." Burch nodded.

"What the hell is it?" Corso mopped his brow with a handkerchief.

"A natural freshwater spring first discovered by ancient Indians," she said. "Somebody, probably the Tequestas, carved a deep well in the limestone bluff above the bay shore centuries ago. There's an arrow marked on a large rock nearby. It's still there, worn smooth by time. Pirates used the spring later and the Spanish used slave labor to improve access to it.

"I was there once when I was little. It's a shallow well with a circular mouth and two stone steps inside that lead to the water's edge.

"It was a favorite gathering place for settlers as early as 1808, one of Miami's first tourist attractions. An old newspaper story reported that the most delicious spring water flows from the rock under the bluff of the shore.

"Its origins are mysterious. No one knows how it got its name. Isidor Cohen, an early Miami pioneer, wrote in his memoirs that 'frequent drinking of the water from that mysterious spring is believed to endow one with perpetual youth.'"

Stone had stopped work to listen. "So you're suggesting it might be what Ponce de Leon was in search of when he sailed into Biscayne Bay in the fourteen hundreds?"

"The Fountain of Youth," Burch said.

"Could be," Kiki said. "Seminole Indians from as far away as Immokalee used to visit the Devil's Punch Bowl once a year and fill containers with the water. Part of some sacred tradition. Reporters would try to interview them, but they refused to talk about the ritual, or their ancient beliefs.

"It's in somebody's backyard now, inaccessible to the public. A damn shame. We've lost so much history," she said earnestly. "It would be terrible to lose this, too."

"One thing I have to say for you," Burch said grudgingly. "You don't give up, or shut up."

Distant thunder rumbled to the west as storm clouds built across the Everglades. The slick face of the bay seventy-five yards away, beneath a downward slope, began to stir as the wind picked up and the air became sweet with ozone.

"Let's look around inside, then get out of here before the storm hits," Burch said.

They took flashlights from the car and climbed the Shadows's sagging front steps.

"Dark as a tomb in here." Stone's voice echoed off empty walls.

The wooden floor groaned and creaked in protest; sounds rustled all around them, and something else, a sort of faint whispering.

"Jesus. This place could use some Feng Shui," Burch said.

Small creatures scurried as their flashlight beams

picked up shadowy images, a large armoire, a heavy dining table, and several other oversized pieces of forgotten furniture.

There was a large eat-in kitchen, a dining room, living room, and what appeared to be numerous bedrooms clustered at the rear of the house.

"A fireplace in every room," Stone noted as they fanned out.

"Look at this." Burch shined his light onto a pine beam above the front door. The words carved there were difficult to make out.

He read them aloud, playing his light across the letters: "'Health and Wealth and the Time to Enjoy Them.'"

"Too bad Nolan didn't get his wish."

"Neither did his father. I have a bad feeling about this place," Nazario said softly. He paused at the foot of a wooden staircase with an ornate banister. "Too many secrets."

"Cubans are too superstitious, always fulla conspiracy theories," Corso complained.

"That's Italians," Stone said.

"No wonder you feel bad vibes. There was a murder here," Burch reminded them.

Corso wheeled to aim his flashlight at the source of a sudden frantic scrabbling. Something furry skittered into a corner. "Shit! What the hell is that?"

Beady eyes glowed red in the flashlights' glare. Ratlike tails, long pink snouts, and rows of sharp, pointy teeth.

"Ahhh, possums," Kiki cooed. "A family."

A mother with nearly a dozen babies blinked at their lights in alarm. But the tiny toylike faces of the babies looked like they were smiling.

"Wish we had some pet food," Kiki said. "They love it."

"Yeah," Stone said. "They used to come to my grandmother's back door at night to eat the food she put out for the cat." He hadn't seen the possums lately, he realized, not for years.

"Maybe," Kiki said, thinking aloud, "we could call the Audubon Society, the Wildlife Federation, or PETA and persuade them to seek a protection order for the wildlife on this property. I think sea turtles used to nest here. If we can spread the news and rally enough animal lovers to block the bulldozers—"

"There you go again," Corso said. "One-track mind. Always scheming."

"I'll try anything to buy us enough time for a response from the National Heritage Trust and their lawyers—"

"Let's check upstairs," Burch interrupted.

"Think they'll hold us?" Corso demanded.

"Sure, as long as you don't practice the polka on your way up," Burch said.

"I'll go first," Kiki offered. "I weigh the least."

Burch handed her his flashlight and they followed her up the creaking stairs.

"It's a Belvedere!" she exclaimed from the top. "Look! This is how they built houses before air-conditioning. The second floor is all one huge room with four-way exposure. Windows all around."

The only furniture left was the remnants of an old double bed.

"Wonder why the widow and kids cleared out so fast after the murder," Stone said on the way back downstairs.

"Probably scared," Nazario said.

"Can't blame 'em," Burch said.

"You know, this is one of the few South Florida houses with a cellar," Kiki said.

"You're kidding me," Burch said. "You sure?"

"Yep, that was where the captain hid his booze. The house sits on a natural ridge above the water table. One of the pictures taken during that 1925 raid showed the basement. It's connected to a tunnel they cut, angled down to the water where the *Sea Wolf* was docked. The smugglers could move contraband in and out without being seen."

"Where's the door to the cellar?" Nazario asked.

"Concealed," she said. "Most likely under the stairwell here, or in one of the fireplaces. That would be the most logical."

"Let's see," Stone said.

He stepped beneath the stairwell, crouched, and pulled up a rotting piece of carpet, exposing a trapdoor. "It's here!"

He yanked at the rusted iron ring. "It's coming loose." With a last mighty heave and a scraping, clanking sound, it yawned open. What lay beneath was as black as a well.

"Looks like it hasn't been used for years." He shined his light down into the opening. "There are stone steps."

"Wouldn't it be something if we found the murder

weapon or some new evidence after all this time?" Burch said. "The detectives didn't mention this in their original reports. Maybe they never knew about it. Let's take a look."

The others followed.

Nazario turned to Kiki, who lagged behind. "Come on." He reached for her hand.

"No. I'm not going down there." Her voice sounded thin and nearly inaudible. "I'll wait outside."

He paused but she was already gone. He shrugged and went after the others.

"This is like one a them horror movies." Corso's voice boomed too loud in the cramped space. "You know, where a girl holds a flickering candle and slo-o-owly goes down into the dark cellar, where the homicidal maniac is waiting with a bloody axe. The audience screams, 'No! Don't go down there!' But the dumb bitch always does."

"If Nolan's killer is waiting down there, he's got a cane and a long gray beard," Burch said.

Ten limestone steps descended into the cellar. Old kerosene lanterns stood in niches on each side. The underground room, only about six feet high, seemed to extend almost the length of the house.

The sighs and whispers had grown louder. Obviously they came from here. The floor sloped toward a hatchlike door at the east end.

"Looks like the tunnel," Burch said.

Stone and Nazario labored together to inch the door open.

"I hope," Nazario said, grunting, "that when it does open, the bay isn't on the other side."

"If it is, let's hope it's not high tide," Stone said.

The door began to give way, releasing the smells of dank air and decaying greenery. "Damn thing does lead down to the water. You were right," Stone said to Kiki. But she wasn't there. He turned. "Where is she?"

"Chickened out," Nazario said. "She's waiting upstairs."

"Scared of the dark all of a sudden?" Corso said skeptically.

"I'll see where this goes." Stone disappeared into the tunnel of sighs and whispers. Crouching, he moved east along the downward slope, stumbling several times over intrusive tree roots that had forced their way through the limestone over the years. Thick cobwebs and trailing roots caught on his clothes and brushed across his face and shoulders. During the descent, he came upon several steplike landings. The tunnel smelled chalky, and of dead fish, leaves, and wet rocks.

"Hey, dawg, let us know what you find down there," Corso called after him.

He was gone for what seemed to be a long time.

"Stone, you okay down there?" Burch finally called into the mouth of the tunnel.

They heard the muffled sounds of his return.

"Sure enough." Stone panted as he emerged. "It goes right down to the bay. But you can barely see day-light down there. I could hear the wind, the water, and the birds, but it looks like the opening is blocked by fallen trees and overgrown mangroves. They'd have to be cleared away before it could be used."

"Too bad they're tearing this joint down," Corso said. "It'd make a helluva Halloween haunted house. We could sell tickets. Make a fortune."

The detectives continued to explore the cellar, their flashlight beams illuminating old wooden shutters, a few rusted tools hanging from pegs, and a pine plank shelf built into the far west wall. The wide shelf, about three feet off the floor, held a wooden chest.

"Look at this," Burch said.

"Maybe it's booze!" Corso's words rang out of the total darkness behind his flashlight beam. "The rumrunner's stash! Think it's still drinkable?"

"Might be." Burch trained his light on the wooden chest. "Doesn't look like a toolbox."

"What do you think?" Stone said.

"It's padlocked," Nazario said.

"You heard Edelman. The man said, 'Help yourself.' The whole place is coming down in a couple days, anyhow," Burch said. "Open it."

Stone used an old hammer to break away the rusted padlock. The hinged lid protested with a groan.

"Something's in here, wrapped in old newspapers." He reached inside.

"Oh Lordy! Oh my God!" He recoiled. His flashlight clattered to the floor. Eerie kaleidoscopes of light and shadow splashed off the walls, floor, and ceiling as it rolled away.

"Shit! Shit! Shit!" He gasped for breath. "Oh shit!"

"What is it? What the hell's in there?" Burch demanded.

"No," Stone groaned. "Oh, no." He scrambled to retrieve his flashlight and, from a distance, trained the beam on the wooden chest.

The light spilled inside, exposing a row of small, neatly wrapped bundles. One was disturbed. From it protruded a tiny, dark, and shriveled human hand.

CHAPTER 4

"Sorry, Sergeant." The chief medical examiner switched off his flashlight. "You're right. This does appear to be mummified human flesh, not a doll."

Burch sighed in the dark.

"The other bundles are suspiciously similar in size and shape, one row on top of the other. There appear to be at least six or seven."

"You don't think . . ."

"No way to know until we get them to the office."

"Son of a bitch." Stone's voice echoed eerily off the walls. "What the hell went on in this house?"

"Told you I had a bad feeling," Nazario mournfully reminded them from the stairs.

"Fetus or full term?" Burch asked.

"Impossible to say. We'll have a better look in the lab."

The medical examiner flicked his light back on, skimming it along the walls of the passageway descending to the bay. "Fascinating. Hear this place has quite a history."

"Which just became a helluva lot more interesting. Let's get organized," Burch said as they climbed the stairs and emerged from under the stairwell. "Naz, call out an ASA. Try to reach Salazar, she's the best. We need a search warrant ASAP. As soon as she draws it up, get it to a judge. Even with the owner's permission, we need to be on the safe side till we know exactly what we've got. God forbid that box arrived here recently.

"Best-case scenario is that it's been collecting dust since the twenties," he said hopefully. "Even if it's homicide, or multiple homicides, nobody'ud be left alive to prosecute.

"Stone, call Donaldson at fire, tell 'em we need a generator and high-intensity work lights down here. And get Ed Baker and the A-team from the crime lab."

"I'll ask for an alternate light source as well, the Poly Light," Stone said as they gathered on the front porch, "to check for hairs and fibers. Doubt if they can lift anything off those limestone walls, but maybe they can get something off the box and the shelf."

"Hey, where the hell is she?" Burch blinked into the sticky summer haze, eyes readjusting to the light.

Kiki Courtelis was nowhere in sight.

"Yeah." Nazario stepped to the porch railing to scan their surroundings. "Our sweet little tour guide is MIA."

"The chick with the briefcase?" The husky uniform officer was tying yellow crime scene tape to a tree. "She just split, took off in a taxicab."

"Go get her," Burch said quietly. "Bring her ass back here! Now!"

The officer ran for his squad car, wheeled it around, then swerved to let the lieutenant's approaching unmarked pass.

"He was in a big hurry," K. C. Riley said, as she joined them.

"Yeah, to bring back Kiki, your new best friend. The M.E. just confirmed the bad news in the basement, we don't know how bad yet. But we turn around and she's gone. Hope you don't mind," he said, "since your grannies go way back and were such good . . ."

"I don't care who the hell her grandmother was." Riley's face reddened. "Do what you have to do."

      •   •   •

Nazario and Assistant State Attorney Jo Salazar returned in near record time, an hour flat, with a search warrant.

When developer Jay Edelman returned to the site of "the most exciting new project in South Florida," police and crime scene vehicles, a fire department truck, the medical examiner's car, and a morgue wagon crowded the winding driveway. Forced to leave his silver Navigator, he hiked up to the house, skirting parked vehicles, stumbling over tree roots, rocks, and branches. He wasn't smiling now.

"Fellas, fellas!" he cried, breathing hard and sweating. Damp circles ringed the armpits of his sea-foam silk shirt; his linen trousers were wrinkled and stained by bushes and brambles.

He waved his arms. "Okay!" he shouted over the din of the generator. "Everybody out!"

"Sir!" An irate uniform patrolman waved him back. "Did you see that crime scene tape across the driveway? Get off the property!"

"I'm the owner! Where the hell is Sergeant Burch?" Edelman stood his ground, red-faced and panting.

Burch and Corso stepped out onto the front porch.

"Fellas, fellas," Edelman greeted them. "What is all this? When I said help yourself, this wasn't what I had in mind. You went way overboard. You have to clear all this out of here.

"Goddammit. Look what all those fucking stones and bushes did to my Ferragamos." He lifted one foot to examine his scuffed shoe.

"Enough is enough!" he bawled as Lieutenant Riley and Assistant State Attorney Jo Salazar joined the detectives.

"What's this?" He held the papers Salazar handed him out at arm's length, then fumbled for his reading glasses.

"A search warrant." Salazar introduced herself.

"Look, lady." Edelman mopped his brow with a monogrammed handkerchief. "I don't care who you are. These people have all got to go. I have heavy equipment coming in first thing in the morning."

"Sorry," she said sweetly. "That won't be possible."

• • •

In stifling heat, under portable floodlights fueled by a fire department generator, crime scene photographers documented the interior and exterior of the wooden chest without disturbing the bundles inside.

Hoping to find transfer evidence from whoever

placed them there, technicians swabbed the parts of the box that might have been handled, seeking fingerprints and possible DNA evidence. They also processed the shelf that held it and the wall behind it. Due to the intense heat buildup, they were forced to take frequent breaks.

Finally, rubber-gloved techs carefully lifted the box, secured it inside a huge zippered pouch, and transported it to the medical examiner's office. Photographers and technicians continued to process the space where the chest had been.

"Stay with it," Burch told Nazario. "Let's just hope they find a date on some a those newspapers they're wrapped in and that it's not recent."

Like a mourner following a hearse, Nazario trailed the morgue wagon to One Bob Hope Road, the Miami–Dade County medical examiner's complex. An attendant logged in the wooden box and assigned a case number to the tiny known occupant.

The detective watched them shoot more photographs, then followed the wooden box to the X-ray room.

The old X-ray machine had recently been replaced by a new top-of-the-line, computerized, digital scanning X-ray machine with excellent resolution and a twenty-one-inch display screen.

The moment of truth, Nazario thought as the chief medical examiner hit the switch.

Nazario held his breath as the outline of the box appeared on the screen. The image revealed the metal hinges on the lid, the broken lock, and inside, rows of tiny skulls, rib cages, femurs, and arm bones.

"We have multiple bodies here," the chief medical examiner told his assistant. "We need six more case numbers, consecutive to the first, for a total of seven."

Nazario sighed.

The process was painstaking.

Each wrapped bundle yielded the image of a tiny human being.

Technicians reexamined the lid of the makeshift coffin again, for fingerprints and DNA. The box's interior was photographed again before the first bundle was removed. Still wrapped, the infant was x-rayed individually, then repositioned several times for X-rays from multiple angles.

Lost children, Nazario thought, watching the procedure followed again and again, seven times over. *Whose babies are you? How long did you stay alone down there in the dark? Who left you there?*

Laid out on two autopsy tables, each infant appeared to have been wrapped first in cloth, then in several layers of now-yellowed newspaper.

"You see a date on any of that newsprint?" Nazario asked.

"I want to wait for a forensic anthropologist before unwrapping them all," the chief said. "Dr. Helmut Newberger over at Florida International University said he'd be here first thing in the morning."

With tweezers, tongs, and careful gloved fingers, the stained wrappings were gently peeled away from the first bundle, revealing the tiny, shriveled, blackened face of the shrunken cadaver.

"Infants dry out faster," the chief explained. "That's why an infant left in a hot parked car will die when an adult would not. The smaller the body, the more rapidly it dehydrates. Since these infants were wrapped in porous materials that allowed the escape of water vapor, they dehydrated and mummified."

"Can you determine race and sex?" Nazario asked.

"That may take a little time," the chief said, delicately stripping away a four-inch-by-four-inch section of yellowed newspaper.

"Let's have a better look at this." He placed the delicate scrap beneath a bright magnifying light.

"Well," the chief said. "No mistaking this."

The detective peered over his shoulder. A partial headline included the initials *JFK* in twenty-four-point type.

"That rules out the twenties," the chief said grimly. "A paragraph on the reverse side mentions an event that occurred in April 1961. Isn't that the year Pierce Nolan was killed? The plot thickens."

"Were these infants born alive?"

"Hard to say. We should be able to determine their maturation by the contents, if any, of their stomachs and the condition of their umbilical cords. We'll take tissue from around the navels, place it in a softening compound, then process it to make microscopic slides of the umbilical cord attachments."

"Will it work with remains this old?"

"They do it with two-thousand-year-old mummies. No sign of trauma so far. The X-rays revealed no fractures."

The cloth used to wrap the remains would be sent to the crime lab for possible identification.

•   •   •

"Don't close that door!" Kiki yelped from inside a small interview room.

Corso swung it shut behind him.

"How's she doing?" Burch asked.

"Pretty pissed," Corso said. "Freaks out when you close the door. Wants to go home."

"Don't we all?" Burch said grimly.

"Bingo!" Stone sat at his computer terminal. "Kiki's got a rap sheet."

"I knew she was guilty of something the minute I laid eyes on her," Burch said, irritated. "I knew it!"

"Had me fooled," Corso said. "She seemed normal."

"Everybody seems normal, till you get to know them," Burch said.

"No major felonies," Stone said. "Trespassing, failure to follow a police order, disorderly conduct, demonstrating without a permit, and resisting arrest without violence. Kiki also has an alias, Lisa Court."

"How 'bout that." Burch stepped into the small interrogation room.

"Okay, Kiki. You've got some 'splaining to do."

She hugged herself as though cold, as he sat down opposite her.

"Would you leave that door open please, Sergeant?"

Her eyes and body language looked odd.

"What's your problem?"

"Open the door."

She wore the expression of a trapped animal. Burch leaned back in his chair, unlatched the door, and left it ajar.

"Happy? Now talk to me."

"Why am I here? I have to leave. Where's Lieutenant Riley? Who had that officer stop my taxicab? What right—"

"I ask the questions." He sighed. "But for your information, when the officer radioed me that you were uncooperative, unwilling to return to the Shadows, I instructed him to bring you here."

"But why? Did Edelman—"

"Edelman had nothing to do with it, Kiki. Tell me everything you know about what we found in the basement."

Her stare was wide-eyed and innocent. "What did you find?"

"Kiki. It's been a long day. Level with me. You knew what we were going to find down there, didn't you?"

She blinked as though puzzled. "No."

"Gimme a break. You insisted we go out there. Why?"

"You know why. To save the Shadows."

"Oh. And you just happened to have information about a secret cellar, and knew where the door to it was located, and then you just happened to decide not to go down there with us because you knew we were about to find a goddamn dead body!"

"A body!" Her mouth dropped, her eyes widened. "Was it a homeless person?"

"No, Kiki. A body that appears to have been there for a hell of a lotta years."

"Captain Cliff Nolan?" Her posture changed and her eyes lit up. "You solved his disappearance? After nearly eighty years! Was he there all along?"

"Kiki, I'm not gonna play games with you," he warned.

"I'm not playing games." She checked her Swatch watch. "For Pete's sake, I have to go home!"

Burch's walkie crackled to life.

"Three thirty-two to four forty-one."

"Four forty-one, stand by." Burch turned to her as he got to his feet. "And you just happened to call a cab after you knew we'd found it? What was your big hurry?"

"Fergie and Di are home alone, since early this morning."

"Sure. I'm Prince Charles and you're the Queen Mother. I've had it with you, Kiki."

He stepped out and slammed the door.

"Leave it open!" she wailed.

"Four forty-one," he said into the radio. "Whatcha got, Naz?"

"Seven," Nazario said. "Cause unknown so far. Could have been live births. Circa 1961."

"Crap. Where you at?"

"Pulling into the station garage now."

"Good, I want you to take a crack at Kiki. She seemed to like you."

•   •   •

Nazario reported to the others in the lieutenant's office.

Salazar whistled and ran her manicured fingers through her curly brown hair. "Edelman won't be a happy camper."

"You're right," Riley said. "We have to go over that place inch by inch, maybe even dig around the back of the house. God knows what else we'll find out there."

"I'll get a temporary restraining order against any action by the builder," Salazar said. "How's thirty days?"

"We can extend it if necessary, right?" Riley said.

"Right. Edelman's gonna hate it."

"I know I do," Burch said. "Jesus. *Babies*. Little babies. You know what the time frame means."

"Nolan had three teenage daughters, didn't he?" Riley asked, face taut.

"Summer, the oldest, was sixteen when her father was murdered." Burch consulted his notebook. "Spring was fourteen, and Brooke, thirteen."

"Nolan was the only man in the house, right?"

Burch nodded. "The son, Sky, was nine at the time."

"Looks like our victim might have been a bad dad, a very bad dad," Riley said.

"Nobody ever looked seriously at the wife or the kids as suspects," Stone said. "Never found a motive, either."

Riley, pale under her tan, toyed with the hand grenade on her desk. "Incest is a motive."

"Think those babies are his?" Salazar said.

"Sick, but not unheard of," Riley said. "Similar cases have surfaced around the country, mostly in rural areas."

"The products of incest buried in backyards or locked in a trunk in the attic." Salazar shuddered.

"Or the cellar," Burch said. "Why hide them if they were legitimate? That son of a bitch."

"According to the background investigations and news clips in the file, Nolan and his wife were always out and about, attending charitable functions, their pictures on the society pages. In the years before his murder, she sure wasn't home pregnant all the time," Stone said.

"Somebody was," Riley said. "Incest sounds like a good motive to me."

"Might explain why the widow and kids split right after the murder," Corso said.

"And hung on to the property," Salazar said.

"Kept it in the family like everything else," Corso said.

"The wife knew," Riley said, thinking out loud. "No way she didn't. Three girls, seven babies?"

"Guy was having himself a field day," Corso said.

"Is the widow still alive?" Salazar asked.

Burch nodded.

"Wonder why she'd sell the place now?" Riley frowned.

"Forty million good reasons," Burch said. "That's what Edelman paid her."

"She's gotta be, what, in her seventies by now.

Maybe she's senile and forgot what they left behind in the cellar," Corso said.

"I don't care how old you are, you don't forget something like that," Riley said. "She knew Edelman's intentions, that he'd demolish the Shadows. Figured nobody would remember the cellar all these years later. The high-rise would go up and the babies would be buried forever under thousands of tons of concrete. Nobody in the outside world would know they were ever born.

"We need to move fast," she told Burch. "Reporters from Channel Four and the *Miami News* are pushing PIO. Word leaked out that we found human remains at the Shadows. They want the story. I'm trying to stall a press release. When it gets out, the story will probably get a lot of coverage."

"In this case it might do some good," Burch said. "Might bring in some leads. Somebody had to know something about those girls being pregnant."

"Or it could put us in the middle of a media frenzy. You need to talk to the widow and the daughters before that happens."

"One of them probably killed him," Burch said. "Or maybe it was a family project. Hell of a thing. Imagine what those females went through for years. Looks like Pierce Nolan was a goddamn monster."

CHAPTER 5

Nazario closed the door to the small interview room. Within seconds, it inched back open. No one came out.

"See, the broad don't like being alone with any guy," Corso said. "Has to tell you something."

Nazario emerged forty-five minutes later.

"Talk to me." Burch looked up from the Nolan file spread out across the conference room table.

"She's telling the truth," Nazario said. "She had no idea what we'd find down there."

"I knew his shit detector didn't work on good-looking women," Corso crowed. "I knew it."

Nazario ignored him. "Kiki's claustrophobic, Sarge. Barely tolerates elevators, doesn't like planes, hates small rooms with no windows." He rolled his sad spaniel eyes toward the interview room. "That's why she didn't go down the cellar stairs with us."

"Makes sense," Riley acknowledged.

"She explain her little rap sheet?" Burch asked.

"She was arrested twice. Edelman was clearing property for a shopping center in the Grove when protesters formed a human chain around a huge, hundred-year-old banyan tree his crew was about to cut down. They were all arrested. She was one of them."

"A tree hugger, too!" Corso said.

"Hardly a public menace," Stone said.

"They call that ecoterrorism," Corso protested.

"Her other arrest was during a protest over on the Beach," Nazario explained. "An art deco hotel was being knocked down so the late Gianni Versace, who owned the building next door, could dig himself a private pool. Both peaceful protests."

"Sometimes that's the only way to change the law or send a message," Stone said, drawing a sharp look from Riley.

"When you said we'd found a body, she thought you meant the old rumrunner. Remember, he disappeared, lost at sea or something, in the mid-thirties, after Prohibition."

"Okay, okay," Burch said. He realized he'd never had lunch. It was nine P.M. No wonder he felt irritable. "One more thing. Did she mention a Fergie and Di?"

"Dogs. Fergie is her Yorkie," Nazario said, his expression serious. "Di is a papillon."

"A what?"

"Some kinda fancy little dog."

"You mean like that one that wears bathing suits with rhinestones—you know, Tinkerbell, Paris Hilton's little dog?" Corso said.

"Nah." Stone frowned. "Tinkerbell's a Chihuahua."

"Somebody from PETA ought to launch a mission to rescue that poor creature," Riley said.

"Right," Salazar said. "The woman wears that dog as

an accessory. Saw it on her lap during a TV interview once. The poor thing couldn't stop trembling."

"Tinkerbell makes a run for it every chance she gets," Riley said, "trying to escape. Saw on the news last week that she got away again on South Beach. But the reward is always so big that people keep bringing the poor thing back."

"Whadaya mean 'poor thing'?" Corso demanded. "I'd trade places with that lucky little pooch anytime."

"Puleeze." Salazar grimaced. "Can you imagine where that dog's been? What it's seen?"

"Exactly. Anytime."

"Guys? Lieutenant?" Kiki Courtelis peered timidly around the door to the interview room.

"You won't forget about me, go home, and leave me in here, will you?"

"No way to forget you," Burch said. "Much as we'd like to. Somebody will be right with you."

"Getting back to Fergie and Di." Nazario lowered his voice. "Apparently, the smaller the dog, the smaller the bladder. And Kiki just got a new carpet. So she was in a hurry."

"Cut her loose. Take her home," Riley said, disgusted. "Pick her brain. Find out what else she knows about the house, its history, and the people who lived there."

•   •   •

Nazario's red Mustang convertible burned rubber, screeching out of the police parking garage.

His passenger clung to the door handle. "Is this how you always drive?"

"Sorry." His foot eased off the gas for a moment. "Want me to put the top down? So the space is not so small?"

"Yes." She sighed and leaned back as the convertible top slowly receded, exposing Miami's big, wide sky awash in Technicolor shades of star-studded midnight blue, streaked by purple, pink, and gold.

"I've traveled a lot," Kiki said softly. "This is the only place you see clouds these colors at night. And see how the crescent moon is upended? Like a bowl upside down. This is the only place in the country where you can see it like that."

She took a deep breath, turned to him, and grinned. "It feels soooo good to get out of your office. How do you work there every day?" She'd returned to her usual feisty, self-confident demeanor. "You need to go green in your cubicles, Pete. Live plants will minimize the effects of electromagnetic frequencies from phones, fluorescent lights, and computers. They'll reduce that geopathic stress. In other words, you don't feel as tired, fuzzy, and depressed with green plants all around you. And everyone knows that fluorescent lights cause eye strain, headaches, and an overwhelming sense of stress and disorder."

"A lot of that's been going around." He raised an eyebrow. "I thought it was from working with Corso."

She had a girlish giggle. "That institutional gray in your office is way too depressing. Bring in some throw rugs and bright colors."

Horns blared and she closed her eyes as the Mustang

careened through a yellow caution light on Northwest Second Avenue.

"We do have a few potted plants around the station," he said. "Personally I could live with more, but forget the throw rugs and bright colors—no way. The gray is working out fine, better than orange. When they built the new station, they made all our cubicles a bright international orange. Hurt your eyes to look at it. Witnesses would get all hyper and agitated after sitting in there for a while. Detectives were taking swings at each other. Two a the secretaries wound up in a cat fight. That last one was a real bad scene."

She frowned. "Maybe some soothing shades of—"

"Look," he interrupted, slowing down as they passed La Esquina de Tejas. "I didn't eat breakfast. We both missed lunch. Want to stop for some Cuban food?"

"No," she said.

"Pizza?" he offered hopefully.

She shook her head.

"Okay." Shot down, he sighed.

"So what's with your alias, Lisa Court?" he asked after an awkward pause.

She laughed unself-consciously. "People on the telephone always mistook my name, no matter how clearly I spoke. I'd arrive at a restaurant, elegantly dressed, trying to look refined and dignified, and the maître d' would shout out, 'Kinky! Your table is ready!' So I started using Lisa, my middle name, and shortening my last name to Court when I made reservations."

"That's it?"

"Yep. When they arrested us at that protest on the

Beach, a policeman asked if I ever use another name, so I told him."

Home was a cottage on Avocado Avenue in Coconut Grove.

"Nice," he said as she directed him into the drive.

"One of Miami Beach's oldest structures."

"Miami Beach? This is the Grove."

"This house was built in 1913, at Nineteenth Street and Collins Avenue in Miami Beach. A judge built it as a fishing retreat. They decided to build a hotel on the site in 1936, and moved the house here for five hundred dollars. It's Dade County pine with insect-resistant cypress shakes."

She was out of the car, fishing her keys from her purse, before he could open the door.

Nazario followed to see her safely inside, where a duet of high-pitched barks had reached a crescendo. Two little dogs burst out the door as he turned to leave.

He glanced back and saw the yellow-pointed Yorkie leap joyfully around Kiki, while the small, long-haired black-and-white dog spun around dizzyingly, feathery ears flying.

"Good girls," Kiki cooed as they danced at her feet.

"You're leaving?" she asked the retreating detective. She seemed surprised.

He paused.

"I thought you were hungry—and thirsty." Hands on her hips, she looked impatient. "Come in."

Uncertain, he followed her. The interior glowed in shades of amber, red, green, and gold. Vibrant Haitian art on the walls, hardwood floors polished to a high gloss, bright throw rugs and sea-grass mats. Big blue and purple glass bubbles, Japanese fishing floats, filled ceramic bowls on tables. Spider plants hung in every corner, their thriving pups spiraling out of control, reaching for the light.

He stood for a moment, taken aback by the warm and welcoming effect.

"No fun eating alone," she said with a shrug. "Stay, and I'll throw something together."

• • • •

He sat on a kitchen stool, listening to music from the stereo, and watched her slim hands, sure and capable, as she worked.

As rice steamed on the stove, she handed him linen napkins, dishes, and silverware. "Here, you can set the table." She nudged him toward the dining room.

"You can wash up in there." She pointed a wooden spoon toward the tiny bathroom.

The tiles were pink, the shower curtain lacy, with framed flower prints on the wall. Pretty little things around the sink included fancy soaps in hand-painted dishes, miniature bottles, and a silver powder box. He lifted the lid to check it out. The delicately tinted powder inside was soft, with a subtle fragrance. It really was face powder.

A white terry-cloth robe hung from a hook on the door. A row of bottles—shampoo, conditioner, and body polish—stood inside the tub enclosure. He paused for a moment to ponder the last item. A white wicker clothes hamper held a swirl of towels, face cloths, and bikini underpants. Victoria's Secret.

Without thinking, he turned the water on in the sink to mask the sound and stealthily opened the medicine cabinet.

Lining the glass shelves: Q-Tips, aspirin, and a box of Midol. He squinted at the label, then moved on. Minipads, panty liners, a bottle of apricot face scrub, a tiny pink razor, sunscreen, powder puffs, toothpaste, dental floss, and hand sanitizer. Nothing suspicious.

He picked up a bottle of silver nail polish. Shimmery Moon, according to the name on the label. As he examined it, Kiki called out, her voice surprisingly loud and close to the door.

"Soup's on!"

Startled, he pushed the bottle back onto the shelf so quickly that the similar little bottles lined up beside it began to topple. He tried to right them but made matters worse. Several fell noisily into the sink. They sounded like marbles bouncing off a tile floor. He cringed.

None broke, but now they were wet. He turned off the water and used a fringed guest towel embroidered with butterflies to dry them. But the impact had loosened the cap on one and Hotsy Totsy, a bloodred polish, spilled into the sink. Hastily, he mopped it up with the guest towel, staining it crimson.

"Hello?" Kiki said from the other side of the door.

"Be right there." He ran cold water over the towel to rinse off the polish, which appeared to harden. He crumpled the towel but it was too wet to stuff in his pocket.

He looked around frantically. Didn't this woman own a hair dryer? He finally hid the towel in the hamper, covering it up with Victoria's Secret bikinis.

Kiki stood there wearing an apron, arms crossed, when he opened the door.

"Find anything interesting?"

He didn't know what to say.

She stared at his hands.

"Were you trying on my nail polish?" she asked, her expression dismayed.

"No." He followed her gaze. The telltale crimson polish had stained his fingertips and seeped into his cuticles.

"It fell. I was trying to pick it up," he said lamely.

"I caught you red-handed. Literally." She did not smile.

"Sorry," he said. "Force of habit."

"You mean you always snoop through people's medicine cabinets?"

He sighed. "I used to work vice and undercover narcotics."

"I guess you weren't very good at it."

"I was," he said. "It becomes second nature. I'm sorry."

"So am I. How sad, to regard everyone as suspect. You should spend more time with normal people, like your family."

"I don't have one." He shrugged helplessly.

"No family? Even sadder. Come sit down," she said. "It's getting cold."

Music played. There were carrots, corn, and peas

hidden in the rice, along with fat, succulent fresh shrimp. They drank La Crema Chardonnay.

He ate silently, savoring the meal.

"Don't interrupt me," she finally said.

He smiled.

"What happened to your family?" she asked.

"I came to Miami alone on a Pedro Pan flight when I was six. My parents planned to follow, but Castro canceled the flights. I never saw them again. My father was arrested. He died behind bars, a political prisoner. My mother died not long after."

"Six? Who took care of you?"

"I grew up all over the country, in and out of orphanages, Catholic children's homes and foster homes."

"That must have been so difficult."

He shrugged, enjoying a mouthful of rice. "I missed the food and the language. I spoke no English and they never sent me to a place where Spanish was spoken. But the same thing happened to thousands of kids; we did fine."

"I grew up in a big, noisy family." She put her fork down. "I can't imagine what it would have been like without them."

"It was okay," he assured her, "especially after I made my way back to Miami and joined the department."

"You don't regret not choosing another profession?"

"I'd do it again, *en un segundo*," he said without hesitation. "In a heartbeat. It is a rare job. You learn about people from all walks of life: big-shot politicians, people who want to fire you, people who love you and want to take you home, people who want to kill you, people who want to bake you cakes and want their kids to grow up to be like you, and people who want your job. It is like nothing else. Cold cases are the best. A real challenge."

She sipped her wine, watching him.

"Sometimes we have to work harder to find a witness than a killer. People die, move away, they are hard to find. Many homicide witnesses live on the dark side themselves and don't want to be found.

"In a fresh murder, time works against you. A case still unsolved after the first forty-eight hours most probably will remain that way. But after a certain point, time turns and it begins to work for you. Compadres who once covered for each other are no longer friends. Sweethearts and married couples break up. People outside the law need to negotiate a deal. Eventually, time works for us."

"I see how easy it is to be consumed by it," she said. "When I researched my thesis, I became hooked on those who came before us. Julia Tuttle, Carl Fisher, John Collins, Major Francis Langhorn Dade, and so many other unnamed heroes, pioneers, visionaries, and villains. I love to research and write articles for historical magazines. That's how I became interested in Captain Nolan and his son's murder years later, all linked to the Shadows. It sounds strange, but I know the stories of many dead people better than those who knew them when they were alive."

"Me, too," he said quietly.

"In a way I guess we both do the same thing."

"But our goals are different. *Lo hago por la justicia.*" Mine is justice.

"History is important, too," she said, "because those who forget the past have no future."

She was stunned to hear about multiple dead infants. Nazario swore her to secrecy. No press release had been issued and the detectives hoped to interview more witnesses before the story leaked out. Most shocking to Kiki was the suggestion that Pierce Nolan may not have been a clean-cut family man and civic-minded citizen.

"He hasn't been gone all that long. Many of his contemporaries are still alive. There's never been a hint, a rumor of anything negative, much less scandalous.

"Everything I've learned," she said earnestly, "everything said by people who knew him indicated that he was above reproach, that his death was a true tragedy for the community. The man might have gone on to become governor, might have changed the history of our city and state."

"How likely is it that some stranger planted those infants in his secret cellar? Some men do lead double lives, *mi amor.*"

"True." She took his big hand in her small one. "I'll get the nail polish remover."

Despite the odor, he enjoyed her daubing at his fingertips with a cotton pad.

They toasted the past, justice, and Miami until the La Crema Chardonnay was gone. Then they took a walk.

"Here, you take Fergie." Kiki handed him the leash. "She's the alpha dog. Di is the princess; she hates to step on damp grass or get her feet wet."

Their leashes were purple, befitting royalty.

"I never had a dog." The detective grinned as they all strolled together.

"You still don't. You can't keep her."

•   •   •

"I don't believe it's nearly two A.M.," he said at her door.

"Thanks for bringing me home."

He turned to go.

"You can call me, you know."

He nodded. "There's something I have to tell you," he said uneasily.

She waited.

"You know that little towel? The one with the butterflies?"

•   •   •

Pete Nazario drove home. Actually, to another man's home. The stately mansion, Casa de Luna, was the residence of multimillionaire W. P. Adair.

But Adair was almost never there. He and other wealthy Miami Beach residents often offered free lodging in servants' quarters, a guest cottage, or garage apartment to police officers, in exchange for security and peace of mind. Craig Burch had lived there when he and Connie were separated and once captured a pair of armed burglars in the act of looting the mansion. When he and Connie reconciled, Burch had recommended Nazario for the job.

Adair, rich, robust, and full of life for a man in his sixties, was touring Europe with his third or fourth wife, a knockout named Shelly, about one third his age. Nice work if you can get it.

Nazario leaped at the chance to save some money. His job was to maintain security and ride herd on the landscaper, the twice-a-week maid, the car washer, and the pool man.

Nazario's apartment, above the four-car garage, had originally been built for a live-in housekeeper and her caretaker husband. The separate entrance was at the top of an outside staircase. Rear stairs inside led down to the huge kitchen of the main house.

Moving in had taken little effort. Nazario's old apartment, which he'd occupied for years, was a furnished one-bedroom near Little Haiti. He traveled light. As a child, anything important to him had always vanished in the next move to a new place with total strangers. Eventually he'd learned to stop wanting things and, as an adult, never acquired many possessions.

He'd arrived with one bag, shaving gear, and toiletries, and his clothes on wire hangers stacked in his car. No furniture. No stuff. No baggage. If he wanted a book, he went to the library. He had always lived that way. *Un lobo solitario.*

Such a lifestyle never seemed lacking, until tonight. After spending time with Kiki Courtelis, he felt like the lost boy he had been. He trotted up the stairs, punched in the code, deactivated the alarm system, and let himself into the small apartment, the nicest place he'd slept in since he was six.

As he peeled off his jacket it occurred to him that he had never had a home. He went downstairs to patrol the grounds, thinking about Kiki as he checked doors and windows. She and her lifestyle were warm and appealing. So why, when he was with her, did he feel like some spaced-out astronaut who had strayed off the planet? He circled the house, walked through the garden and past the pool. Casa de Luna, on nearly two acres, was one of Miami Beach's largest private residences. Satisfied that nothing was amiss, he returned to his room.

Alone.

CHAPTER 6

"O.J. is free, searching Miami golf courses for his ex-wife's killer, but Martha Stewart is behind bars." Jo Salazar reached for a garlic roll.

"Go figure." She licked her fingers, eyes rolling in ecstasy. "These are so good! What is it with judges? Whatever happened to the concept of creative sentencing?"

"Right," Riley said. "Instead of jail time, she could've done so much righteous community service." They were devouring green salad and drinking red wine while waiting for their mushroom pizza at Mario the Baker's.

"I used to tape her TV show," Riley confessed.

"You, too?"

"How lame are we? Fans of a convicted felon," Riley said.

"She could have been sentenced to teach child-rearing classes to welfare mothers," Salazar said. "How much child abuse and neglect might that have prevented? Her classes could have been made into training films. They could've been used for years, could have affected still-unborn generations."

"You're preaching to the choir, Jo. What about Habitat for Humanity? Part of her sentence could have been community service, teaching recipients how to take care of their new homes. Most never owned or even lived in a house before, don't have a clue about upkeep, what to do with a yard, or how to start a garden. She could've taught them how to decorate on a shoestring, as well. They could have presented the tapes of those classes to the new owners along with the house keys."

"Exactly," Salazar said. "And she could've taught people in low-income neighborhoods how to cultivate community vegetable gardens in vacant lots, then how to prepare the produce they grew."

"No limit on the skills she could've shared with the have-nots. How to knit, sew, crochet, how to make their own clothes. She could have taught inner-city young marrieds how to make a home together. Instead they assign Martha to scrub the floor in the warden's office. They blew a once-in-a-lifetime chance to tap into a treasure trove of talent. Why aren't we judges?" Riley demanded.

"Because somebody has to catch the real bad guys and put them away." Salazar wolfed down another warm, fresh roll, drenched in olive oil and garlic and sprinkled with parsley.

She caught Riley's expression. "I do watch my calories," the prosecutor said defensively. "I watch them on my fork as I shovel them into my mouth."

Riley laughed. "I didn't say a thing. Whoever thought when we were roommates at the police academy a hundred years ago that we would wind up still like this."

"Look at me now," Salazar said, "an old married lady with two kids, who I hope to God are in bed. Their father promised me they would be. You can't believe how they can actually manipulate that man into letting them stay up as late as they like. They know how to wrap him around their fingers."

"I wonder who they learned that from?" Riley said.

"And look at you . . ."

"Yeah, me," Riley said quietly. "Spinster with a gun . . ."

"Spinster?" Salazar nearly spit up a fork full of romaine. "Are you crazy? Did you date that studly FBI agent Conrad Douglas yet?"

Riley looked wistful. "No, he came by my office the other day. He's a nice guy. We had coffee and shot the breeze about some investigations. But I just can't. Not yet."

"You knocked his socks off." Salazar reached across the table and squeezed Riley's hand. "Time's a wasting, Kath. You may not find another Kendall McDonald. But you'll find another man just as choice in his own special way."

"He was the one, Jo, since elementary school. I still expect to see him at the station, around the next corner, or on the elevator. I expect to hear his voice when the phone rings. It's so hard to believe he's really gone."

"Probably that damn closed-casket funeral. They give no sense of closure, you don't really get to say good-bye."

Riley bit her lip.

"Sorry, Kath. I'm just saying you can't stay off the market forever. Life goes on. Hey, here comes the pizza!"

• • •

"You're sure they said to paint it red?" Burch squinted at the fire-engine-red walls.

Connie nodded. "The Feng Shui consultant, the bagwa, said it's the room best positioned for passion and love."

"But it's the goddamned laundry room."

"I know." She frowned. "Architects are not in tune with the elements. The bagwa used the Tibetan Divination system. I added crystals and live plants in the bedroom and rearranged the furniture, but unless we change rooms with Jennifer . . ."

"What's Jennifer's room got to do with it?"

"The bagwa said it has the highest sexual energy in the house."

"Crap."

He'd been worried about that. "Where are they?" he asked, looking around.

"Jenny went to a movie with Lindsey and Heather. Craig Jr. is at softball practice under the new lights at the park, and Annie is at a sleepover at her new best friend, Tara's, house."

"We have to start keeping better tabs on them." He followed his wife into the kitchen. "They're growing up too fast. Man, I hate summer. This is the most dangerous time of year for kids. Do we know Tara's father? Is he a stepfather? Who is this guy?"

"I think you had a beer with him at the block party last year. Did you miss lunch?" she said. "Poor baby, are you hungry?"

He nodded.

She ladled her homemade mushroom gravy onto the meat loaf and popped his plate into the microwave.

"Summer," he told her, "is when most teenagers have their first sexual experience. No school. Time on their hands. Slam-dancing hormones, and the next thing you know . . ."

"I think our kids are trustworthy," Connie said.

"Were we?"

She hugged his neck as he sat at the table. "We turned out okay, didn't we?"

The microwave beeped and she placed the steaming plate in front of him.

"That outfit Annie had on this morning, those little shorts and that top that shows her belly button. We can't let her walk around looking like a prosti-tot. She's only eleven."

"Why don't you tell me what you really think?" Connie smiled coyly from across the table. "Have you noticed that we're home alone for a change?" She cocked her head, smile fading. "What are you working on? What kept you so late?"

"A case, Con, a cautionary tale of what can happen to little girls, even at home with the parents who should protect them, much less out among total strangers.

"They're so smart," he agonized, "with cell phones, computers, and electronics, so sophisticated that it's scary—but they're still little kids." He buttered a roll, sopped up some thick gravy, and savored the taste. "Ahhh, this is great, Con."

"I know something even better."

He put his fork down as her bare foot caressed his thigh. He caught her instep and caressed her toes.

"I can't help worrying about the kids," he confessed, "especially after a day like today. Why do they call them the echo generation? I don't remember anything like it in the past. No surprise that their pop star icon has the initials B.S. I want that poster out of Annie's room."

"Think inspirational thoughts about a happy, healthy, and fulfilling evening, sweetheart."

*   *   *

"What's this?" Shiny pistils and stamens bristled from planters in every corner of their bedroom.

"Remember?" she said. "I told you I rearranged some things. The kids helped."

"But where's—"

"Bedrooms should be kept free of clutter, so the chi can flow freely."

"I don't even want to know what that means. Why is the bathroom door shut? And why'd you move the bed?"

"If a doorway and the head of the bed share the same wall, it can make you restless and disturb your sleep. If there's a door to the bathroom, it should be kept closed."

"Nothing's disturbed my sleep so far. But walking smack into the bathroom door in the middle of the night just might do it."

"You're still unenlightened, sweetheart." She pulled her sunshine-yellow T-shirt off over her head. "From now on we are all about living in harmony with nature. You'll see. Relax and feel the vitality. Would you rather try the utility room?"

"No way." He watched her unbutton her shorts.

•   •   •

Jennifer returned home shortly before midnight and went straight to the refrigerator. Her dad joined her for Oreos and a glass of milk.

"How's your summer been so far, sweetie?"

"Swell, Daddy," she said.

"Good. Jen," he said. "Tell me, what kind of things are you thinking about sex these days?"

"Euuuuw, Daddy!" She made a face and fled to her room.

CHAPTER 7

"What this place needs is more green plants." Nazario eyed the few limp specimens in the homicide office. "The place would be healthier, less stressful."

"Eu tu?" Burch said. "What the hell is this?"

"Green is good," Corso agreed. "Your wife would agree, I'm sure. How's Connie doing?"

"Baked her homemade meat loaf last night with the mushroom gravy. I swear, it's better than sex."

Stone grinned and shook his head. "Sarge, my grandmother makes grits into little hand-molded dumplings. The crackling brown coating on her Southern fried chicken is beyond belief. So are her biscuits and cornbread, her sugar snap peas, her corn and scallions with butter, and her hush puppies with tomatoes and corn, but *none* of them are better than sex."

"Yeah, showing your age, Sarge, or maybe your sex life needs a little boost," Corso said.

"I'm about to give you a little boost, right out that window. 'Better than sex' is nothing but a goddamned figure of speech." Burch frowned. Corso had been in the lieutenant's office again, their heads together, when he arrived that morning. What the hell was it with those two?

"Ever tell you 'bout how I made Officer of the Month?" Corso was regaling Stone and Nazario with his war stories. "I made it twice. My ex-wife stole the plaques.

"See, right out of the academy you have to do a year in uniform, it's mandatory—*unless* they need a fresh face in Narcotics. I did eighteen months in Narcotics. Drinking and buying dope every night. We worked undercover six P.M. to two A.M. What a life! They'd give us three hundred dollars, city money, and tell us to go hang out on the strip. The hotel owners loved us. They wanted us there. We'd drink in the hotel bars. We were supposed to nurse one drink all night, but the bartenders knew who we were and kept pouring us more.

"The security guard at the Holiday Inn was an old geezer, a retired Baltimore cop. 'Pops,' we told 'im, 'anytime you need anything, call us. Anytime.' We never shoulda said that, 'cause he called us every god-damned night. One night he says he can smell marijuana smoke in a couple's room. Wants us to come kick down the door and arrest them. So we knock, then kick down the door. The toilet is flushing fast and furious.

" 'Where's the marijuana?' we ask. 'There is no marijuana,' this smart-ass punk says. All we find is residue in the toilet, that's all. He keeps giving us lip. So we grab 'im and hang him over the eleventh-floor balcony by his heels. 'See that pool down there?' we tell 'im. 'We're gonna drop you in it. Maybe you'll survive, if you don't hit your head on the bottom.'

"He's screaming bloody murder.

"We hear a call go out on the radio, a possible suicide, somebody threatening to jump off a balcony at the Holiday Inn. They're dispatching uniforms. I jump on the radio. 'We're in the neighborhood,' I say. 'We'll handle it.'"

"So," Stone said. "What happened?"

"We handcuff the guy, Baker-Act 'im, and commit 'im to County for a three-day psych evaluation.

"The hotel manager writes the department a letter of commendation. I get called in, honored for pulling the guy off the balcony and saving his life. I made Officer of the Month.

"Loved that gig. But one night, we're drinking and shooting at the statues in the garden at the Tahiti Motel and a new sergeant shows up. 'What the hell are you doing?' he says. 'Gimme your guns.'

" 'Wait a minute,' we say, and keep shooting till they're empty. 'Okay,' we say, 'you can take 'em now.'

"He didn't turn us in. But we were cocky. Got more aggressive and nasty. Kept throwing chairs through lobby windows. We would say it was part of our cover." He shrugged.

"The inevitable finally happens. I land back in uniform, taking orders, all that nitpicking shit. They kept saying, 'Write more tickets. Write more tickets.' So I set up a roadblock right across the street from headquarters. Wrote thirty, forty tickets a day. Defective equipment, driving too slow, no blinkers, no inspection stickers, dirty license tags. Wrote one guy four tickets, one for each balding tire. Citizens' groups start marching on the station, demanding to see the chief."

Corso smiled fondly at the good memories.

"Enough," Burch interrupted. "Now that our role model has inspired us to achieve greater heights in police work and public relations, let's get down to it. We're under the gun on Nolan."

"The ME said they took DNA samples from the infants' femurs," Nazario said.

"Good, but I gotta say," Burch said, "if it turns out to be what it looks like, I have little to no sympathy for the victim. Those girls were his own goddamn daughters."

"I know how it looks, Sarge," Nazario said. "But what I hear from Kiki and read in the old news accounts, and the original reports, the victim was straight arrow."

"Aha," Corso said. "Now it's *Kiki.*"

Nazario ignored him.

"You got another explanation for what was in that house? Let's hear it," Burch said. "In this business, the most logical explanation is usually the right one. I'm not saying we don't give it our best shot, but it won't make my day to charge some female with shooting her rapist, or her daughter's rapist, forty-plus years ago. So, before we step into that mess, let's go through Stone's case and see what we find."

• • •

They settled into the conference room and passed around copies of the file.

Stone sat stoic, rereading reports already seared in his memory. He watched the others study the photos and the medical examiner's report and wondered if they would reach the same stomach-churning conclusion he had.

Corso finally broke the silence. "I'm thinking that this wasn't no robbery."

"I agree," Nazario said solemnly.

"Right," Burch said. "The wounds make you think of one word—and it sure isn't robbery."

"*Ejecutados*," Nazario said. Executions.

The others nodded.

"After they were hit and down, there were additional head shots," Burch said.

"The coup de grâce," Corso said. "Two different guns." He cocked his head at Stone. "Wazup, dawg? What was your old man into? Making book on the side? Bolita? Doing a little loan-sharking? Was he into loan sharks? Prostitution? Did Pops have a rap sheet? What?"

"No." Stone sat stony faced. "I'm not bullshitting you. He was a small businessman, an entrepreneur. He and my mother worked long hours, seven days a week, trying to build a business, a future."

"Girlfriends? Boyfriends? Love triangle? Come on, dawg, hadda be something," Corso went on.

Stone's eyes flashed. "They were always at work or at home, together. Churchgoing people. They met young, up in Mississippi, on some freedom march or something. You know, a civil rights thing," he said, recalling stories he'd heard as a child. "They were hardworking, God-fearing solid citizens."

Burch planted his elbows on the table and leaned forward. "Where do you want to start, Stone?"

"I've thought for years about the police officer who delivered the death message to our house that night. He said he was first at the scene, but it was too late, nothing could be done for them. Reports in the file confirm that he found them.

"That man is why I'm sitting here today. It was raining and dark. This cop knocks at the door. My grandmother lost it. She started screaming. I was a little kid. He picked me up. Held me. Said everything would be okay. I always remembered him. Big and strong, a kind man. A good guy, what I wanted to be when I grew up. I saw him again at the funeral. He smiled and gave me a little salute. He's the one who made me want to be a police officer, to go to the academy someday. I couldn't remember his name. After I graduated I expected to find him here. Looked for him every day my first six months on the job. I knew I'd recognize him when I saw him, even though it was twelve or thirteen years later. But I never did. He must've retired.

"Ray Glover, badge number seven thirty-eight, it says in the file. According to Personnel, he quit seven months after the murders. I think it makes sense to sit down with him first. See if he agreed with the original detectives who attributed the murders to a pair of armed robbers who were hitting small businesses back then. Were those stickup artists ever caught? If so, were they cleared in this case? Were they involved in any actual shootings? How many cases, if any, did they cop to?"

"I can do that," Nazario said. "What's your grandmother think?"

"She's all hinky. Doesn't like to talk about it."

"Bad walk down memory lane? Or does she know something she won't say?" Burch asked.

"I'll find out for sure." Stone's words rang with a certainty he didn't feel.

"Do that. Try to find Glover today. Nazario will check out those old robbery cases. Me and Corso will work Nolan, talk to witnesses."

•   •   •

"I was with Pierce Nolan the night he was killed."

The detectives were seated in the living room of Richard Temple's palatial Coral Gables home.

"It was at the Dupont Plaza Hotel," Temple said. "A dinner meeting of the Fine Arts Association. Pierce was hell-bent on bringing more culture to Miamuh." The retired bank president chuckled. "I'm sure his wife, Diana, had some influence there. Not that Pierce didn't have a taste for the finer things in life himself. That was how the two of them met. He supported the Opera Guild, was eager to see Miamuh have its own ballet company, philharmonic, and symphony hall. He'd be pleased at the cultural climate we have heah today. Would have been achieved years sooner had that man not been cut down in his prime. After the meeting we retired to the hotel bar for a drink as usual. He always drank Scotch."

"Anything controversial come up at the meeting?" Corso asked.

"Not at all." Temple rested his hands on his cane. "We said good night, Pierce took off his jacket, threw it into the front seat of that big Buick he drove, and went off. Never saw him alive again. An assassin waited. What a tragedy. Pierce had nowhere neah achieved his full potential. He had an uncommon knack for bringing people together, could have gone on to accomplish anything. His killin' turned this town on its ear, a terrible loss to the community. The man was a local hero."

"Yeah," Burch said. "Heard he had quite a reputation."

"How many drinks did you two have in the bar?" Corso asked.

"One, as was our custom. Mainly an excuse to talk. I'm not even sure Pierce finished his."

"Any arguments in the bar?"

"No." He waved away the question, dismissing it with a clawlike arthritic hand. "The original investigators asked the same things, covered it all pretty thoroughly. I spoke with them often, trying to assist. Apparently I was the last known person to see him alive. A large reward was offered but it brought in no useful information."

"Was he the sort of man who would argue with another driver in traffic?"

Temple frowned at Corso. "You have to remembuh that the term *road rage* didn't exist in that Miamuh. Back then, we had no rush hour, no traffic to speak of. You could drive anywhere in Dade County, from one end to the other, in twenty minutes. It was a different Miamuh and Pierce Nolan was a gentleman."

"You mentioned the wife, Diana. Any trouble in the marriage?" Burch asked.

"Oh no, not at all. I'm sure Diana felt stifled down heah from time to time, but the loving relationship they shared more than compensated, I'm sure. She was raised in New York and Paris, a beautiful woman, educated at the Sorbonne, a vibrant socialite, debutante of the year when she came out. She was well traveled, played the harp, spoke several languages. She and Pierce met during one of his New York trips. She was one of the most sought-after young women in New York. He was a handsome, dashing fellow, an athlete and a war hero, interested in bringing the latest plays, dance troupes, and fine arts to Miamuh. I understand it was love at first sight. But he was wedded to Miamuh, his roots were heah. In those days, for a woman like her, this was a cultural wasteland. Not even a place heah to find the designer clothes she was accustomed to wearing. She and the girls, when they were old enough, took shopping trips to New York and Paris several times a year."

"So she was bored in the marriage?" Burch said.

"Not at all. They shared the challenge, worked together to improve the cultural climate and raise a family. Diana wasn't the sort to sulk or become bored. She was a woman of action and accomplishment. First rate at golf and tennis. They adored each other. My late wife and I were married for fifty-two years and I loved that woman dearly, but I must say I envied what those two shared."

"So it was all peaches and cream, huh?" Burch sounded skeptical. "How was his relationship with his daughters?"

"The girls were a delight, beautiful and musically talented like their mother. They all had a sense of joie de vivre. Diana always dressed them in white. They had those bright blue eyes like Pierce, and his black hair."

"Ever hear rumors that one or more of the girls might've been pregnant or had a child out of wedlock?"

"Outrageous!" Temple jerked back in his chair at the thought, his expression indignant. "Absolute nonsense, sir! They were very young. Pierce was protective of those girls, loved them so dearly. I doubt if a young man could get neah them. I nevuh saw a better father. He gave up politics to spend more time with them. Took them on trips, taught them to swim himself, used to carry them on his shoulders when they were little."

The detectives perked up, exchanging glances.

"And as they got older?" Burch said.

"Traditionally the father presents his daughter to society, has the first dance, and then the young man who is her escort cuts in. But when Summer, the oldest, came out, well, the young man nevuh had a chance. Pierce just waltzed and waltzed that beautiful girl around the floor until her head was spinning. What a beautiful picture that was."

"Yeah, I bet," Corso said.

"A pity," Temple said sadly, "that so many glorious traditions become lost to time."

"Have you been in touch with Nolan's widow through the years?" Burch asked.

"A few letters as Pierce's estate was being settled, but it ended there. She was high spirited, energetic, and active, her husband's death a terrible shock. Especially the manner in which it happened. I don't believe she ever recovered. Any thought of returning to Miamuh for even a visit was probably far too painful. I don't believe any of the children ever returned heah, either.

"Apparently she decided to cut all ties. Never heard from her again. The last I knew, she lived in San Francisco. Wasn't sure she was even still living until I read in the financial section of the newspaper that the Shadows had been sold to a developer and she was listed as the seller."

He sighed. "Miamuh was a kinder, gentler place then, before all the immigration, drugs, and crime. To that community, Pierce's murder was the crime of the decade, the crime of the century. Even more so than the Mosler murder later. Everyone was in a state of shock. If a man of Pierce's stature could be killed, then no one was safe."

"Who do you think killed him?" Burch asked. "And why?"

"That's a question I would dearly love to see answered before I die. His death is one of those nagging, unanswered enigmas that preys on my mind late at night. Who? Why? I do have one simple suggestion for you gentlemen. Instead of covering the same turf so thoroughly plowed by your predecessors, it might be more beneficial for you to branch out, be more original, and seek other avenues of investigation. In simpler words, why waste your efforts in a berry patch already picked dry?"

"Any original avenue or new berry patch you'd like to suggest?" Burch asked.

The old man shook his head thoughtfully. "You're the trained investigators, gentlemen. That's your department."

Temple struggled out of his chair, leaning on his ornate cane as he saw them to the door.

"Ain't he in for a shock when this story hits the headlines," Corso said outside.

"I need to talk to the widow before it does," Burch said.

●   ●   ●

Diana Nolan's officious secretary was persistent. She insisted she had to know the precise nature of their business with her employer before putting the call through.

"Her husband's murder," Burch said bluntly.

The Widow Nolan sounded wary. "Why would you call about that after all these years?"

"There's been a new development in the investigation," Burch said.

She said nothing.

"Mrs. Nolan?"

"Yes, I'm here."

"We'd like to interview you and your daughters."

"Brooke is here in San Francisco. I've been estranged from the others for years." Her voice sounded brittle.

"And your son?"

"Sky rode away on his motorcycle one day. He hasn't kept in touch."

"How long ago was that?"

"I don't recall precisely. Sometime in the early 1980s, I think."

"More than twenty years ago?"

"That sounds about right."

"And you don't know the whereabouts of your older daughters, either?"

"I didn't say that. My attorney must have their addresses. We've been in litigation."

"What sort of litigation?"

"Various family matters over the years, too personal to discuss with strangers. I'm busy now. Is there anything else?"

"The new development in the case—aren't you curious?"

"Oh," she said, as though absentminded. "Certainly."

"It was triggered by your sale of the Shadows."

Silence.

"The house is about to undergo demolition. So we went out to take a look, hoping to find some new clue to your husband's murder."

"And?"

"We did. In a box, in the basement."

She said nothing.

"Do you remember that box in the basement?"

"I never liked going down there. I was afraid of rats."

"Do you know what we found in it?"

"I'm not really interested. How would it have anything to do with my husband's death?"

"We hoped you could tell us."

"Frankly, I have no idea what you're talking about. I haven't set foot in that house since August 1961. If you have any further questions, you can direct them to my attorney. I'll give you his number."

"Something wrong, Boss?" Corso caught Burch's expression as he hung up.

"Nah, just shell shock from talking to the Mother of the Year."

•   •   •

"Admittedly, they are not your typical family," said Mark Sanders, Diana Nolan's San Francisco attorney. "They keep me busy."

"Any criminal matters?" Burch asked.

"No. Any reason to believe there might be some now?"

"A good chance," Burch said. "A very good chance. We need your client to be more forthcoming." He asked about her history of litigation.

"All in the family. Paranoia, accusations, spite suits, and countersuits. They've been at it since my father first represented her thirty-five years ago. No sign of a truce. They'll fight to the death and the survivors will sue the estate."

"Is her son a litigant?"

"No, oddly enough. He ran, escaped the madness. I don't think he's spoken to any of them in years. It may stem from the trauma of the father's murder. People react to tragedy in different ways. Instead of making this family closer, it tore them apart. Sad, isn't it?"

Summer, he said, had pursued an acting career after the move to California. "Appeared in quite a few movies during the late sixties and seventies. Never the lead, but had some impressive credits."

"Anything I'd know?"

"A Western with Richard Widmark, the title escapes me, a horror flick starring Vincent Price, and a small role in an Elvis movie, among others. Her screen name was Kathryn Ashley."

"Why didn't she use her real name? Summer Nolan sure has a ring to it."

"My client," he said proudly. "We sued to prevent it. She didn't want the family name disgraced. You know, emotional distress and all that. Probably wasn't a winnable action but my client insisted, and it delayed Summer's pursuit of her first movie role long enough that her agent advised her to simply acquiesce and change it."

"Sounds pretty small and petty."

"That's nothing, for them.

"Summer was a gorgeous woman in her prime. Still was when I last saw her in court. They all were. My dad always said it was a shame they were all so unhinged. He used to try to gather them together in one room for mediation. Talk about hormones, he said. Whoooh."

Spring, he said, now lived at the Villages, a huge self-contained retirement community in central Florida. Summer lived in San Antonio and Brooke, the youngest, in San Francisco. "But don't presume by that that she and her mother speak. They have a love-hate mother-daughter relationship. At each other's throats, filing defamatory lawsuits today, dismissing them and taking a cruise together tomorrow.

"With the sale of the Miami property injecting an

infusion of forty million dollars into the mix, I'm clearing my calendar for the next round of complaints," he said happily.

• • •

Maude Wells was society editor at the *Miami News* in 1961. They found her in a Miami Beach nursing home.

"I remember them so well," she said from her wheelchair. "A beautiful family, exquisite lineage except, of course, for Pierce Nolan's father, that rascal of a rum-runner. But even at that, it was a fascinating marriage of Florida pioneer stock and New York society aristocracy. Stunning creatures, the entire family. The cameras just loved them. At every event photographers just flocked around them. The girls went to Cushman School. Excelled in everything."

"Ever hear any nasty rumors? Any gossip?" Corso asked.

She raised her eyebrows.

"Everybody we've spoken to said if anything was going on in Miami back then, you knew about it," Burch said.

"That's not the sort of column I wrote, young man," she said, smiling coquettishly. "But that doesn't mean that my ear wasn't always to the ground.

"Pierce broke a lot of hearts. Every eligible girl in Miami was writing to him, baking him cookies and sending packages when he was in the service during World War II. And when he came home wounded, everybody wanted to play nurse. But then he went off to New York and came home with his beautiful bride."

"Did their daughters miss a lot of school?"

"Only when they traveled, but they were top scholars nonetheless. Diana taught them so much. She was so accomplished."

"How did the girls and their father get along?" Burch asked.

"Those darlin' girls were all little tintypes of their mother. Pierce couldn't have loved them more."

"Now, that's what we're talking about," Corso said. "You think Pierce Nolan might have been . . . having unhealthy relationships with his daughters?"

"Oh, dear God, no!"

"Ever hear any talk about his sex habits?"

"I'll have you know that Pierce Nolan was no sexual predator, although I can assure you that most girls and women in Miami would have been absolutely delighted to accommodate him had he been."

"Did you attend his funeral?" Burch asked.

"Of course. Everybody who was anybody did. Heartbreaking, not a dry eye. Diana looked beautiful in black. The poor thing was so devastated she had to be held up at one point. The girls all wore white. People couldn't stop talking about the murder. It was such a sensational story. Some friends were upset that the widow left town so quickly, just a week or so after the funeral, and didn't stay to keep up the Shadows the way Pierce would've wanted. He loved that place. But it was understandable under the circumstances. Diana wasn't from here to begin with, didn't share his roots. And she hated gossip. I'm sure she hated the idea of people pitying her and the girls, talking, and watching their every move."

•   •   •

"I thought she was gonna stroke out when I asked if he was having sex with his daughters," Corso said in the parking lot.

"That's the problem with that whole damn older generation," Burch said. "They all live by that old axiom about only speaking well of the dead. If a guy's a son of a bitch, they're too damn genteel to say it. They're covering for him."

"Or," Corso said, "somebody else was diddling his daughters."

•   •   •

Summer answered her own phone.

"I was only sixteen at the time," she said.

"Builders are about to demolish the Shadows," Burch told her.

"Sad," Summer said. "How much did she get for it?"

"No secret," Burch said. "It's public record that your mother sold it for forty million dollars."

"Unbelievable."

"How was your relationship with your father?"

"Ask my mother."

"How is it that you're estranged?"

"Ask her," she said, and hung up with a bang.

• • •

Burch called Spring, at the Villages, and asked the same question.

"Ask my mother and sisters," she said peevishly.

"I already talked to your mother and Summer," he said impatiently. "Now I'm asking you."

"What did they say about me?" she demanded.

He sighed. "Do you remember the limestone cellar under the Shadows?"

He heard her quick intake of breath. "Cellar?"

"That's right. Where your grandfather, the rum-runner, stashed his booze."

"Ask my mother, but she'll lie, of course. She always does."

"Why?"

"She needs no reason. The woman has a fertile imagination and an evil mind. Even when she has no reason to lie, she will. Don't believe a word she tells you."

"You in touch with your brother, Sky? Exchange Christmas cards or anything?"

"Not that I remember."

• • •

Brooke operated a small high-end boutique in San Francisco.

"My mother said you called her." Her voice was a shaky whisper. "You have to talk to her lawyer. I can't say anything. I was only thirteen."

"You're not thirteen anymore," Burch said. "Your mother still tell you what to do?"

"I can't—"

He heard a rush of breath just before she hung up. He didn't know if her gasp was the prelude to a sob or a laugh.

●   ●   ●

"I can't believe we're all talking about the same people. Everybody describes them as the all-American family," Burch told his lieutenant during a team meeting. "In reality they're the most evasive, secretive, fucked-up bunch of dysfunctional suspects I ever talked to. They're all covering up something."

"Go see some of these people in person," Riley said. "Start with the daughter who lives in Florida. Take Nazario with you, and do it in a hurry. The press is pushing for the story."

"Just talked to the medical examiner's office," Nazario said. "The babies all appear to be healthy live births. Four girls, three boys."

"Christ," Burch said. "Live full-term babies."

"The umbilical cords were all healed or nearly healed. They had dried milk in their stomachs," Nazario said. "Causes of death still under investigation. No trauma or obvious birth defects. They're pushing the lab for speedy DNA results."

"Good," Riley said. "We'll need samples from members of the Nolan family. What else have you got?"

"The infants were wrapped in cloth and newspaper.

The newspapers were local, the cloths were dish towels and thin cotton baby blankets," Nazario said. "The lab deciphered the labels on the towels. The manufacturer's still in business and keeps good records. Sears stocked and sold that pattern between 1959 and 1973, when it was phased out. We had two Sears stores back then, as opposed to six now. There was the old downtown store on Biscayne Boulevard and the one that's still on Coral Way.

"I've got some info on Stone's case, too," he added. "The armed robbers, the initial suspects, had ironclad alibis. Two nights before the murders at Stone's Barbecue, they got into a running gun battle—with each other. They were free-basing cocaine and got into an argument over who was gonna drive the car to their next stickup. The argument escalated into a gunfight. Twenty-four hours before Stone's folks were killed, one of them was dead in the morgue and the other was in jail, held without bond on homicide charges."

"Darwin was right," Burch said.

As the detectives left her office, Riley called Burch aside. "Have you heard from Stone?"

"He's tracking down Glover, the first cop at the scene in his case. I'll probably hear from him any time now."

"I tried to raise him on the radio," she said. "No answer. Keep him on a shorter leash. This case is way too personal for the kid. He needs backup and supervision. His worst trait and his best is that he's like a runaway freight train."

"Hey," he said. "What the hell's going on? Look at that."

Every phone in Homicide was ringing. Every line lit.

CHAPTER 8

One of the old-timers told Stone that Ray Glover had been close to a onetime partner in patrol, now retired and living in Steinhatchee, near the Gulf.

"Haven't heard his name in years," the retired cop said when Stone called. "Didn't stay in touch. I rode with Glover, can't say anything bad about him. Not a bad guy. Maybe that was his trouble, a little too idealistic. Most rookies lose that in six months. Not him. He was one a those do-gooders, saw everything in black and white, couldn't make adjustments, you know. Why you looking for him after all this time?"

"Some questions about an old case of his," Stone said.

"Not surprised. Ray left under some kinda cloud. Heard scuttlebutt he was a troublemaker. No paper on it. Nothing official. Heard he moved up somewhere around Orlando. That's the last I know."

Stone felt a surge of energy. He could drive to Orlando in four hours.

No Orlando phone listing for Raymond H. Glover. Stone found a 1989 address and phone number in a database of old city directories. The number wasn't good anymore, but he called three neighbors. One remembered him. "An ex-cop. Miami, I think. Young fella, friendly enough. Stayed around here for just ten, eleven months, worked security at Mouse World, then moved on. A little paranoid. Said not to tell anybody where he was going. But you're official, right? He asked me to make sure his mail was forwarded to a post office box over in Mount Dora."

Stone tracked Glover from Mount Dora to Kissimmee and from there to Sarasota, on to Cedar Key, up to Ocala, and then west to Immokalee.

A woman answered at the last number listed for Glover in Immokalee.

"Is this the Glover residence?"

She hesitated, as though uncertain. "Yes."

"Can I talk to Ray?"

"No." She sounded flustered. "He, he's not here." Her voice faded.

"When do you expect him?"

"I— I'm not sure. I don't know." She spoke quickly, in a Southern accent, the words so soft he could barely hear them.

"Is this his wife?"

"I have to go now." She hung up.

Despite her reticence, Stone was elated. Immokalee was about 115 miles from Miami, a little more than two hours away. He checked an unmarked out of the motor pool, made sure the gas tank was full, and hit the road.

He considered stopping to tell Gran but decided against it. He'd tell her after he'd made progress, so she would see he was serious. Besides, he was in a hurry.

He took the turnpike north, then Alligator Alley due west, flying low, glad to be alone. He'd waited a long time for this day. He tried to picture Ray Glover's face almost twenty years older.

However he had aged, he knew he would recognize the man any time, any place. He would ask for his help, but more than that he wanted to tell Glover what he had meant to him, to let him know that he had changed one life forever. It was important, he felt, to express how in life's vast tapestry, a small kindness or a few words can resonate through the years.

He stopped for a cup of coffee and took it with him, checking the time all the way.

He'd sit across from Glover, seek information, and pour out his heart. The man might not remember him. If so, he'd say, "But I remember you, Officer Glover. That's what counts."

Visualizing their meeting, anticipating their conversation, Stone raced toward the sun. If he made good time, he might even arrive early enough to buy the man dinner. Even if he wasn't home, finding Glover in a small town like Immokalee should be no problem.

He made good time until a tanker truck jackknifed, rolled over, and spilled diesel fuel onto I-75 near the Big Cypress Indian Reservation. Trapped in gridlock with countless other hot and frustrated motorists, Stone despaired. Twenty minutes after traffic finally began to move, an Everglades brushfire again slowed motorists to a crawl through dense, eye-stinging, foglike smoke.

Closer to Naples, he hit rush-hour traffic. It was

nearly sunset when he rolled into Immokalee; then he had trouble finding Glover's address.

He was surprised that it was a trailer park. He drove slowly through the narrow lanes, watching out for speed bumps, loose dogs, and small children. A few residents, drinking beer as they barbecued outside, stared suspiciously. All were white. Some of their trailers were in good condition, with small, neat flower beds; others were in states of disrepair, rusted, with sagging awnings.

One of those belonged to Glover.

The day had wound down, the curtain of darkness had fallen. Streetlamps had bloomed. Stone parked, stepped over a bicycle chained to the trailer, and approached the door. There were lights inside and voices. He thought he smelled hamburgers frying and frowned regretfully, remembering his hopes for dinner.

He thought of his grandmother, imagined telling her every detail when he got back to Miami.

She'd be impressed by his persistence, his progress. She'd help him.

His heart beat faster as he knocked at the narrow door.

The voices stopped. The lights blacked out inside. Startled, he knocked again. Only silence.

"Hello?" He rapped sharply on the glass portion of the door. "Ray Glover?"

He knew they were in there. He'd heard them. He'd waited so long. He'd driven so far.

"Mrs. Glover?"

"Go 'way. I'm calling the police." It was the woman, the same thin, small voice as on the telephone.

"Mrs. Glover, I *am* the police. Detective Sam Stone, Miami P.D. Here, I'll slide my business card under the door."

He did so, then reached for his badge case. He hopped up to the top step to display it at the window when a bloodcurdling, high-pitched shriek came from behind him.

A skinny wraith burst out of the darkness, wildly swinging a baseball bat. Shocked, thrown off-balance, Stone nearly fell off the narrow steps. The first swing narrowly missed his midsection. He felt the rush of air as the second just missed his head. He stopped the next swing with his left hand, winced, then grasped the bat with both hands.

"Police! Drop it!" he shouted. They scuffled for a moment, until Stone tripped his attacker, wrenched away the weapon, and knocked him to the ground. Panting, the bat in one hand, Stone planted the other on the bony chest of a scrawny boy of about twelve and held him down. The barefoot kid had a runny nose and tears in his eyes, but kept kicking and flailing.

The trailer door flew open and a woman scrambled out screaming, "Don't hurt him! Don't you hurt him!"

"I don't plan to," Stone said, perplexed. "What's wrong with you people?"

She was a skinny redhead with lank hair and pale skin.

"Calm down, ma'am, I'm here to see Ray Glover. All I want is five minutes of his time."

"I called the police." She stared at him, her gray eyes haunted.

"Fine," he said. "They'll confirm who I am and set your mind at ease." He didn't feel as confident as he sounded. This part of Florida was more like the Deep South than Miami.

He took his hand off the boy's chest and reached down to help him to his feet. The boy didn't respond. He'd stopped kicking and just lay there panting.

"Son, you can't go around attacking people with baseball bats," Stone said. "That could land you in a world of hurt and trouble." He held the bat up. "This thing is for hitting home runs and winning baseball games."

The boy stared up at him, expression uncomprehending, like a frightened animal.

"Come on, baby." The woman helped the youngster to his feet and held his hand.

"You the one who called?" she asked Stone.

"Yeah, that was me."

Fellow trailer park residents, who'd gathered to gawk, began to wander away.

Stone thought it was because the excitement was over, then saw the approaching police cruiser, blue light spinning. He sighed. He should have brought another detective. Even Corso would be better than nobody. Nah, he thought, watching the two cops step out, that would probably end up three against one.

The deputies were young and overweight, in starched uniforms that were too tight and uncomfortably creased. He wondered how they could ever run should the need arise.

"Ha there, Katie," one said with a smirk. "Whatcha'll

got going on heah this time? Who's your friend?"

Stone identified himself.

"Miamuh? Thought all they hired down there was Cubans. Empty your pockets, boy. Right there on the hood a that car."

Stone was frisked, his gun and badge case confiscated.

"Look, Reggie," the other one said, "how his hand's all swoll up. Looks like the kid got hisself in a good lick."

They confirmed that Stone's unmarked was registered to the City of Miami.

Humiliated, Stone stared balefully at the redhead.

"Reggie," she finally said to one of the deputies. "Ain't nothing wrong here. This fella's an acquaintance. I was half asleep, got scared when there was a knock at the door, and Jimmy went off half-cocked. You know, 'cause of all the burglaries 'round here." She turned to Stone. "Since the last storm, looters have been breaking in right and left."

The cops insisted on confirming Stone's identity with his supervisor. Eventually, as neighbors began to wander back to watch, they reached K. C. Riley.

"*She*"—the deputy gloated, exchanging glances with his partner as he handed Stone the phone—"wants to talk to you."

"That you, Stone?"

"Right, Lieutenant."

"You okay?"

"Sure, fine." He flexed the fingers of his swollen hand.

"Are you sure? Can they hear me?"

"Not at the moment."

"Good. I don't know what the hell you think you're doing over there, Detective. But I *will* see you in my office bright and early in the morning. Got that?"

"Sure thing, Lieutenant."

"Watch your ass. Now let me talk to them."

Stone handed the phone back.

He heard her voice but couldn't make out the rapid-fire words. The deputy reacted as though his cell phone had suddenly become red-hot and blistered his ear.

"Ooo whee," he said as he snapped the small phone shut. "You work for that woman?"

Stone nodded.

"You have muh sympathy. No wonder Miamuh's a mess. Anything you need, Detective, let us know."

He winked at the woman. "And you know that goes for you, too, Katie."

She shook her head as they drove away.

"Can we talk?" Stone asked.

She nodded. "But ain't nothing to tell. Is your hand hurt bad?"

"It'll be okay," he said.

He followed them into the trailer, making sure the boy wasn't behind him.

"Where's Glover?" The inside of the trailer was drearier than the exterior. He was surprised that Glover hadn't kept it up better.

"He's not here." She shook her head. "I kep' the phone number even though it was in his name. I knew I shouldn'ta done it, it'ud just bring trouble. But if I wanted to change the name on the account, the phone company 'ud want a new deposit and I couldn't afford it."

The boy went to the small refrigerator, took out a can of Coke, turned on the TV, and sat down in front of it.

Katie sat at the small table.

"He's not living here?" Stone sat opposite her and flipped open his small notebook. "Where can I find him? Is he still here in town?"

She nodded. "Oak Land Memorial Park," she said softly. "He's in the second row south a the reflecting pool."

Stone blinked. His hand suddenly throbbed.

"Dead?" he whispered.

She nodded, eyes pained, and shoved back her dull red hair.

Stone felt the wind knocked out of him, as though he'd been sucker-punched.

She mistook his expression. "I'll get you somethin' for it." She went to the fridge and returned with a box of frozen peas. "This'll help." She put the box across the knuckles of his left hand and wrapped a towel around it.

"Thanks." He swallowed. "When did Ray die? What happened? You sure we're talking about the same man?"

She took a framed five-by-seven photo from a shelf. Stone held his breath, hoped for a moment it was all a mistake, then sighed. Ray Glover and Katie were seated at a table together in the photo. The occasion looked festive, a wedding or a holiday celebration.

Their tilted heads touched each other as they faced

the camera, his arm around her. Her face wasn't as thin then, her upswept hair looked shiny, and she smiled shyly. Ray Glover smiled, too, but there was something different about him. Something Stone didn't remember. Despite his smile, the man's eyes looked lost, hunted.

Stone stared at the image of the man he'd expected to break bread and share talk with tonight. Why hadn't he come sooner?

Katie took the picture from him and gazed at it for a long moment.

"He's kilt." A tear skidded down one freckled cheek. "They kilt him. Left him to die like an animal in the road."

"Who?"

She shrugged. "They never caught 'em. Nobody knows. But Ray knew. He knew and I never listened."

A hit-and-run, she said. Ray had gone out jogging, as usual, at eight A.M. He never came back. They found him in the roadway near the jogging path he used most mornings.

"I never believed him," she said. "He wanted to move again. I didn't wanna go this time. He said it was too dangerous to stay here."

"What danger? Was he threatened?"

She nodded. "Something hanging over him. He never said what. From back when he was the law, I think."

They had met in Orlando. She was from Medlin, Georgia, a twenty-year-old cocktail waitress with a drug problem. He helped her kick cocaine, saw her through re-hab. When he left town, she went with him. Again and again. They never married. He said it wouldn't be fair to her until he cleared something up. He never explained what that something was.

He was killed fourteen years ago, three years after leaving Miami. Dead at twenty-seven, a year older than Stone was now.

"I can't believe he's been gone all this time," he said miserably, the box of frozen peas still melting on his hand.

"Did you know him?"

"I met him," Stone said bleakly. "He made a big impression. He's the reason I'm a policeman."

Her fingers curled together on the tabletop. "He'da been pleased to hear that," she said softly. "I didn't know him when he was a law officer, but that was his happiest time. Then something happened—something went wrong."

"What did he tell you about it?" Stone said urgently.

She shook her head. "Not much. Ray was ambitious, wanted to get ahead. He was trying to investigate something and it all backfired on 'im. That's all I know. Was a lady used to write 'im sometimes. They'd talk on the telephone from time to time. But that was years ago."

Stone glanced at the boy, engrossed in the TV.

"Mine," she said. "Born a couple years after Ray got kilt. His daddy's not in the picture. I made some mistakes. But I'm blessed to have him. He's all I got. He came three months early and had to stay in the hospital a long time. He's a sweet boy. Slow, but a real sweet nature."

Stone recalled the boy's shrieks, his crooked teeth gritted as he swung the bat.

"He's very protective of his mom," she said. "I'm so lucky. I've got him, and I had Ray."

Katie said she now waitressed at the IHOP just off the highway nearby. "You hungry? We was just making burgers."

The burgers sat congealed in grease, in the now-cold frying pan.

"No," Stone said. "I want to take you and your son out to the best restaurant in town, but I have to work tonight and then get back to Miami. I'm not sure when, but I'll be back."

She walked him to the door, the TV blaring in the background. The boy never looked up.

She picked up the business card Stone had slid under the door. Squinting, she scrutinized it.

"Look at that," she said in her small, soft voice, when he was halfway out the door. "You have the same last name as that lady, the one Ray used to talk to on the phone, the one who wrote him letters."

CHAPTER 9

HOUSE OF HORRORS, the headline screamed. Under it, the slightly more restrained subhead in the afternoon paper read: *Seven Dead Infants Found.*

"I like it." Corso displayed the front page proudly. "Didn't I tell ya? That place woulda made a perfect haunted house. It says we made 'a grisly discovery.'"

"How'd they get the story?" Nazario demanded. "Had to be Edelman."

"A reporter called PIO a couple hours ago, said the paper was gonna go with the story and needed a quote from the department," Burch said. "The chief told Riley to speak for us. She gave Padron bare bones, no pun intended, for a press release but asked him to try to persuade them to hold the story one more day. They didn't."

"Bet that brightened her day," Corso said. "You know how she feels about the press."

Lieutenant Riley's quoted comments were terse.

Cold Case Squad detectives were investigating both the 1961 murder of Pierce Nolan and the discovery of the dead infants. Whether the two were related had not yet been determined.

"Pick up your phone," Emma, Riley's secretary, called to Burch. "It's PIO."

Burch gritted his teeth and answered. Padron told him that Edelman had already called the police three times since the paper hit the street to report trespassers, reporters, television news crews, and sightseers with shovels all invading the Shadows.

"That's still a goddamn crime scene," Burch barked irritably. "Notify the uniformed lieutenant in that sector. If the crime scene tape has been taken down, put it back up. Arrest anybody who violates the scene, including that son of a bitch Edelman."

"Wonder how he likes having his exciting new condo project renamed the 'House of Horrors.' How ya think it'll affect pre-construction sales?" Corso chortled.

The phones continued to ring nonstop. "Take that file into the conference room," Burch told Nazario, "and study it till you know chapter and verse. We're gonna have to hit the road, go talk to members of that family eye to eye."

•   •   •

Pierce and Diana Nolan sat in elegant straight-back chairs. The girls, in billowy white dresses, posed gracefully around them. The boy, Sky, sat on the floor at their feet. Nazario tried to read the faces in the formal family portrait, circa 1960.

Summer had big, dark fringed eyes, lush hair down her back, and a tiny Scarlett O'Hara waist. The detective's eyes lingered on her as he wondered. The other girls were as slim. Diana, also serene in white, was slender and nicely proportioned, despite being the mother of four.

Summer, alone in her room, music playing, heard the shotgun blasts, first one, then another, shatter the night, according to her statement.

In their shared bedroom, Brooke was occupied by homework left by her math tutor, while Spring chatted on the telephone with a classmate.

The housekeeper, Sandra Martin, forty-seven, had gone home at six P.M. after preparing dinner. Housekeepers always know a family's secrets. Nazario did a computer check, trying to locate her. He found her death certificate, dated 1979, natural causes.

Sky, who was supposed to be doing his chores, was hiding instead, playing explorer in the tunnel.

Diana Nolan was writing a letter at the dining room table, classical music playing on the stereo, when she thought she heard her husband's car. She went to the front window, she said, then went to look for Sky.

Investigators noted that blood droplets and smears had been found on and in the shrubbery on both the west and south sides of the house. The blood was human, A-positive, and was believed to have come from the killer. The evidence, small traces on leaves and grass, was now unavailable for DNA testing. It had been lost or discarded, possibly in the move to the new station years earlier.

Nazario closed the file and took the elevator down to Missing Persons. No unresolved missing-baby cases reported in Miami that summer of '61. His phone rang as he returned to his desk.

"Hi, it's me," Kiki said. "Edelman was just on Channel Four, absolutely apoplectic. I thought something was wrong with my TV, his face was so red. Accused you of trying to delay his project."

"Me?"

"The whole police department. Claims I put you up to it."

"Thanks, I'll let the lieutenant know."

"Okay, but before you go, would you like to have dinner at my place tonight?"

"No, thanks."

"You can wear my nail polish," she coaxed.

"Cut that out." He grinned.

"Tomorrow night?"

"Nope."

"Okay," she whispered, shot down.

"No way. Not when it's my turn to take you out."

"Oh! Okay."

"But first thing in the morning I have to go outta town and I'm stuck reading statements tonight. I'll give you a jingle as soon as I get back."

He thought about her as he drove home to Casa de Luna. He parked in the shadowy driveway then trotted upstairs to his empty apartment.

But the place looked far from empty. The door stood ajar. A dim light shone from inside. He'd left no lights on.

He drew his gun and nudged the door open with his foot. A chill rippled along his spine.

The light came from the bathroom. It was enough to see that the bed he'd made that morning was disturbed. More than disturbed. Occupied. A naked woman lay facedown, tangled in the sheets, her soft brown hair spilled across his pillow.

What the hell was this? He'd seen no strange car in the driveway.

Was she alive? Was she alone?

He approached cautiously, gun still in his hand.

She was breathing, snoring gently. Relieved, he checked the bathroom. She'd used it, had scattered his toiletries about. He pulled the shower curtain back, checked the closet. No sign of anyone else. He walked lightly to the staircase leading down into the main house.

A light had also been left on in the futuristic stainless-steel kitchen. Cautiously, he descended the stairs. He found the kitchen in disarray, but not as though a thief had been stacking appliances to steal; it was as though someone had simply made a mess trying to find something to eat.

He checked the entire house. Nothing seemed missing, all the other windows and doors secure.

He stole back up the stairs half expecting her to be gone, a mirage, a fantasy, a figment of his imagination.

But she still snored gently in his bed.

This could be trouble. Serious trouble. He was alone with a naked intruder who could say anything. To protect himself, he should call the Miami Beach police. This was their jurisdiction.

Instead, he turned on the bedroom light. She did not react. Her underwear, a T-shirt, and a pair of blue jeans lay on the floor. He looked for her handbag but couldn't find it.

What if she started screaming?

It was easy to see she wasn't armed. The thought struck him that this was every man's fantasy: arrive home after a hard day on the job and find a beautiful, naked woman in your bed.

So why did he have such a bad feeling? Because, he thought, fantasies never happen in real life. Not to him, anyway.

She didn't look homeless. Golden highlights streaked her silky hair and her manicure, though chipped, looked professional. Two shiny gold studs sparkled in the ear he could see. A thin gold ring winked from one of her toes and there was a tattoo on her left ankle, a blue half moon. No jailhouse tattoo, he noted on closer examination; it was professionally done.

He sighed and put his gun on the dresser, out of her reach.

He took out his badge case, stood over the bed, and gently tapped her on the shoulder. Her skin was soft. He detected the smell of liquor.

"Excuse me," he said.

She groaned and rolled over without opening her eyes.

"Hello?" he said. "*Hola*. Ma'am?"

She moved over to make space for him on the bed.

Was this a joke? Was he being set up? He scanned the room for peepholes, cameras, or Alan Funt.

This didn't make a damn bit of sense.

He wondered what Kiki would think.

"Wake up, ma'am. Wake up. I'm a police officer. I need to see some ID."

Her eyelids fluttered, as though disturbed by the latter.

"Hummmmhhhhff," she protested, eyes squeezed shut like a child unwilling to get up and go to school.

"Rise! Shine! Show me your identification."

Her eyes slowly opened. They were hazel, flecked with gold, the pupils dilated.

"Who're you?" she mumbled. Dazed and pale, she propped herself up on one elbow.

"You first," he said. "I live here."

"Me, too. Used to."

"What's your name?"

"Fleur Adair."

"You know W. P. Adair?" he said.

She nodded numbly.

"This is his place."

"My father." She grimaced at the word, as though pained, then squinted sleepily at Nazario. "You Shelly's boyfriend?"

"Shelly?"

"My stepmother."

"Hell, no. I'm security here, keep an eye on the house when they're out of town. The old man didn't say anything about you coming in."

"Doesn't know." She pushed back her hair and tried unsuccessfully to sit up.

"You, uh, want a robe or something?"

"Okay," she said affably, eyes closing.

He had no robe. Neither did she, so he gave her one of his shirts, a guayabera.

"How'd you get in here without setting off the alarm?"

"Tol' you, I used to live here. He always uses his birthdate, or my brother's, as the code, and he always hides spare house keys in the cabana and under the statue of the sprite by the fountain in the garden."

Nazario frowned. He had to have a serious talk with Adair about security.

"Is he still married to Shelly?"

"Right, they're in Europe."

"Crap." She fell back on his pillow, eyes closed.

"Don't go back to sleep."

She didn't answer.

"I've got their number if you want to talk to them."

"No!" Her eyelids fluttered in alarm. "Don't tell 'em I'm here."

A definite red light. "Why, if you're his daughter?"

"Shelly hates me. I'm not allowed in the house." She licked her lips. "Got a cigarette?"

"No. They're not good for you."

There was no humor in her laugh. "I need a drink."

"I don't have any booze here, either."

"There's plenty downstairs."

"You helped yourself, didn't you? Knew where the key to the liquor cabinet was, too?"

"No. Had to bust the lock."

"*Coño*, you shouldn't've done that. I'm responsible. Your ID—where is it?"

She shrugged. "Stolen, in Atlanta."

"I need proof that you are who you say."

She shrugged again.

He stood over her, arms folded, waiting.

"I know." She brightened. "If they're still there." She

swung her legs over the side of the bed, wincing at the sudden movement.

He persuaded her to pull on her blue jeans before they descended the inside staircase into the kitchen. She led the way, padding barefoot, down the long hall to her father's study.

Numerous framed photos of Adair and his wife Shelly adorned his massive mahogany desk. Dressed for skiing, sailing, and for fancy dress balls.

"Oh, shit, that's her." Fleur picked one up. "Would you believe that Shelly was my roommate at college? I brought her home for Thanksgiving. Now she's in and I'm out."

She gazed sad-faced at the photo.

"Where's *your* picture?"

"Lessee, unless she threw them all out, should be some in here." She fumbled with a highly polished cabinet door.

"If that's locked, don't force it!"

"Don't worry." She pulled out a heavy leatherbound scrapbook.

"Look." She turned the pages, finally stopping at a family photo. "There I am. I was seventeen. And here I am with my dad on my eighteenth birthday."

Nazario's eyes went from the photos to her face and back again.

"That's you, all right."

"My mother moved to Seattle after the divorce. My father suggested I go live with her after Shelly said she didn't want me around. She said I made her uncomfortable. Then Mom married her personal trainer. He's a lot younger than she is, and she felt uncomfortable with me there."

Fleur took off with a boyfriend, a grunge musician from Seattle, she said. His band worked various gigs around the country, but the jobs ran out and their bus broke down in Atlanta.

The musician boyfriend asked Fleur to call her mother for money. She refused. They argued, but he apologized later the same evening and fixed her a drink in their motel room. Twenty-four hours later, she woke up bruised and sick, with a splitting headache. He was gone, with whatever money and good jewelry she had.

"The only thing I feel bad about," she said mournfully, "was my watch. My dad gave it to me on my eighteenth birthday."

"What did the cops do?" Nazario asked indignantly.

"I didn't call them." She shrugged. "I brought it on myself. It's not like it never happened before."

"*Dios mío, niña.* You got to pull your act together. How'd you get here from Atlanta?"

"Hitched."

"*¿Qué?* That's dangerous!"

"A trucker brought me most of the way. Nice guy."

"You're lucky to be alive! Please don't ever do that again. You using drugs?"

"He had some pot."

There was little food to speak of in the huge stainless-steel kitchen or in his apartment refrigerator, and she was hungry. He ordered a pizza.

While Fleur showered, Nazario called Sonya

Whitaker, W. P. Adair's longtime secretary/bookkeeper, at home.

"Fleur's there? Is she okay?"

"A little down on her luck," Nazario said. "Think the old man would mind if she spent the night?"

"Do what's right, Detective. Fleur's not welcome right now, thanks to Shelly. But blood is thicker, you know. Between you and me, Fleur will still be W. P. Adair's daughter long after his current wife is gone and, hopefully, long forgotten. I watched Fleur grow up. The poor kid got a raw deal.

"But don't mention her to Shelly, or to him, if they call. I'm the sole survivor from his original staff only because I know enough to stay out of that woman's way."

Fleur's color began to look a little better as they ate, though she insisted on beer with her pizza. He'd ordered salad, too, and a side of eggplant parmigiana.

"So, your name, it sounds French."

"They named me for the place where I was conceived. A town where artists congregate. It's where Vincent van Gogh cut off his ear."

"Nice." He frowned. "Look, you can stay here tonight. But that's it, unless you talk to your dad and he tells me different. I have to leave early in the morning. I'll be back tomorrow night or the next day. By then you gotta be outta here."

"Sure." She put down her fork and bit her lip. "Don't worry about me. I'll go to work tomorrow, find myself a place."

"What kinda work?"

"I go to parties."

"You mean you—"

"No. I'm not hooking, if that's what you're asking."

She explained as he rinsed the dishes in his little sink. When he turned, she held his gun in her hands.

"Cool," she said. "Is this real?"

"Hey!" He snatched it from her.

"I was just looking at it," she protested. "It's beautiful."

"Yeah, a work of art. But it can do ugly things."

When he went downstairs to check the property, he took the gun with him, unloaded it, and locked it in the glove compartment of his car.

●   ●   ●

"Why'd you come up here to go to sleep when you grew up in the main house?" he asked.

"I don't have a room anymore. My dad always kept my old bedroom for me, no matter who he was married to. But when Shelly redecorated, she got rid of my stuff. She made my room into a giant closet for her evening clothes. Has her collection of Judith Lieber evening bags on display, like art, in glass cases. So tacky.

"Besides, I always liked it up here." Her expression waiflike, she glanced around the familiar room. "When I was little and my parents were fighting, I'd sneak up here and sleep with Maria, our housekeeper."

Nazario gave her a T-shirt to sleep in.

"Take my bed. I'll sleep on the couch in the next room."

She tumbled into bed, then patted the spot next to her. "There's room right here."

"Look," he said firmly, "your father trusts me with his property. I can't take advantage of his daughter."

"You're not taking advantage," she protested. "I'm not sixteen years old, I'm twenty-four."

He shook his head. "You're making me uncomfortable."

"Sorry." Her voice sounded small. "I always do that to people. I don't mean to."

"I didn't mean it that way. It was my poor choice of words."

She didn't answer, alone in his bed.

He sighed and said good night.

He was nearly asleep when she came into the room and curled up next to him.

"What are you doing?" he grumbled.

"I don't wanna be alone. Just hold me."

He sighed. "I don't like being put into this position."

She began to whimper.

He got up, went to find a blanket, covered her, then sat down next to her. "Okay." He put his arm around her. "Get some rest and together we'll work things out for you, I promise."

CHAPTER 10

"Sorry to trouble you so late, but I have to go back to Miami tonight," Stone explained.

"No apology necessary, Detective." Dr. Peter Jensen, the Collier County medical examiner, fumbled for his key. The building, adjacent to a hospital, was minuscule compared to the Miami–Dade County Medical Examiner's sprawling complex. "Right now I welcome any reason to return to the office. My mother-in-law and her sister are paying their annual visit. They've been with us for the last ten days. Four more till they say adios."

Jensen, tall and bookish, with salt-and-pepper hair, tugged at his lower lip. He might remember the case, he said. When he pulled the file, he was sure.

"Yes, sir. Rang a bell when you mentioned that the victim was a former Miami law enforcement officer. That one struck me as out of the ordinary at first."

"How so?"

"He was the first dead jogger to come in here wearing a gun."

"Ray Glover was armed when he was killed?"

The doctor raised a thoughtful eyebrow and nodded. "A .25 caliber automatic weapon, fully loaded, as I recall. On a sunny spring Sunday, mind you, in this bucolic area with little crime or traffic. He wore it concealed in a cloth body holster. You know, the ones that wrap around the rib cage and fasten with Velcro. Unnoticeable under a baggy T-shirt.

"Unusual. Thought it might be worth looking into, an indicator of foul play or even suicidal tendencies, psychological problems, or paranoia on the victim's part.

"But there was a logical explanation once he was identified. Our dead jogger was a former Miami law enforcement officer, from a city where the violent crime rate had been enormously high.

"Wearing a gun was obviously his habit, a sign of the times and the environment to which he'd been accustomed. Probably wore a weapon routinely, the way I wear a wristwatch."

"Can I see the pictures and the autopsy report?"

"Certainly." The doctor shuffled out the eight-by-tens like oversized playing cards.

"Did you injure your hand, Detective? It looks swollen."

"A small mishap. It's fine." He picked up one of the photos. "Did you go out to the accident scene, Doctor?"

"No," Jensen said. "It was a Sunday. After church we brunch with friends at the country club. I think I got a call but the deputy said he didn't require my presence." He peered through his reading glasses at a document from the file.

"According to the report, the victim remained unidentified until late Sunday afternoon when one Katie Abernathy called the hospital to ask if there had been any accidents. Said her live-in boyfriend had never returned from his morning jog. She was referred to the sheriff's office, then came in and made the positive ID. I took my first look at the body on Monday." He leafed through the pages to the autopsy report.

"Ankle fractures and a grill pattern higher up on the thigh indicated that he was erect, on his feet, when hit, then went airborne. His head struck the windshield or roof of the vehicle that hit him, resulting in a scalp laceration and a depressed skull fracture. Then he fell off to the side. Typical scenario in pedestrian versus car fatalities.

"He had other fractures and internal injuries, but the head injury was the primary cause of death."

Stone stared at the grotesquely sprawled corpse on the blacktop and remembered the husky young cop whose strong arms had lifted him up on the darkest night of his childhood.

"I understand they never found the car or driver," he said. "Was there much physical evidence?"

The doctor frowned at a printout. "Flecks of white paint on the victim's clothing and in his hair, possibly from a GM vehicle, and bits of glass and plastic from a broken headlight and turn signal lens embedded in his skin. Nothing much good without a vehicle to match it to."

Stone frowned. That should have been enough to identify a make and model, he thought. "This was a divided stretch of roadway?"

"Yes, sir. Still is. Northbound. Drive it every day myself. There's a gully, a big, wide, grassy median that separates it from the southbound lanes. Joggers often use the bicycle path, which is about three feet off the roadway. That's where this fellow was hit. See here, in this photo? You can see the scuff mark made by his running shoes on impact."

"The road looks straight."

"Like an arrow," Dr. Jensen said. "Due north."

"So the weather was clear, the road straight, and he was jogging several feet off the pavement. How do you think he happened to be hit?"

The doctor shrugged. "Anybody's guess. Distracted drivers take their eyes off the road for all sorts of reasons. To retrieve a dropped cigarette, change the radio station or CD, make a call, swat an unruly child. Might have swerved to avoid another vehicle, or an animal darting across the roadway."

Stone frowned.

"Maybe the driver had been out drinking all night and was impaired," Jensen said. "Could be why he didn't stop."

Stone rubbed his chin as he studied the pictures, one at a time. "Who found him?"

"A woman passerby called nine-one-one from a pay phone at a Texaco station three or four miles north of the scene. Saw a dead body in the road as she drove by. Said she didn't stop because she was late for church. Deputy drove out to check her story and, sure thing, there he was."

"He's hit by a northbound car," Stone said, thinking aloud, "hurled off to one side, lands out in the roadway. But if he was thrown to the side, how did he get tire impressions on his clothes and his skin?"

"Let me see that." The doctor examined the two photos Stone handed him. "Often, after a pedestrian is hit, other motorists run over the body."

"Right," Stone said. "But the lanes are northbound. Look at the impressions. You can see where a tire backed up, rotating his T-shirt down toward the pavement, dragged his clothing downward across his skin. Then there's another impression. . . ."

"He should not have tire marks." The doctor's eyelids fluttered behind his glasses.

"But here," Stone said. "It looks like a wheel depressed the side of his torso—it's even more obvious in the morgue pictures—mashing it down as a tire backed up and over his body."

They stared at each other.

"I see what you're suggesting." Jensen ran his fingers through his thinning hair. "Maybe my first instinct, my gut reaction, was right." He got to his feet to study the photo more closely, under a high-intensity lamp.

"You know," he said, almost as an aside, "that I am at the mercy of the police investigators. Some are better than others. The deputy who handled the scene was convinced this was a simple hit-and-run accident."

"Was he a trained, full-time traffic homicide investigator?"

"No, not much call for one in these parts back then."

"Do you mind if I borrow the file for a consultation with our chief medical examiner? He's an expert on pedestrian-crash reconstruction?"

"No, not at all," Jensen said. "I'd be extremely eager to hear his conclusions. Give my regards to your chief. I did an internship in his office years ago, the high point of my professional career, the greatest learning experience I ever had. In Miami, pathologists see cases they wouldn't see in a hundred years anywhere else."

"Not always, sir," Stone said. "Sometimes pretty bizarre things happen in places you'd least expect."

He signed a receipt for the file and left, a man in a hurry. As he pulled out of the parking lot, Dr. Jensen emerged from the building and waved him down.

"I just checked our log for that date. That same Sunday a local boy dove off a pier into the lake and fractured his neck. Drowned before anyone realized he was in trouble. That evening a light plane crashed. A local county official, his wife, and daughter, coming home from a family reunion in Mobile. Killed all three. Might be a slow day in Miami, but for this office it was a full house.

"I have an assistant now, but back then I was the only doctor, running a one-man office."

"Sure," Stone said. "I understand. Sometimes things fall through the cracks."

He found his way back onto Alligator Alley, then drove east through the dark, his mind racing far ahead of his headlights.

CHAPTER 11

His grandmother's bungalow was dark, the street quiet. It was three A.M. She was an early riser, but Stone was too impatient to wait. He rang the bell, then knocked. She appeared at the door more quickly than he expected, blinking out into the glare from the motion-detector lights he had installed beneath the eaves on each side of her house.

"It's me, Gran."

"Sonny, are you all right?" She wore a thin house-coat over her nightgown. "What's wrong?"

"Hope I didn't scare you. Sorry to wake you."

"You didn't. I don't sleep much anymore."

He followed her inside.

"You're up early."

"Haven't been to bed yet, Gran. And it looks like I won't be for a while. I drove over to Immokalee."

He thought he glimpsed a flicker, a slight reaction in her eyes, but might have been mistaken. The living room was dark, and the only light came from her bedroom and outside the windows.

"You want some breakfast?"

"I'da gone to Denny's if I wanted breakfast. I'm not

hungry, Gran. Don't think I will be for a long time. I could use some coffee, though. It's gonna be a long night and I need to talk to you."

She pulled her cotton wrapper closer around her, slowly tied the belt, then shuffled into the kitchen in her pink slippers.

He sat at the kitchen table, watching her as though she were a stranger.

She set the steaming cup in front of him. "Sure you don't want me to fix you some eggs?"

"No," he said impatiently. "I didn't come here at three A.M. for eggs. Sit down, Gran, please."

Eyes wary, she sat across from him.

"Gran, remember the police officer who came here to bring us the news the night Momma and Daddy died? His name was Ray Glover."

She sighed, pursed her lips, and gave a slight nod.

"He's dead, Gran. Ray Glover's dead."

"Coulda told you that." She shrugged. "Man's dead and gone for years, God rest his soul. That why you drove all the way over to Immokalee? I coulda saved you the trouble."

"But you didn't, Gran." He stared at her accusingly. "Why?"

"Was none a your business. It had nothing to do with you, boy."

His lips tightened. "Yes, it did. It had everything to do with me. What else didn't you tell me?"

"Drink your coffee, Sonny, 'fore it gets cold."

He took a sip. His stomach churned and he put the cup down.

"Glover's death was no accident, Gran. I think he was murdered."

She nodded slowly in agreement, her eyes knowing.

"You knew?" he said, in disbelief.

"Only thing that made sense to me."

"Damn, Gran. You talked to him! You wrote to him! Tell me about it."

"Nuthin' to tell."

"What did you talk about? Did he say why he left the department? Did he know why Momma and Daddy were killed? Why did you stay in touch? What did he tell you?"

She averted her eyes. "Now, Sonny. It was a long time ago. Most days I can't remember what somebody tol' me last week. And even if I did, it's none a your concern."

"They were my parents!" His voice rose angrily.

"I did the best I could for you. Still do."

"I know, Gran," he said more gently. "But I can't stand you keeping secrets from me. You always helped me when I needed you."

"I won't help you get killed like your father!"

"What does that mean?"

"Nuthin'." She shrugged infuriatingly.

"Why are you so stubborn?"

"Not me! It's you. Too stubborn for your own good!"

"Whatever happens, I'm pursuing this anyway." He sprang to his feet, and forgetting his bruised hand, slapped his palm down so hard that coffee slopped from his cup onto the tabletop. He winced at the sudden pain.

"Sonny, what's wrong with your hand?"

"Nothing! What do you care? I won't give up! Whether you help or not, I won't quit. With you or without you! How can you be so cold?" He stormed out, slamming the door behind him.

She remained huddled, a small figure, in her chair and didn't look up.

•   •   •

They had never exchanged such angry words. Never. Even when he was a teenager he'd been respectful, aware that she didn't put up with, or deserve, any sass.

They always shared, able to talk about anything, open and direct, never devious or evasive. Stone drove to the station, read through his notes, the Collier County file on Glover's death, then highlighted every mention of Glover in his parents' homicide file. At six A.M. he got on the phone and tracked down Bill Rakestraw, the department's best traffic homicide investigator.

Stone's energy flagged, sucked dry by remorse. His grandmother was so frail. She had been his rock, had raised him all alone on a housekeeper's salary, had taught him a love of reading and justice, had cultivated his curiosity. They had explored and experienced every-place in South Florida that a bus could take them, even places where they weren't always welcome. She had always told him, "You can't be what you can't see."

She had opened the world to him, made him the man he had become. He wanted to make her proud, to care for her the way she had cared for him. She was all he had. He never wanted to hurt her. That was the last thing he wanted to do. Yet he had shouted and slammed the door.

He checked his watch. He still had time to apologize, to try again to explain why he had to do what he was doing.

He drove back to the little bungalow where he'd grown up.

She didn't answer the door. He didn't think she'd gone out yet. He called out. No answer. She might be watering her herb garden, he thought. She always said early morning was the best time. He went around to the back of the house. She wasn't there.

As he returned to the front, he paused to peer in the kitchen window. Perhaps she was in there, listening to the radio, and hadn't heard him.

Something caught his eye. One of her pink scuffs on the kitchen floor. Then he saw her, lying next to it, face-down.

CHAPTER 12

"Sergeant Burch," Emma said shrilly, hands on her hips. "Will you *please* pick up your phone."

"Who is it?"

"Greta Van Susteren."

"Tell her I like her show and she should call PIO. We didn't come in early today to talk to the press."

Moments later, Emma was back.

"Your phone," she said. "Answer it."

"No."

"All right!" She marched back to her desk. "A man says he knows who killed Pierce Nolan. I'll tell him to call PIO."

"Probably a wacko nutcase." Burch reached for his phone. "Newspaper stories always bring them out of the woodwork."

"Thanks for taking my call." The man sounded lucid, soft-spoken, and slightly apologetic.

They always do at the start, Burch thought.

"I read the story in the newspaper."

So did half a million other readers. Burch wondered if they'd all call. The story had now taken on a life of its own, spreading across the nation via wire services, network television, radio, and the Internet. Hundreds more like this one would soon be calling.

"I don't know anything about the dead babies."

Burch nodded and rolled his eyes.

"But I know who killed Pierce Nolan. It's been on my conscience all these years. I have no reason to keep it a secret any longer."

"Okay, pal, who did it?" Burch picked up a pencil.

"My brother. My younger brother, Ronnie. Ronald Stokoe. That's S–t–o–k–o–e."

"And what makes you think your brother murdered Pierce Nolan?" Burch doodled on a desk pad and wondered if Greta Van Susteren believed in Feng Shui.

"He was there, at the Shadows, that night," the man said. "He called home from a pay phone down on Bayshore Drive. He begged me to come pick him up. His clothes were all torn and bloody. He was totally panicked, never saw him so scared. He said something terrible had happened."

Burch stopped doodling and printed the name Ronald Stokoe on his pad.

"What was he doing up at the Shadows? Why was he there?"

"He wouldn't say then, but I know. Those young girls. The Nolan girls. Ronnie's had a problem all his life, since he was eleven. His thing was window peeping when he was a teenager. Then he started climbing in the windows to steal the underwear of the women he watched. After that he'd climb in windows to wake them up, or hide in a closet and wait for them to come home. He's been in and out of jail on sex charges all his life. He was just paroled from prison a couple of years ago after a rape conviction."

"Pierce Nolan was killed more than forty years ago. How can you be sure we're talking about the same night?"

"As I drove Ronnie away, police cars and an ambulance, with flashing lights and sirens, went flying past us in the opposite direction, going to the Shadows. The next day it was all over the news. I was in the army then. My military records will confirm I was home on leave when it happened."

"What's your brother's date of birth?"

"May tenth, 1944. He was seventeen then."

"Where's he staying?"

"At home, my folks' old house over near Mercy Hospital."

"Why didn't you report this before?"

"To protect our parents. I kept quiet for them. They were in poor health. It would have killed my mother. There was just the two of us kids. He was the youngest, their favorite, my little brother. He begged me not to tell anybody. Promised to straighten out. He was bleeding. I took him to a clinic, a place up in Miami Shores where they didn't ask any questions. They patched him up."

"What made you call today?"

"My parents are gone now. I saw the news story and decided there was no reason to protect him anymore. It's not worth it. Ronnie was always in trouble. He broke my parents' hearts over and over. They bailed him out, hired lawyers and shrinks. They'd go see him in jail and in prison. They worked hard all their lives. Any money they ever managed to put aside for their own retirement, they wound up spending over and over to bail him out of trouble.

"I was the oldest. I never gave them a moment's grief. Do you know that when they died, they left the house, all their assets, what little they had left, all to him?

"They wrote in their wills that I was a wonderful son, capable of taking care of myself. That's why they left everything to Ronnie. He needed it more, they said. They left him everything it took them a lifetime to accumulate. He was in trouble again in a heartbeat. I'm tired of covering up for him. He's never changed."

"When you picked him up that night, did he have the gun?"

"No, I never saw it."

"Did he have access to a shotgun?"

"My father had guns he'd used for hunting. I think there was a double-barreled Remington. I was away in the service for four years. By the time I got out, the guns were gone, along with a whole lot of other stuff, that Ronnie either stole, or had been sold by them to help get him out of trouble."

Leonard Stokoe sounded resentful, weary, and truthful.

"Is your brother home now?"

"Probably. He can't hold a job."

• • •

Ronald Stokoe's adult record began at age eighteen.

"Look at his rap sheet!" Riley unfurled a printout as

long as she was tall. Scores of arrests over the years: multiple counts of loitering and prowling, trespassing, window peeping, indecent exposure, masturbating in public, lewd and lascivious conduct, breaking and entering, assault, indecent assault, attempted sexual battery, and rape.

"And these are just the times he got caught."

Riley had been a rape squad lieutenant for years. Stokoe was right up her alley.

"About the only crime he's never been arrested for is homicide," she said. "And that may be an oversight we can remedy. Postpone your trip upstate," she told Burch, "until we have a better take on Stokoe. The escalation of his offenses makes sense." She pored over his record. "Many rapists start out as Peeping Toms, but as their fantasies progress it's not enough to merely look in a window and fondle themselves. Eventually invading a home to masturbate in a woman's underwear is not enough, they need to touch the woman herself.

"This could be the break we need," she said, "especially with the press hounding us. They just live to make us look bad.

"He's on parole," she said. "Go find him, bring him in for a little chat."

She smiled and went back to her office.

Maybe things are looking up, Burch thought, and absently snatched up his ringing phone.

"Hey, Doc." He listened for a moment, his expression changing.

"You're not serious. They musta made a mistake at the lab. You're sure? My God!"

He sat stunned for a moment after hanging up.

"I don't believe this." He got to his feet. "That was the chief ME," he told Corso and Nazario. "They pushed through the DNA tests on the dead babies. None of 'em are related. Every single one of them had a different mother and father."

"How can that be possible?" Nazario said.

"So Nolan wasn't . . ." Corso said.

"We're back to square one," Burch said.

"Kiki was right all along," Nazario said. "She insisted that he was no monster. Sarge, let's talk to Sky. He was playing in the cellar, in the tunnel, when his father was shotgunned outside. He might remember if the box was there before the shooting. If not, somebody else hid them in there after the family cleared out."

"Kid was only nine then," Burch said. "My son is thirteen and can't remember where he left his shoes ten minutes ago."

"It's worth a shot," Nazario said.

"But if somebody brought the box in later and the Nolans know nothing, why are the women all so goddamn evasive? They're hiding something. They gotta be."

Riley emerged from her office. "What? Why are you guys still here? Nothing better to do than stand around with your mouths open? I said to go find that suspect. And has anybody seen Stone?" She sighed, annoyed. "I'm having a bad day."

"Take a number," Burch said.

CHAPTER 13

"Gran! Gran!" Stone dropped to his knees on the floor beside his grandmother and felt for a pulse. She was breathing. He turned her over gently and she opened her eyes.

"Gran, are you okay? I'm sorry. I'm so sorry! Talk to me. Please talk to me."

Did she have a stroke? Had she been taking her blood pressure medication? He'd neglected to remind her lately as he usually did. It was critical to act quickly if it was a stroke. What had her doctor said? Stone tried frantically to remember the questions that can identify stroke symptoms.

"Gran, smile. Can you smile for me?"

The corners of her mouth turned up. Her gaze was fond.

"Good. Good." No facial weakness. "Now try to raise both arms."

She raised her right arm, then her left.

No arm weakness.

"All right now, sweetheart. Try to speak. Say a complete sentence, just a simple sentence."

"For pity's sake, Sonny. Just help me get up."

"Excellent, very good." Her speech wasn't slurred.

"Gran, tell me, who's the president of the United States?"

"Dubya. I mean it, Sonny. Quit your silly questions and help me up."

He opened his cell phone to punch 911. "I want Rescue to check you out."

"No need," she insisted, sitting up. "I don't want them busting in here, disturbing the neighbors with all that noise and fuss. It was so hot up there. Jus' had a little weak spell. I'm fine."

"Sure you're all right?" he asked doubtfully.

"I'm fine. Jus' felt a little weak and lost my balance when I stood up."

He picked up her pink scuff, helped her to her favorite chair, lifted her feet onto the footstool, and slid the slipper onto her foot. "Did you take your medication?"

She hesitated, uncertain. "Maybe I forgot. I wasn't sure and I didn't want to make a mistake and take it twice."

"I'm calling the doctor."

"Don't you go bothering him, he's a busy man."

"I'll go get you one of those pill dispensers that have sections marked with each day of the week," he said. "You can see exactly when you took your medicine last. I meant to buy you one before.

"What did you say you were doing when you felt weak?" He brushed what looked like a cobweb off her shoulder. "You said hot. Up where?"

She looked guilty. "I went up into the attic crawl space. It's so hot and dusty. . . ."

"What?" The only opening to the crawl space was in the top of her bedroom closet. "You climbed the stepladder and went up in there? You promised you'd never go up a ladder when you're home alone. What if you fell? Whatever you want up there, you know I'll get it down for you."

"Didn't want you getting yourself all exercited before I saw if it was still up in there. Shoulda throwed it away or burnt it. Meant to a long time ago."

"What?"

"An old box a your father's papers. Maybe something there can help you. Maybe not. After the funeral I went over to the barbecue store to clear out your mama and daddy's things. Put 'em all in one a them cardboard file boxes and stored it up in the crawl space."

"What's in it?" he whispered.

"Papers, a lot of business papers." She shrugged. "Ray Glover, he went through 'em before I put 'em up there. Said I should hang on to 'em."

He followed her into the bedroom and winced at the old six-foot stepladder still standing in front of the closet. A dusty cardboard file box sat atop her neatly made bed.

"You might find somethin'." She bit her lip. "You know I'm so proud of you, Sonny, but sometimes I'm scared for you, too."

"Sure, Gran. But I can take care of myself. You taught me how to do that."

Her smile was sad. "I don't want to lose you the way we lost your daddy and Annie. I'm jus' scared—for you, not me. I been arguing with myself.

"I pray to God every day to keep His hands on you. I don't want to fuss with you anymore, Sonny. Don't want you believin' I don't care. I'll do what I can."

"Atta girl." He gave her a gentle hug. "I have to go to a meeting now, but I won't turn off my cell phone, no matter what. I'll keep it on vibrate. If you don't feel well, call nine-one-one right away, then me. Want to go through these papers together later?"

She shook her head sorrowfully. "I hope I'm not makin' a terrible mistake," she whispered. "I made so many. Take it outta here, Sonny. I don't want to see it."

He locked the file box in the trunk of the unmarked and drove to the medical examiner's office.

Rakestraw was already there.

He'd been called out to a fatal accident before dawn.

"Traffic stopped," he said, his thin face morose. "College kid in a Ford Focus didn't."

Bill Rakestraw took every traffic death personally. That's why he's the best, Stone thought.

He filled in Rakestraw and the chief medical examiner and left the Collier County medical examiner's file with them.

His beeper had already sounded. Four times. He went straight to the office.

Nazario and Corso were waiting for the elevator as Stone stepped off.

"Dawg! You are in so much hot water!" Corso said. "The lieutenant's gonna whup your ass."

"Hear about the DNA results?" Nazario asked grimly.

"Yeah, at the ME's office. Hell of a thing."

"We're going to bring in a suspect right now."

"Good luck," Stone said absently.

"You're the one who needs it, dawg."

∙ ∙ ∙

"Where the hell have you been!"

K. C. Riley was red in the face and on her feet. "Glad you could make it, Stone. Oversleep? Glad you slept like a baby! I didn't. What in hell did you think you were doing over there in goddamn redneck country? Nobody even knew where you were! I expect better from you. Since when are you the Lone Ranger?"

"Sorry, Lieutenant. I didn't oversleep. Haven't slept yet. I left word with your secretary that I had tracked down Ray Glover."

"Sure, but you neglected to mention he was on the goddamn other side of the state. Had he been in Baghdad, I suppose you'd be there, ducking bombs and bullets, without asking my permission."

"Let me tell you what I found, Lieutenant. Glover's dead. I think he was murdered."

"Don't screw with me, Stone."

"I'm not."

She cocked her head at him, sat down, and listened. Before he finished, she called in Burch.

"Holy crap," he said after hearing everything. "Where is this one going?"

"Let's find out," the lieutenant said. "Good work, Stone."

CHAPTER 14

The metal door handles were as hot as a stove. The detectives gasped as they slid into their unmarked, a blast furnace exposed to the ruthless summer sun on the rooftop level of the parking garage.

"Now I know what a corpse feels like being rolled into the crematorium," Corso said.

Nazario felt the heat searing his lungs, turning his bones to ash. He rolled down the windows, turned on the AC, and floored it, steering gingerly with his fingertips until the wheel cooled off.

"I swear to God you ain't driving on the way back!" Corso bellowed as they circled around and around in a dizzying spiral descent to the street. "Never shoulda got in the car with you. I know better."

"What, you expect to live forever?"

"No, but a few more weeks would be nice."

"Yeah, might be nice to get married first," Nazario said.

"Then it'll just seem like forever. Hey!" Corso yelped as a concrete retaining wall loomed in the windshield. "How the hell'd you get your driver's license? Mail-order from Havana?"

"I don't like those insinuendos. Tell me when I had an accident! Name one."

Heat rose in waves off the blacktop as they hit the street.

"You Cubans are all alike. Too macho, no sense a humor."

•   •   •

Ronald Stokoe lived in a tree-shaded, one-story, concrete-block, fifties-style South Florida home, attached to a one-car garage. The mailbox tilted at a precarious angle, its door hanging open like a parched tongue. The paint on the north side of the house was dark with mold, in need of pressure cleaning. Large round brown patches in the weedy, overgrown lawn signaled that the chinch bugs were in charge.

Stokoe answered the door shirtless, barefoot, and in need of a shave. A TV blared in the background.

"Chinch bug inspector!" Corso flashed his badge. "Sir, you got a serious problem."

"What are you talking about?" Stokoe said.

"Miami police," Nazario said.

"Ahhhhh!" Stokoe slapped his head and spun around in frustration. "What the hell is this? Harassment? Because I have a record, right? What's going on?"

"A good-looking blonde wants to see you," Corso said. "That's the good news. The bad news is she's our lieutenant."

"Can we come in?" Nazario said.

Stokoe stepped back reluctantly.

"Did my parole officer send you? Look, I only missed two appointments."

"Oh, ain't that nice to know?" Corso shot a triumphant look at Nazario. "Thank you very much." Eyes roving, he stepped into the living room.

"Sir," Nazario said, "I think you should get dressed, put on a shirt—"

"Am I under arrest?"

"We just want to talk to you down at the station."

"Who are you with, what unit?"

"Homicide, Cold Case Squad."

"What you talking about? You got me mixed up with somebody else! Did my goddamn neighbors call you?"

"Do they have a reason to?" Nazario asked mildly.

Chastened, Stokoe said, "What if I don't wanna go?"

"What do we *have* here?" Corso boomed triumphantly from a corner of the living room. "Well, well, well. Naz, lookit this. Our buddy here's got a green thumb."

Six small marijuana plants were thriving in an egg carton beneath a blue light.

"Sorry, pal. Gotta confiscate these and take you in. You got no choice about coming downtown now."

"They're strictly for medicinal purposes," Stokoe protested. "I been in ill health. Had a gallbladder operation a couple months ago," he said, pulling on a shirt in his bedroom.

Corso put the egg carton in the trunk while Nazario watched Stokoe dress. "Your lieutenant really a blonde?" Stokoe ran a comb through his thinning hair and daubed on some cologne. "Okay," he said, "how do I look?"

•   •   •

"You got to be kidding!" Stokoe exploded when Burch asked where he was the night of August 25, 1961. "Are you crazy?"

His initial reaction simmered down as the gravity of Burch's question began to sink in. Something changed in his eyes.

"We're not kidding. We're dead serious."

"Number one," Stokoe said. "The statute ran out a long, long time ago on anything that coulda happened back then." His confidence restored, he leaned back in his chair and grinned at them.

"Wrong. It never runs out on first-degree murder."

Stokoe's mouth opened, but he said nothing.

"Want to tell me about Pierce Nolan?"

"I don't know what you're talking about. I don't have to talk to you."

He shut down, silent and unresponsive. Burch left him alone and found Riley and Corso in her office.

"Stokoe's playing cute, doesn't want to cooperate."

"Okay," she said. "Let me take a crack at him."

"He's all yours," Burch said.

"I'd like to give that guy an attitude adjustment," Corso said, cracking his knuckles.

•   •   •

Stokoe smiled up at her. "Hey, they sent in the blonde. I was hoping they would. If more cops looked like you, I wouldn't mind visiting here more often."

She smiled back as his oil-slick eyes roved boldly over her cream-colored blouse and form-fitting slacks.

"Call me K.C."

"Yes, sir, ma'am." Stokoe gave a charming little salute. "You can call me Ron."

"Okay, Ron. I hope bringing you down here so abruptly wasn't inconvenient." She took the chair opposite him.

"An imposition, but I got to meet you. Wish I'da had time to shave. Always wanted to meet a babe who owns her own handcuffs." He winked.

Riley chuckled.

"I see here, Ron," she said, frowning at the folder in front of her, "that you did some time for rape."

"A misunderstanding," he said. "Strictly consensual, I swear. You know how it goes, some women get crazy. It was one a those she said, he said deals. I took a bad rap. Had a lousy lawyer."

"She was fifteen years old," Riley said. "You went in a window. It says here her arm was broken, a spiral fracture from being twisted. Tsk, tsk, Ron, I'm surprised at you."

He sighed. "She was into rough sex. She wanted me, she told me she did."

"Ohhh, so that explains it." Riley sniffed the air. "What's that smell?" She looked around the room, puzzled.

"I think they call it *Le Male*. It's French." His sly smile returned.

"No, Ron, I don't think it's that." She wrinkled her nose. "I think it's your breath."

He blinked, smile fading.

"How bad is your breath? How backward is your brain? And how little is your penis, Ron? It must be terribly small. You must have needed tweezers and a magnifying glass to find it every time you pulled it out to wave at little girls. Want to wave it at me? I could use a laugh today. I bet I've seen bigger dicks on little kids," she said casually, then smiled.

"Your own hand probably rejects your pathetic little pecker, you ballless bastard." She shook her head sadly and continued her role of bad cop, very bad cop, with no good cop in sight.

●   ●   ●

"Hey, Sarge, listen to this," Nazario said. "Not only did we run down the owner of that clinic in the Shores, but they're still in business, just down the street. Had all the old records. Unbelievable! Stokoe did show up there that night. Suffering from scratches, mosquito bites, and a gunshot wound, a shotgun pellet the doctor dug out of his left shoulder."

"The blood out there that night was his!" Burch said.

"Without a doubt. Damn, wish we had it for DNA. We coulda positively nailed him in court."

"DNA wasn't even on the horizon then. But if Stokoe was the shooter," Burch said, "how'd he get hit?"

"Ricochet maybe, or when he and Nolan wrestled over the weapon."

"Damn, he looks good for this! What a break," Burch said. "What'd I tell ya? Despite what the lieutenant says, sometimes putting it in the newspaper works."

"Yeah. . . . Listen, Sarge, there's something I didn't wanna bring up in front a Corso." He filled Burch in about Fleur Adair.

"She shows up, naked, in your bed?"

"Swear."

"You didn't do the nasty with her? Tell me you didn't."

"Could have. Didn't. Wouldn't. You recommended me for that job, Sarge. Adair trusts us with what belongs to him."

Burch sighed in relief.

"Did you know that promoters pay pretty girls just to go to parties at South Beach hotels and clubs?"

"Party girl is her profession?" Burch said. "Used to call 'em B-girls. This close," he said, squeezing his thumb and forefinger together, "to prostitution."

"She's not a bad girl. Poor kid's a broken cookie." Nazario shook his head.

"If she's on the outs with her father, you gotta get her outta there."

"No problem. She promised to be gone by the time I get back."

"What do party promoters pay girls for something like that?"

"Didn't say, but it must be enough to make a living."

"Even if that's all she does?"

Nazario shrugged. "They party down every night in South Beach. Says she gets a bonus to be a human table."

"The hell is that?"

"A girl who lets rich guys eat sushi off her naked stomach."

"Sounds like ptomaine city to me. Jeez, you see a big, beautiful house, the fancy cars, the big bucks, and think the people who live there and their kids don't have a care in the world. Uh-oh."

The door to the interview room slammed shut.

"Over to you." Riley went into her office and closed the door.

•　　•　　•

"Let's go pick up the pieces," Burch said.

Stokoe's body language and cocky demeanor had changed. Slumped in his chair, he rocked back and forth.

"I don't want to talk to her anymore!" He jabbed a finger at them. "Jesus God, what kind of woman is that? I don't wanna see her again!"

"That can be arranged," Burch said. "If you cooperate . . ."

"Sure, whatever you want to know. I'll tell you the whole thing. Just keep her the hell away from me."

After being advised of his rights, Stokoe said, "I went up there that night to see Summer Nolan. You shoulda seen 'er. She was so beautiful that cars would wreck when she walked down the street. But meaner than a snake."

"Mean?" Nazario asked.

"Had an attitude. Pretended not to see you. Wouldn't give me the time of day."

"She was only sixteen," Burch said.

"So? I was seventeen, perfect for her. I'd say hello, she'd look the other way. Followed her home once. Then I started going up there almost every night. I'd ride my bike or take the bus.

"I'd watch her, through a bedroom window. She used to dance. All alone, in her room. I'd stand on a rock and watch her. Used to get off. She hadda know I was watching. She'd undress. Sometimes she'd touch herself."

Stokoe licked his lips, eyes dreamy. "She wanted me. She knew I was there, hadda know. But I was scared shit-less of her father. He was a big guy, a big shot. I'd been caught red-handed, so to speak, once before, down in the Roads section. The judge gave me one more chance. It was my third or fourth one. I couldn't afford to get caught again. I didn't wanna go to Youth Hall."

"So that's why you shot Pierce Nolan when he caught you that night."

"Hell, no!" Stokoe jerked back in his chair. "I never shot nobody. I have scruples. I was a victim. Think I'd be sitting here talking to you guys if I killed anybody? I'd be lawyered up and outta here. Hope you catch the guy who did it—you can charge him with assaulting me, too."

"Sorry," Burch said. "There's that pesky statute of limitations again. So what happened?"

"That was one hot, steamy night. Summer was alone in her room. She was waiting for me. I knew it. She had music on the radio. She took off her dress first, real slow, in front of the mirror. She was swaying back and forth. Started doing ballet exercises, bending and stretching. Really sensuous shit. Hadda know I was there. She starts dancing, barefoot, in a little slip. I'm jerking off, fantasizing about what I'd be doing to her if I was in there. I was really excited, but it was taking me longer. She had Patsy Cline on the radio, singing 'Crazy.' I'm whaling away and, Shit! I hear his car coming up the driveway. Almost there, I had to quit. Hated leaving her but I didn't want him catching me. Son of a bitch was a big guy, an athlete. So I ran down behind the hedge, figuring I'll circle around behind his car and split once he goes in the house. But something's moving on the far side of the driveway. I don't know what it is. I'm thinking maybe they got a dog. So I freeze, outta breath, take cover, and wait. Nolan gets outta his car, starts to walk inside, then stops and yells something at me. I'm thinking, Oh shit.

"Then from the other side of the house I see a burst of red flame and hear the blast. I'm in the line of fire, behind Nolan. We both get hit. I take a shotgun pellet at the top of my shoulder, by my neck. Hurts like hell. Nolan's staggering around, making noises, trying to call for help and, all of a sudden, somebody charges outta the dark right toward 'im and blasts him again. Point blank. I'm bleeding like crazy. All I want is outta there. I run around behind the house to get back down to Bayshore Drive. Then I hear somebody, something else, running, too. Ahead of me, breathing hard. The guy with the gun. He's in front of me, there's all kinds of screaming behind me. I'm too scared to stop. I know they'll blame me. I just had the dam run-in with the juvy judge. I keep going, falling, getting cut and scratched up by the branches. I get down to the highway and don't know what to do. I call somebody from a pay phone, ask 'im to pick me up. Need a doctor to dig the goddam shotgun pellet outta me. I still got the scar. If I shot him, how the hell did I get shot?"

He leaned back in his chair and studied their faces.

"I'll take a polygraph," he offered, "but only about the shooting. Nothing else. Any time, any place. Tell my parole officer I cooperated. A hundred percent. I don't want no hassle from him. Got that? I'm telling you the truth here.

"How'd you find me?" His expression grew wiser. "Did my goddamn brother throw me under the bus?"

"You saw the gunman?" Burch asked.

"It was dark as hell out there. I was a kid. I was scared. He's crashing through the bushes ahead of me. I thought if he turned and saw me, he'd shoot me, too."

"What did he look like?"

"Taller than me. Had a long gun, a long stride. Heard his breathing. I was praying he wouldn't turn around and come after me."

"Was he black, white? What was he wearing? Did he say anything? Did you hear his voice?"

"Nah. Never said a word that I heard. It was dark as hell. If he'da turned around so I could see him, I probably woulda had a heart attack. Never saw his face. Didn't want to."

"When did you lose sight of him?"

"When we got down onto Bayshore, he ran left. I took off to the right, to the pay phone at the service station on the far side of the highway."

"You sure it was a guy? Was it possibly a female?"

"No, no way it was a woman. I think he had a car. Heard the door, then heard it start. I was scared he would turn it around and come after me, but he didn't.

"Until my . . . ride came, I stayed in the men's room at the service station. Didn't want the guy with the gun to come back looking for me. Didn't want anybody seeing me. My face and arms were all scratched to hell and bleeding. I had splinters, thorns, scrapes, and everything else you could imagine, and was bleeding like hell from that shotgun pellet."

"Did you go to the hospital?"

"No, my ride took me to a clinic in the Shores. We used to get our shots there cheap when we were kids. Get patched up every time we got hurt. I think the law said they had to report gunshot wounds back then, but since this was only a pellet, I don't think the doctor reported it.

"I tol' 'im I got hurt when a bunch of us guys were target-shooting at a fishing camp out in the 'Glades. That it was an accident. I sweated it for a long time, whenever there was a knock at the door, when stories about the Nolan murder ran on TV or in the newspaper. Nothing happened, till now.

"The story in the newspaper, is that what brought you to my door? I don't know nothing about any babies. Don't know what the hell that was all about."

"All the nights you watched Summer, ever see her father in her room?" Burch asked.

"Yeah. Once. She was dancing, had music on the radio. He must've knocked, because she turned off the radio and ran to put on a robe. It was him. Her father came into the room. He looked so big and tall next to her. They sat on the bed for a while, talking. Then he got up, kissed her on the forehead, and said good night.

"Then she sat down at her little desk and started to do her homework."

"That was it?"

"Yeah. I scouted around looking in some of the other windows. The younger girls were always on the phone or in their books, and the mother . . . she was something, too. Always wanted to catch the mother and father together, doing it. But she always drew the curtains before she got undressed. I caught her in the shower once, but it was that rippled glass that blurs everything. All you see is an image, but sometimes that's a turn-on."

"You ever tell anybody what you were doing up there?" Burch asked. "Anybody else ever peeping at those girls?"

"Hell, no. I wouldn't have been up there if I didn't think I was alone."

"You ever hear about any of the Nolan girls being pregnant?"

"No way. Far as I knew, they were untouchable little virgins. Funny. Never saw Summer again except for her picture in the paper at his funeral, but years later I saw a girl who looked just like her, uncanny resemblance, in a cowboy movie. She got abducted by Indians. That little fantasy kept me going for a while.

"Went to see it two or three times, read the credits, some girl named Kathryn or something. Had me going, reliving all that shit, all those hot nights."

"We'll arrange a polygraph," Burch said, "and call you."

"Right," Nazario said. "We want you to go home. Think hard about that night, then write down everything you remember, even the smallest details."

•   •   •

"He's telling the truth," Nazario said sadly, outside the interview room.

"Crap," Burch said. "I really wanted it to be him."

CHAPTER 15

Rusty paper clips held some related papers together, others were loose and faded. Tax forms, canceled checks, receipts, and bills from vendors.

A snapshot of his parents, his father's arm around his mother, both beaming from behind the counter at Stone's Barbecue.

There were pamphlets on how to operate a small business and directions on how to apply for Small Business Administration loans, along with the application forms.

Optimistic booklets on how to franchise a business. Framed pictures of Jesus, Martin Luther King Jr., and John F. Kennedy that had hung behind the counter, along with articles and inspirational quotes on how to succeed in life, love, and business, clipped from magazines and newspapers. Some of the passages were highlighted. One read, "You never know how high you can fly until you spread your wings." It all made him want to weep. There was nothing here about why anyone would kill them.

He went through business cards from wholesalers and from area organizations that had ordered food for employee luncheons, picnics, and special events. There were receipts for ads his father had placed in a small weekly newspaper for "the best barbecue in town."

A small leather-covered telephone book full of alphabetically listed numbers, mostly friends, relatives, purveyors, and customers. Stone recognized his mother's neat, legible handwriting.

Tucked inside the front cover was a snapshot of himself, Sam Stone Jr., smiling at age three from his grandmother's lap. He was surprised at how young Gran looked in the photo. Next to it, a wallet-sized copy of his third-grade picture taken shortly before the murders.

He felt despair. He saw nothing here that could help, only a painful history of dreams and lives cut short. He knew he would keep every scrap of paper as long as he lived—in remembrance of them. But he would have to look elsewhere for clues to why they died.

He sighed and closed the address book. Taped to the back was a small form, one of the preprinted paper meal checks presented to customers with their orders. This one had not been used. All that was written on it, in his father's handwriting, was a name, Asa Anderson, and an out-of-state number with a 601 area code. The meal checks came in books, consecutively numbered, so it appeared that the name and number had been written on this one sometime shortly before the murders.

He checked the area code. Mississippi.

They had no relatives there.

He dialed the number. The woman who answered knew no one named Stone and had only had the number for six months. He tucked the snapshots of his parents, and him with Gran, into his wallet and closed the box.

Online, back at his computer terminal, he located a database with old Mississippi city and telephone directories and began to research who that number was listed to in 1987.

He got a hit. Surprisingly, it was not to a man named Anderson.

In 1987 that was the telephone number of the Criminal Division of the U.S. Justice Department in the Southern District of Mississippi.

What did that have to do with his father?

He found the current number, called, and asked for Asa Anderson.

"I don't show anyone by that name on any of our personnel rosters," a young woman drawled.

"Okay, can you put me through to the person with the most seniority in your office, somebody who was on staff in 1987?"

"I've only been here a year," the woman said. "But I guess that would be Mildred. She's been here at least a hundred years, but don't you dare tell her I said that."

"I won't," he promised.

Mildred proved talkative. "Oh sure, I was here in 'eighty-seven. I started here as a clerk right outta high school. Now I'm the office supervisor."

"I'm looking for Asa Anderson."

"Sure, I remember him. One of our investigators, retired 'bout five, six years ago. Top-flight. Nice fella."

"Is he still around?"

"What did you say your name was again? What department are you with?"

There was a long pause after he told her.

"Do you know where he's at now?" Stone asked.

"Sure thing. Think he's at Eagle Lake, up in the Delta. Has a fishing cabin up there."

Stone sighed in relief. At least the man was still alive. This was probably nothing. For all he knew, Asa Anderson had vacationed in Miami and enjoyed Stone's Barbecue. But why didn't he leave a business card? Why was his number simply scrawled on a blank food check? That indicated that the man must have called and that his father, busy behind the counter, jotted his number down on the first handy scrap of paper. Why did somebody from the Justice Department in Mississippi call his father? Or mother?

"You have his home number?"

Mildred was suddenly guarded. "Sorry, don't think I'm allowed to divulge that information. Gotta take another call now."

Stone called back, asked for Human Resources, identified himself, and got Anderson's number.

He called several times throughout the afternoon. The phone rang endlessly, no answering machine. He wondered if he had the right number. Shortly after five P.M. a man answered.

"I'm looking for Asa Anderson, former investigator for the Justice Department field office in the Southern District of Mississippi."

"You've got him," the robust voice replied cheerfully. "What can I do you for?"

"Glad to finally catch you. My name is Sam Stone. I'm calling from Miami."

"Sam Stone? From Miami? Is that what you said? You bastard! You sick son of a bitch! Who the hell is this?!"

"Excuse me?" Stone said.

But the line went dead.

CHAPTER 16

"Go, go, go!" K. C. Riley waved them toward the eleva-tor. "Before the chief changes his mind. You know how hard it is to squeeze travel money out of the budget."

"Stokoe looked so good," Burch mourned. "I really thought we had our guy for a while. Thanks for soften-ing him up."

"Anytime," Riley said. "Now go. Bring back some answers."

The trip to interview Spring Nolan at the Villages had blossomed into a cross-country itinerary. The Villages, San Antonio, Frisco, and Oxford, Ohio.

"It would be a hell of a lot easier if the members of this family would live in the same state," Burch said. "But they can't stand to be that close to each other."

As he confirmed their Orlando flight, every other phone line in Homicide was busy. Word had leaked out that a person of interest had been questioned in the Shadows case. Inquiring minds wanted to know.

The detectives suspected Padron, the public infor-mation officer, of tipping the press, trading favors with certain reporters.

"Nazario!" Emma waved. "Pick up your phone. Your lady friend."

"*He* has a lady friend?" Corso hooted. "Since when?"

"Pete! I'm so glad you're there!" Kiki sounded excited.

"We're on our way to the airport," he said. "To see some of Nolan's family."

"Perfect! Perfect! You won't believe what I found! I think I've solved the mystery!"

"Shoot," he said, expression skeptical. "We need all the help we can get."

Burch caught his eye, pointed to his watch, and frowned.

Nazario covered the mouthpiece. "Hang on a sec, Sarge, this might be important."

"You know that a number of Irish fighters fought against Franco during the Spanish Civil War, right?" she said.

"Never mind," he told Burch, and got to his feet. He grabbed his jacket.

"Look, Kiki, I gotta go."

"Wait! Pete, this is huge. The family may know the truth."

"The Spanish Civil War?" He lowered his voice so Burch couldn't hear. "Wasn't that back in the thirties? The one where Ernest Hemingway—"

"Right. It all makes sense," she crowed, heady with excitement.

"All right. Spit out the short version. We have to catch a plane."

"Okay! I went to the South Florida Historical

Museum to do some research and stopped to see an exhibit by David Beale, the famous Spanish Civil War photographer.

"He shot group photos of Irish soldiers in the International Brigade. A face in one of them stood out. The caption included the name Clifford Nolan. It was the same one that caught my eye. Captain Cliff Nolan, the rumrunner, the man who built the Shadows!

"It fits," she said. "All was not forgiven after Prohibition ended in 1933. The feds still wanted to prosecute Nolan for the deaths of the two lawmen killed in that gun battle off the Jersey coast. Federal murder warrants had been issued. Old records show several attempts to serve the outstanding arrest warrants on him. He would have been taken to New Jersey to stand trial. He faced the death penalty or life in prison.

"He knew he couldn't dodge federal agents forever. So, in 1936, Captain Cliff started the rumor that he and the *Sea Wolf* had been lost off the Cuban coast. Then he went off to join the Irish members of the International Brigade and fight fascism in Spain."

"That sounds pretty far-fetched," Nazario said. "A good old boy. A South Florida pioneer going to—"

"No, it isn't," Kiki said confidently. "Nolan was born in Ireland. Even though his parents brought him to America as a child, he still had relatives there, had cousins in the Brigade. It makes perfect sense. He must have felt that by the time the war ended, things would have blown over here and he could come home. His wife, Pierce Nolan's mother, must have been in on it.

Cliff wouldn't have left his wife and young son alone, wrongly believing he was dead. Pierce and his family might have known his father was still alive as well."

"So, why didn't he come back?"

"I think he may have been killed. A number of the Irish soldiers died in that war. I'm looking for casualty lists now. I'm so excited, Pete. It's a major find, the last chapter of a major saga of early Miami finally unfolding."

"Good for you, Kiki. We'll bounce it off the family. I'll let you know. Can't wait to see you. I'll call you from the road.

"What a woman," he said, hanging up. "And she cooks, too."

$\bullet \quad \bullet \quad \bullet$

"Nice try," Burch said en route to the airport. "Wrong mystery. Wish you'd put her to work on a case *we* need to solve."

"To her, a Miami historian, this is big, very big. How often do you get to solve a seventy-year-old mystery?"

"How often do we get to solve anything? That's our problem. If nothing else," Burch said grudgingly, "maybe we can use it on Diana Nolan as an icebreaker."

Between business travelers and families bound for Disney World, the Orlando flight was full.

An energetic little boy behind them tapped Burch on the shoulder to announce that he was four.

"He's really only three and a half." His father frowned apologetically as he tried to restrain the squirming child in his seat.

"Why does he do that?" his mother asked peevishly.

"He's in a hurry to be a big boy," Burch said. "Right, son?"

"Vincent," the father warned when Burch again turned his back, "you're bothering that man in front of you. Next time he'll turn around and smack you—and I'll let him."

"Vincent," they heard the man say minutes later, "they're going to make you get off the plane and leave me and your mom here alone. You don't want that, do you?"

The flight was only thirty minutes, less time than it had taken to pass through airport security.

During the approach to the Orlando airport, they saw hundreds and hundreds—thousands—of what looked from the air like blue roofs, tarps covering damage to homes as far as the eye could see. Some blue roofs were in huge clusters in a single development, with adjacent developments almost unscathed, indicating the erratic paths of whirlwinds spun out of the storm—or the shoddy work of certain builders. A few roofs were covered with new wood, under reconstruction, but very few. Brown forests of uprooted trees were everywhere.

"Look at all that misery down there," Burch said.

"We could be next," Nazario said grimly.

"It's not if," Burch said, "it's when."

They shared the restless anxiety of all Miamians, living on the edge, knowing that today is borrowed time and tomorrow is uncertain.

"How often can you dodge the bullet, or catch it in your teeth?" Burch said. "Something will zero in on us, sooner or later. Mother Nature on a rampage, out of the sea or the sky, lightning, hurricanes, or tornadoes, terrorists at the Turkey Point nuclear plant or the port, or El Loco with a gun. Sooner or later, something's coming for us."

Behind them, Vincent apparently committed some unforgivable infraction. "Okay, Vincent." The father's voice was raised. "Get off the plane. Now. You heard me."

"This," Burch said, "I gotta see."

•   •   •

The detectives could discern no sign of storm damage at the airport. An ultramodern monorail whisked them into the terminal through a lavishly landscaped Disney-like vista. The Villages was more than an hour's drive away, but near the car rental counter, they spotted a driver holding up a VILLAGES SHUTTLE sign.

From his running commentary en route, they learned that the Villages had its own radio station, daily newspaper, several movie theaters, nine golf courses (two of them championship), six supermarkets, hard- and soft-top tennis courts, archery and air-gun ranges, banks, a hospital—and a hospice.

Every evening, free entertainment in the town square, ranging from jazz to country-western to rock and roll. Residents boarded trolleys, drove golf carts or their own cars, and could choose from more than 250 clubs and activities.

The most popular sports, the driver confided, were

bowling, golf, and pickleball, a fast-paced cross between Ping-Pong and tennis.

The local lifelong learning college offered year-round classes on any subject one could want, without tests or stress.

"The energy here is unbelievable," said the silver-haired driver as they passed Rollerbladers in their eighties and seniors waterskiing without boats, clinging to electric pulleys as they skimmed across a controlled water course.

"It's like Disney World for retirees," Nazario said.

"Or the Evil Empire," Burch said. "Listen to this."

He read a list of residents' rules and requirements from a brochure. "No fences, no hedges more than four feet tall. No boats, trailers, or disabled cars allowed in a driveway for more than three days. No clotheslines, etc., etc."

The Villages sprawled into three counties, with fifty thousand residents already, the driver said. New houses were being built at a rate of four hundred a month. "A few weeks ago you could see a lake right over there." He pointed to a row of new homes. "But this new section went up in front of it overnight. Now you wouldn't even know there was a lake."

The detectives took the trolley to the address of Spring Nolan Grayson and her husband, a retired insurance executive. The sprawling house, a top-of-the-line model called the Sanibel, according to the brochures, had a golf cart outside and twin Lincolns in the garage.

Spring Nolan's hair was a soft salt-and-pepper. Wearing casual golf clothes, she looked like the mother of the girl she had been, the one the detectives had seen only in old photos.

She knew about the dead infants from the news accounts, she said.

"I have no idea who they might be."

"You can appreciate, I'm sure, that we'd like to return them to their families for decent burials," Birch said.

They talked in a screened-in lanai with a view of a serene lapis lake beneath a Wedgwood sky.

"Ask my mother how they got there," she suggested sweetly.

"Are you saying she knows?" Nazario asked.

"I can't speak for her," she said.

"Did your family have problems before the murder?"

"That's the hell of it. I didn't think so. Our childhood seemed idyllic until that moment. Everything after the loss of my father—the change in my life, the changes in my mother—was shocking, so totally out of character with all that happened before."

"How did your mother change?" Burch asked.

She sighed and rolled her eyes, as though she didn't know where to begin. "From a vibrant, vivacious, warm, and outgoing woman, which is how I remembered her, to a vicious, paranoid, accusatory, abusive . . . I can't even go on." She held up her hand for a moment, as though shielding herself from her own dark thoughts. "I don't want to be upset."

"Did your father ever molest you, any of your siblings, or your friends?" Burch asked.

"Never!"

"Do you believe the others will give us the same answer?"

"Of course! Though, as I said, I can't speak for anyone else. Brooke is emotional, so weak and impressionable that if she's told anything often enough, she'll believe it."

"Do you have any theories about where those infants came from?"

"I don't think I should answer that, gentlemen. I'm doing my best to be helpful and courteous, but both my therapist and my husband felt I shouldn't even see you. Stirring up old wounds and painful issues from the past isn't healthy. Anytime I hear from anyone in my family, it's a definite setback."

"Is that why Sky left?"

"My brother was lucky in that respect, yet in another way, I always pitied both him and Brooke because they're the youngest. They had less time during their formative years with both parents and a lifestyle both healthy and perfect. It was a time when the future held nothing but promise. Then it changed, and as a result, none of us ever achieved our full potential.

"Brooke fancies herself a fashionista, a businesswoman, owns some little boutique that couldn't survive without financial help from our mother. She's never mustered enough strength to cut the apron—or purse—strings. Never will.

"We were all affected by what they now call posttraumatic stress disorder. They had no name for PTSD then."

"Did you know that a Peeping Tom was stalking

your sister Summer in the months before the murder?" Burch asked.

"No!" Her hand flew to her heart.

"He watched her through her bedroom window. He was there that night."

"Did he kill my father?" She looked pale.

"No," Burch said. "We believe he was a witness. He saw it happen."

"Who did he say did it?" She leaned forward, eyes intense.

"We don't have a positive identification of the gunman yet."

"It was a man?" Her voice dropped to an incredulous whisper. "A man shot my father?" She looked stunned.

"You thought it was a woman?"

She said nothing for several moments, processing the information.

"We never knew." She regained her composure, her true emotions behind a bland, courteous, and evasive mask.

"The prowler who was peeping at Summer said he thought she knew he was watching her. Did she ever confide in you that she thought someone was out there?"

"No. But I wouldn't be surprised." Her lips curled into a sneer. "Summer the exibitionist. She always danced as though no one was watching. Everyone did, of course. No one could take their eyes off her. She thrived on attention."

"Did some acting, I hear."

"Nothing of any note."

"One more thing," Nazario said. "Was the family aware that your grandfather, Captain Cliff Nolan, fought in the Spanish Civil War, that he wasn't lost earlier, off the coast of Cuba, as people believed?"

Her sudden peal of high-pitched laughter startled them both. She clapped her hands in girlish excitement. "Oh, how rich, how wonderful! Please do be sure to tell my mother you know that!"

"We may be back," Burch said at the door.

She did not answer. She had turned away, still laughing.

CHAPTER 17

Stone waited five minutes, then redialed.

"You telling me you're a ghost? Who the hell are you?" Anderson's voice shook with anger.

"I told you. You're welcome to call me back at Miami P.D. Check with my sergeant or my lieutenant. I need to know why my father had your name and telephone number back in 1987, shortly before he and my mother were murdered."

Anderson paused for a long moment.

"I'll be damned. I do recollect now that they had a little boy. That you?"

"Right. Detective now, on the Miami P.D. Cold Case Squad."

"Humph. Time sure flies. Had me going for a while. What can I do for you?"

"We're investigating my parents' case. It's still open. How did you know my father?"

"You mean your folks' homicide wasn't solved?" He sounded surprised. "I understood at the time it was a robbery. Some stickup men that had been hitting small businesses. That's what I was told by your homicide investigators."

"No. It's still open. The robberies were solved but this case was unrelated."

"Damn. Wish I'da known that. Sorry for my initial reaction to you. Thought it was some kinda sick practical joke. That case has always been a sore spot for me. A real piece a bad luck.

"We put a helluva lot of time and work into it. It was really going somewhere. Your folks had agreed to talk to me, to give statements and then testify at trial in an old case."

"What kind of case?"

"Homicide. You know there've been a string of civil rights–era cases reopened and successfully prosecuted in recent years—the church bombing that killed those little girls in Birmingham, the murder of Medgar Evers in Jackson, Mississippi.

"Your folks were the only hope we had of putting together a successful prosecution in another one. I worked with a task force in the civil rights section of the criminal division. Took us quite a while to track them down. We were elated after I talked to your dad. I was delayed a couple a days in getting down there. When I did, I learned they were both gone, killed during an armed robbery at their business. I met briefly with the detectives."

"There's no mention of that in the case file."

"Guess they didn't think it relevant to their investigation."

"You sure you had the right people?" Stone asked, puzzled. He had thought he knew everything about his parents. "What kind of homicide are we talking about?"

"Let me verify who I'm speaking with first and I'll tell you."

Anderson called back minutes later through the main Miami Police line.

"We were trying to reopen a 1972 case. During that summer of 'seventy-two, civil rights volunteers from all over had come here to launch a voter registration drive in the black community. The local Ku Klux Klan types resented the Freedom Riders from out of state, said outside agitators had no business coming in to stir up trouble. Things got pretty hot."

"Wait a second," Stone said. "I remember, that's how my mom and dad met. She and some classmates from New York had gone down to Mississippi to help. My father and a few friends went up there as well. They met in Mississippi. They had a lot in common. Both had taken part in demonstrations, sit-ins, wade-ins at segregated beaches, that sort of thing. After that summer, I don't think they were ever as involved. But I never heard anything about a murder. What were the facts?"

"A black man, a young fellow from Pennsylvania, was dragged from his car and shotgunned. The suspects were three white police officers."

"Oh." The word sounded hollow.

"The rights workers used to travel together for protection. Four cars in a convoy were headed for the county seat to open the registration in the morning. They'd already been threatened by police, who'd ordered them out of town, escorted them to the city limits. Three of the cops continued to follow them in two patrol cars.

"When they stopped the third car, occupied by Ernest Wendall Hill, age twenty-one, on an isolated stretch of road, the drivers of the first two carloads fled. The fourth vehicle was occupied by Sam Stone and his then-girlfriend, Annie Oliver. Stone pulled over, unwilling to leave their friend behind. They saw Hill dragged out of his car. They witnessed him being beaten, kicked, and then dragged to a ditch at the side of the road where he was shot multiple times. Stone drove off in a panic. If he hadn't, he and Annie probably would have wound up in the ditch that night, too, and we wouldn't be having this conversation.

"But they saw it and could identify the killers. They were the same cops who had stopped and threatened them earlier. They fled in fear, went to Miami. They were scared. Can't say as I blame them. Who do you go to when it's the police doing the killing?

"Investigators learned over the years that the police officers were responsible and there'd been talk, rumors of witnesses. We were itching to prosecute. Put a cold case team together and worked it by process of elimination. Contacted every civil rights organization and former volunteer we could find, checked marchers' names in newspaper accounts, books, documents, jail logs, and hospital records. A tedious process.

"Eventually we honed in on Samuel Stone. And, lo and behold, the former Annie Oliver, the second missing witness, was now his wife. I spoke to your dad at length twice, and once with her. They felt safer, given the years and the geographic distance, but were still reticent, said they had a family now, and mentioned you.

"I promised to protect them if they would give sworn statements and testify at the grand jury and at trial. They said they could identify the officers, had even heard them call one another by name. Guess you don't forget those things, even after fifteen years. When I first made contact with your dad, he promised to discuss it with his family, his wife and his mother.

"He called back and said they had all agreed it was the right thing to do. They hoped to see justice. Our office was jubilant. We had such high hopes of making that case. Can't tell you what a blow the loss of your parents was to us."

"You weren't suspicious that they were killed right after they agreed to cooperate?"

"Seemed like a tragic twist of fate at the time," Anderson said. "After all our efforts to find them. I hear what you're saying now, man, but it was fifteen years after the fact and a world away. No way the suspects could have known the Stones were about to become a threat to them."

"How can you be so sure? Can you be certain there was no leak in your office?"

Silence at the other end of the line. Stone could hear the man breathing. "Let me tell you about a Miami police officer by the name of Ray Glover," he said quietly. "I think he tried to investigate my parents' case on his own and stumbled into something."

When he finished, Anderson sounded excited. "You've gotta get on the horn and talk to Ashton Banks, the cold case investigator who took my place. Ash will be super-interested in your information. This opens everything wide up again. We couldn't make the original homicide case without your parents' testimony, but if this all pans out, we could still prosecute them for conspiracy, the murders of your folks, and if what you suspect about Officer Glover is true, we could nail 'em for that as well. Those sonsabitches ain't home free yet."

"Where are the suspects? You sure they're still alive?"

"One of the original trio died awhile back. Natural causes. The other two are still around, about sixty years old now. One has a son, a sergeant on the same goddamn police department. Give Ash a call, hear? Got a pencil? I'll give you the direct line."

CHAPTER 18

Stone thought the number was a direct line but a woman answered.

He assumed she was a secretary, identified himself, and asked for Ashton Banks.

"You're talking to her."

"Sorry, I didn't know you were a woman."

She laughed. "I know far more about you, Detective Stone, than you do about me. I've been waiting on your call."

"You spoke to Anderson?"

"Certainly did. He burned up the phone lines after you two talked. That old warhorse is ready to abandon retirement, charge back in to work, and commandeer his old desk. He's on his way down here right now to lend a hand. Let's talk."

She wanted copies of both files, Glover's and his parents'.

"Is your grandmother still living?"

"Saw 'er this morning. She gave me a box of my father's old papers. That's where I found Anderson's number."

"Good, I'll come on down there and take her statement."

"I'm not too sure about that," he said. "She's pretty gun-shy, closemouthed about the past. Gran raised me. We're close and she worries. She's getting on in years. She's fragile and I don't want her stressed out or put at any kind of risk."

"I'll be gentle," she said confidently. "She may be more help than you realize. I can be down there in a day or so. We can get to work, brainstorm, and I can take her statement."

"Look, I'm closer to her than anybody in the world. If I can't persuade her to talk to me about it, what makes you think she'll talk to you?"

"Because I'm *not* closer to her than anybody in the world."

"Like I said, I don't want her put at risk."

"She'll be protected."

"That's what they told my parents."

"I need to come anyway so we can get this show on the road. Overnight me copies of both files. I'll read them on the way. How's Thursday?"

"Great."

He hung up the phone and whispered, "Thank you, Jesus."

CHAPTER 19

"It's something I always wanted to see," Burch said.

"Me, too," Nazario said. "I read a book about it when I was a kid."

"Look, is that it?"

"It's a lot smaller than I thought it would be."

The detectives had arrived at the San Antonio airport too late to drive to Summer Nolan's ranch outside the city, so Burch had asked the taxi driver to drop them at a hotel near the Alamo.

The historic landmark, surrounded by desert willows, live oaks, cedar elms, and redbud trees, was closed for the night, but lights blazed outside at two A.M. and throngs of people stood gazing at the old fort. The two detectives joined them.

"Are you Texans?" asked a tall man in his twenties, wearing a plaid shirt and blue jeans.

He seemed genuinely sympathetic when they said they weren't. "Too bad," he said.

"You visit here often?" Burch asked.

He nodded. "I try to drive down from Dallas at least twice a month. I just like to be here."

People were always there, he said, no matter the time, day and night.

"That's nice," Nazario said later. "The way people treat it like a shrine, with respect. No graffiti. No garbage. Nobody selling cheap T-shirts. If the Alamo was in Miami, you know what would stand on that site now—the sixty-story Alamo condominiums."

"You're starting to sound like Kiki," Burch said.

"She grows on you," Nazario said.

San Antonio was as hot as Florida, even hotter, as they drove out to Summer Nolan's ranch in the morning, but this heat felt dry and invigorating, not like Miami's humid, soggy, wet blanket.

What took their breath away was Summer Nolan.

"You're Summer?" Nazario said when she opened the door.

"Yes." The same spirited girl in the old photographs, the same lush dark hair, pillowy lips, high, chiseled cheekbones, and brilliant blue eyes.

She hadn't aged. Burch decided it must be a top Hollywood secret, how to stay young and beautiful forever. "You're exactly like your pictures!" he exclaimed.

She laughed. "That's the other Summer. My mother. I'll get her."

Summer Nolan, the original, still looked good for a woman her age. She wore silver and turquoise jewelry, an Indian-style skirt, and a peasant blouse.

"I saw one of your movies," Nazario said as she led them into an air-conditioned patio with spectacular views. "You were on the wagon train and the Indians—"

"The best thing I can say about that one is that we

shot it on location not far from here. That's how I fell in love with this part of the country."

"Musta been quite a career," Burch said.

"Not really," she said easily. "It was actually mediocre, thanks in no small part to my mother. She didn't want an actress in the family. She always has to be queen bee, the center of all attention. She even sued to stop me from using my own name and called gossip columnists and casting directors to spread malicious rumors about me." She sighed. "Acting was good therapy for me when I needed it most."

Though friendly, she remained vague and evasive about the past, until Burch mentioned the Peeping Tom.

Her body froze, her blue eyes widened.

"His name is Ronald Stokoe. He went on to build a longtime career as a sex offender."

"Did you arrest him?" she whispered.

"No," Burch said.

"Why not!" Fists clenched, she sprang from her chair at the hand-carved wooden table. "Why didn't you?"

She stared at them, then slumped back into her chair and folded her hands in her lap. "Guilt is such a terrible thing." Her voice cracked. Tears sparkled, caught in her heavy, dark lashes. The tilt of her head, the mournful, downcast look, reminded Burch of her image in the forty-year-old funeral photo that had appeared in the newspaper. The grieving wife and daughters of the deceased.

"I've lived with guilt my whole life," she said, her voice a monotone. "It's like a shadow you can never shake, no matter what you do, who you love, or what you accomplish. It's always there, just over your shoulder."

"You felt guilty?" Burch said.

She nodded slowly. "I knew a stranger was out there," she said, her words a shaky whisper. "Sometimes I could hear him breathing. I wasn't afraid. He was my audience and I danced, I performed for him. I was a foolish, romantic young girl with a head full of fantasies—that I was Salome, Jezebel, Mata Hari.

"He killed my father when he came home and caught him watching me that night. I've always known it was my fault." She stared at them accusingly. "Why didn't you arrest him?"

"He didn't do it," Burch said.

"My God in heaven! If he didn't, who did?"

"We don't know. Your Peeping Tom was a witness. He saw the killer run."

"Oh my God!" She rested her head on the table and began to weep. "Oh my God! I can't believe it," she gasped between sobs. "I knew it was my fault but couldn't tell. I was too ashamed. My father was murdered because of me. I felt so guilty."

"You were wrong," Burch said solemnly. "We want to find the man who did kill your father. Maybe you can help. And as a mother, you know how important it is to identify those little babies and give them proper burials. It's the right thing to do. We still need to know how they figure into the case, whether they were even related to the murder."

"My mother always believed they were." Summer wiped her eyes with her fingers.

"Do you know how they got into the cellar?" Nazario asked.

She nodded, eyes regretful. "We put them there."

"Wait a minute," Burch said. " 'We'?"

"Yes."

"Ma'am," Nazario said quickly. "I have to advise you of your rights before you say anything more."

He did so, and she waived her right to have an attorney present.

"I have nothing to hide anymore," she said softly.

Tears streamed down her face as she spoke.

"It was the day after the funeral. My mother hadn't slept. She was restless, shaky, crazed by grief and disbelief, desperate to know why it happened and filled with a manic energy. She hated the publicity, the police, the pity. And I couldn't talk to anyone. I was desperate to keep her from finding out it was my fault.

"She began to go through my father's things, tearing them apart, looking for answers, for a sign, for anything.

"She found two keys and a receipt for a storage unit he rented a few days before his death. She didn't want to tell anyone until she saw for herself what was in there. We all had to go. She was afraid to leave any of us alone.

"I don't know what she thought she would find. I don't think she knew, either. It was one of those storage places in an industrial area, a loading dock and a row of cubicles, each about the size of a small room. Spring and I went inside with her. Sky was somewhere out by the car. Brooke was behind us, at the door. She had allergies and was afraid there might be dust inside.

"The only thing there was a padlocked wooden box,

about the size of a hope chest. My mother used the second key to open it.

"I was right beside her when she saw them. So was Spring.

"'Oh my God! Oh my God!' she said. 'Girls, you have to help me!' She slammed the lid down and locked it so Sky and Brooke wouldn't see what was inside. Then she backed the car up close to the unit. Spring and I helped her put the box in the trunk of our car and we took it home, to the Shadows. My mother sobbed and shook all the way. We helped her carry it down to the cellar.

"She kept telling us to be brave, to be strong. No one must know about it, she said. It would ruin us, our reputations, the family name, forever."

"Did she know where the box, the babies, came from?"

"She assumed the worst, that my father was responsible, he'd been unfaithful, a pervert, a baby killer who'd somehow brought on his own death. I never told her his murder was my fault.

"A few days later, she suddenly announced that we had to leave the Shadows. Immediately. That day. We packed up a few things and left. As far as I knew, they were still down there, in the cellar. All these years.

"As soon as we left, she began to accuse my sisters and me of terrible things. She was horrible to Sky. Her treatment of him became worse and worse as he got older because he looked just like my father. I knew I deserved the abuse but the others didn't. Poor Sky," she said mournfully.

"Spring has always had sexual hang-ups because of the things our mother accused us of. I think she and Brooke always suspected that our mother killed our father because of what was in the box. Brooke was always very fragile, physically and mentally. I kept my guilt to myself. Lord knows what poor Sky thought, if anything. He was just a little boy."

She agreed to a DNA test. "Do they have to draw blood?" She shuddered. "I hate needles."

"No, it's much simpler," Burch assured her. "A crime lab technician from the local police department will just swipe a Q-Tip inside your cheek, between the gums and your teeth, and seal it in a glassine envelope. It's called a buccal smear. Then we'll take it back to Miami for testing."

They arranged to have a court reporter from the local state attorney's office take Summer Nolan's statement recounting how the infants' makeshift coffin was moved to the Shadows.

"Did I commit a crime?" she asked at one point.

"Technically, yes," Burch said. "But nothing that would have been prosecuted, even then. It's a misdemeanor to interfere with a dead body, but you were a juvenile at the time. We just want to put a record together in the event that someone is eventually prosecuted. We don't even know yet how they died."

"There's another mystery I hoped you might clear up," Nazario said. "Captain Clifford Nolan."

"My grandfather," she said. "He died when my father was still a small boy."

"Lost in a storm off the Cuban coast?"

"No." She smiled wryly. "Halfway around the world. I know you won't believe this, but he was killed in the Spanish Civil War in 1937, at the battle of Jarama, trying to stop the fascists' march on Madrid."

"I do believe it," Nazario said.

"My mother wouldn't allow his name to be spoken in our home. She considered him scandalous. Only her relatives were respectable. But my father and I were close and we shared secrets. I was the oldest, his favorite. When I turned sixteen, he gave me a few old love letters his father had written to his mother from the front, and the medal she was sent after he was killed. My mother would have destroyed them, given the chance. My father knew I'd keep them."

"Did you?" Nazario asked.

She nodded. "They contain nothing of great historical import, mostly about how he missed her, my father, Miami, and the Shadows. He believed he was doing the right thing, that the war was for a noble cause and he was making amends for anything he'd done before. If the federal authorities believed him dead he thought he, and the charges against him, would be forgotten and he could eventually come home. There wasn't a great deal of communication between Washington, D.C., and Miami at the time. His plan might have worked, but the false report of his death became a self-fulfilling prophecy."

Nazario told her about Kiki Courtelis.

"Have her call me," Summer said. "I'll share whatever information I have."

As the detectives left, she asked a question of her

own. "What do I do now? The secrets I kept burned holes in my heart for my entire adult life. All those years wasted. Where were you? Why didn't you come sooner?"

Craig Burch replied with another question. "Why the hell didn't you tell the truth that night?"

She nodded. "I was afraid my mother would hate me forever but, of course, she did anyway. I feel free now. The burden's been lifted from my shoulders, but now I want to know who did kill my father, and why."

"So do we."

On the way to the airport, Burch said to Nazario, "Let's see what little brother knows."

• • •

"I never knew the Cincinnati airport was in Kentucky." Burch scowled down at peaked rooftops in dark shades of gray, unlike Miami's pastels. Below, a tug pushed a huge barge up the Ohio River.

"Look at the traffic!" Nazario said.

"Where?"

"There isn't any!"

Nowhere in sight was anything like Miami's wall-to-wall gridlock.

To reach Oxford, Ohio, they had to drive through parts of Indiana and Kentucky with rolling hills, bright blue-green grass, and small brick-trimmed houses set back from the road behind sweeping lawns.

Sky Nolan had fled his past, taking refuge in rural farm country with maple trees, sheep, cattle, silos, and corn and soy bean fields.

As their rental car roller-coastered up and down steep hills and around blind, hairpin curves, the detectives, accustomed to South Florida's flat terrain, grew queasy. The rental actually seemed airborne at times, until Burch ordered Nazario to pull over and relinquish the wheel.

Sky Nolan, now in his early fifties, met them in a crowded coffee shop frequented by students. A youth at the counter wore a T-shirt proclaiming that MIAMI WAS A UNIVERSITY WHEN FLORIDA BELONGED TO SPAIN. Beneath, in smaller letters: *Miami University   Oxford, Ohio   Established 1809.*

Sky was handsome and easygoing, with a smile like his father's.

"Ironic, isn't it?" he said after shaking hands. "This is a college town. Miami University, the closest I've come to Florida since age nine."

He apologized for meeting them in a public place.

"One of my hard-and-fast rules for years," he explained. "I don't let my family, or any discussion about them, into my home. Self-defense."

A local teacher and football coach, he'd married late, he said, and still had three young children at home. "Luke, the oldest, is nine, the same age I was when I lost my dad."

"It took guts, real character, to just walk away from your family's money," Nazario said.

"It was survival. Believe it or not, I was nearly thirty before I realized that to survive, both mentally and physically, I had to walk away from all of them. Not walk, actually, run. Took me another ten years to get my act together and start building a normal life."

"How much do you remember about your childhood?" Nazario asked.

"That my mother was crazy about my father—until he died. Then she was just crazy. She hated him, *really* hated him. Maybe because he'd left her alone with us, or for some more sinister reason. Unfortunately, I looked just like him. Same smile, same eyes. That didn't bode well for our relationship.

"I remember the night it happened like it was yesterday. I was in the cellar with a lantern, playing pirate in the tunnel.

"I didn't want to do my chores. I heard my mother call me again and figured it probably meant my father was home and it was time for me to surrender.

"I went up the stairs and had just emerged from under the stairwell when we heard an explosion in the night.

" 'What was that?' my mother said. She went to the stereo and turned off the music—Vivaldi, I think. I've never been able to listen to it since, to this day.

"As she walked toward the front door, I thought I heard my father's voice calling her, then we heard the second explosion. 'Oh dear Lord,' she said. 'Your father!'

"Summer came out of her room and said, 'What was that?'

"My mother ran outside screaming.

"I followed her and our lives were never the same again. By the time I reached them, she had blood all over her dress. She was screaming, 'They killed him! They killed him! My God! Oh my God!'

"Our lives changed from day to night in that moment. My mother was hyper, trying not to fall apart which, of course, she kept doing. She sobbed, shrieked, and howled like a banshee all night long."

"Where were the other girls when the shots were fired?"

"Brooke and Spring were in the music room watching a television show when I'd last seen them. I think it was over and they'd gone to their room to listen to music, or whatever. They never let me in there.

"My mother found something in my father's effects a few days later. Made us all go with her to a storage unit.

"I was playing around outside. My mother and the girls came out, all crying and shaky. She said what my father left in the storage unit would be a disgrace, a disaster for us all. She kept talking about the family name." Sky laughed heartily.

"I don't know what family name she was trying so hard to protect. My damn grandfather was a smuggler, a rumrunner for God's sake. My dad used to tell me stories about him, when Mother wasn't around. We used to talk a lot. I was the youngest, the only boy, his favorite.

"They brought a box, like a chest, out of the storage unit and took it down to the cellar. I kept asking, 'What is it? What's in it?' Nobody would tell me, and all of a sudden the cellar was off-limits. I'd played down there all my life. The girls, too. We used to hide down there."

"Hide from what?" Burch said.

Sky pointed his coffee stirrer like a gun. "Hey, don't you start in, too. You sound like my mother. All us kids would hide down there from time to time. From each other, from our parents when they wanted us to do chores or homework. We'd play hide-and-seek. Typical kid stuff.

"But all of a sudden it was forbidden. So naturally, I went down there to snoop the first chance I got. The box was on a shelf. Padlocked. I was trying to get the lock open when she caught me.

"She freaked, went totally crazy. Said we had to get out of the house, started to throw our clothes in the car. I didn't want to go. I was surprised that the girls didn't put up an argument or balk, too. They knew something I didn't and seemed all too willing to get out. My mother drove us away from there like somebody possessed. We never slept there another night, never went back. It was like we were on the run from the Shadows. From that thing in the cellar."

"Did you know what was inside?" Nazario said.

"Hell, no. Nobody would ever tell me. But I do now." He shrugged. "I read the newspapers. Back then I had all kinds of fantasies about what was down there."

Like his sister, Sky agreed to give a DNA sample.

"Have you seen my mother yet?"

"Our next stop," Nazario said. "Any message?"

"No. I'm over it. Every once in a while I get letters from their lawyers wanting me to testify in one of their lawsuits against each other. My father had established trusts for us in his will. He named my mother as administrator. We were all at her mercy financially. The girls periodically sue her for breach of fiduciary duty, her handling of the family money. And she files outlandish complaints against them. I never respond. I'm done. I was done a long time ago." He paused for a moment to reflect. "But no matter what your relationship is with a parent, you regret when they are gone from your life.

"The Shadows," he said as they stepped out onto the street. "Is it still standing? I read they planned to knock it down. If it's still there, I'd like to go back and see it one last time."

"If you're serious, don't put it off," Burch advised.

•   •   •

The detectives skirted yellow crime scene tape to enter the posh high-rise San Francisco apartment building where Diana Nolan lived. The shrouded corpse of a jumper awaited removal from the bloodstained sidewalk.

The detectives exchanged alarmed glances. "You don't think . . ." Burch said.

They were relieved when a uniformed maid said they were expected and that Diana Nolan was out on her penthouse terrace plucking roses from her private garden.

Pierce Nolan's widow, now eighty, had delicate, almost childlike features. She wore a woven straw hat with a round brim to protect her from the sun. With her hat and curls she resembled a wrinkled, wizened Shirley Temple.

She brought in an armful of roses in lush, velvety shades of pink and red and handed them to the same maid, who waited while she peeled off her gardening gloves. She took them as well.

Diana Nolan ordered tea, then settled herself into a plush red chair as though preparing to hold court.

"I believed in truth and beauty," she told them imperiously. "I was the belle of New York, debutante of the year. Walter Winchell wrote about me in many of his columns. So did Dorothy Kilgallen. I was photographed at every opening night on Broadway, at the Metropolitan Opera, and at the ballet. I would have been the Paris Hilton of my day except, of course, that my parents and I had style, class, and good breeding. You should have seen our listing in the Social Register. My friends were Gloria Vanderbilt and Cary Latimer, but then I met Pierce Nolan and isolated myself in Miami for him. I lamented the lack of culture there, but did it all for the love of the wrong man. That was the great tragedy of my life.

"He had a dark side I never suspected and it brought an end to him. If he was that perverted, I *knew* what must have happened in our own home, a place built by his father, a notorious adventurer and criminal. When I asked our daughters to tell me if their father had ever touched them, they denied it. To this day they refuse to admit it. Deny, deny, deny." Her voice grew shrill. "They lie and lie and swear to each other's lies. They all lied to me, starting with him. They are obviously their father's children, as was he. The apple never falls far from the tree.

"I believed our life was idyllic. Despite the backwater climate in Miami, we had music in our home, took trips to New York for the opera, the shows, and the shopping. I tried to bring style and grace to Miami. I believed that love would compensate for what my surroundings lacked. I was so naive.

"Our children, all of them damaged goods, damaged by their devil of a father, repaid me by lying. They grew up greedy, ungrateful, and grasping. Lucky sperm, demanding money because of a mere accident of birth."

"I thought Sky hadn't asked for anything since he left years ago," Nazario said.

"He'd better not plan to in the future, either. He's so like his father. God knows what double life he leads wherever he is. Now that I'm rid of that cursed house and know it will be destroyed, my attorneys and I plan to see to it that none of them ever see a dime of that money. Not one deserves a cent."

"What we want is to solve your husband's murder and identify those infants," Burch said. "Did you know they'd be there when you took your children to the storage unit that day?"

"Of course not. No one was more shocked than I."

"Do you have any idea who they were?"

She shook her head.

"It seems impossible that seven infants could be found in a house occupied by only one family, yet nobody in that family has a clue who they were, or where they came from."

She shrugged. "Obviously they were bastards. Who the mothers were, how many women there were, over what period of time, I have no idea. My husband had to be the father."

"No," Burch said. "He wasn't."

"What are you saying?" She looked startled. "Who else would have fathered them? Pierce rented that unit, he paid for it. He clearly hid them there shortly before his death. And just as clearly a killer took revenge for his reckless philandering."

"No," Burch said again. "You're wrong. We haven't made it public yet, but DNA test results show that none of the infants are related. None shared the same parents. We've taken DNA samples from both Summer and Sky. They'll tell us if your husband was related to one, but we believe it will show that he wasn't the father of any of them."

"That's preposterous!"

"No. Now, knowing this, do you have any idea where they came from?"

She was silent.

"Sometimes," she finally said, her voice less shrill, "I wonder what Pierce would look like today, had he lived. Would we recognize each other if we passed on the street? His memory burns like a flame in my soul, but my heart was broken forever."

She swore she knew of no other motive for his murder. She had no jealous admirers, he had no financial or business problems. Like everyone else had told them: Pierce Nolan had no enemies.

Burch checked his watch as they rose to leave. "When we spoke to Brooke, she agreed to meet us here. Do you know where we can find her?"

Diana Nolan looked up, startled.

"You just missed her," she said slyly.

•   •   •

The shocked detectives conferred with the police down on the sidewalk.

"The way the mother took the news, dry-eyed and

calm, almost as though she expected it, struck me as odd," the San Francisco detective said. "But people react in different ways." He shrugged.

"All she said was that her daughter suffered from periodic bouts of depression and they'd been involved in a series of long-running family disputes. The daughter apparently left the apartment upset after they exchanged words today. Instead of leaving the building, she took the stairwell to the roof.

"An employee up there to repair a flagpole saw her. He yelled to her but said she didn't hesitate. Dove off, arms out, like she was trying to fly."

CHAPTER 20

Stone feared she'd missed her flight.

Miami International Airport was chaotic as usual, a cacophony of languages, police whistles, and the blaring horns of taxis, shuttles, and impatient drivers. He had said he'd pick her up. It made sense. She didn't know the city, it would give them more time to talk. He could drive her right to the station, take her to lunch later, then drop her off at her hotel.

He tried not to stare at a beautiful, sophisticated-looking black woman in a tailored blazer and continued to scan the streams of arriving travelers in search of Ashton Banks.

He felt a light tap on the shoulder.

"Detective Stone?"

It was the beautiful woman, skin like chocolate, black hair pulled back, big eyes alive with intelligence and anticipation. Stylish and smart-looking, she stood about five feet four inches tall, no more than 110 pounds, with a wide mouth and thick eyelashes.

"You're Ashton Banks?"

"That's right. Call me Ash. You walked right by me."

"I didn't know you were black." He hated himself

when he heard what he said. What he really wanted to say again was, *Thank you, Jesus.*

He was glad he'd worn his good jacket and had taken the time to put on that industrial-strength goop so his hair didn't walk through a door before he did.

She flashed a megawatt smile. "For a detective, you sure don't know a lot of things, do you? Let's go meet Gran."

He warned during the drive that his grandmother would be hostile. "She refuses to talk about it. She's afraid something will happen to me."

"Can't blame her." She gave him a sly once-over.

Was she flirting? Was the instant attraction mutual? Nah, he couldn't be that lucky.

"Particularly after what happened to her son," Ash said.

•   •   •

They found Gran picking herbs in her garden. She looked up as they exited the car.

"Gran, I want you to meet someone."

"I see you've got basil, chicory, and parsley," Ash said before he could even introduce them. "Is that peppermint? Bless your soul. People usually grow spearmint."

"That's right," Gran said. "Sonny likes it in his iced tea."

"Sonny?" Ash cut her eyes at him, amused.

He winced. "Nickname," he muttered, "from childhood."

"I live in an apartment," she told Gran, "so all I have

is a little window-box herb garden. I mostly grow catnip for Snugglepuss."

As the two women talked fertilizer, a rare and refreshing sudden summer breeze clapped the palm fronds together overhead.

"I do love that sound." Ash shaded her eyes and looked up.

"The palm trees are clapping their hands for God," Gran said, nodding.

"Nice line, Gran," Stone said.

She shot him a withering, sidelong look. "That's from Psalms, boy. When did you quit reading your Bible?"

"Yeah," Ashton Banks said. "When?"

"You two are ganging up on me. I can't win."

After the garden tour, they went inside.

"So you're a Cold Case girl from Mississippi," Gran said as she added peppermint leaves to the iced tea. "Guess that means you and Sonny have a lot in common. Are you married?"

Stone rolled his eyes but held his breath for the answer.

"No, I'm not. It's hard to build a social life when I'm always working. Why? Is there someone you'd like me to meet?"

"Maybe," Gran said coyly. "Very good-looking, a little bit spoiled, but a good boy."

"Gran!" Stone interrupted, embarrassed.

She smiled up at him. "What do you think, Sonny? Wouldn't she and your cousin Robert make a handsome couple? I bet they'd hit it off."

"Robert?" he said, startled. "No way! I wouldn't wish him on any woman."

"How did they happen to name you Ashton?" Gran was asking.

"It was my maternal grandmother's maiden name. She had no brothers to carry it on, so my mother gave it to me."

"That's nice." Gran nodded. "I like remembering family. Very nice. If I ever was to have any great-grandchildren," she said, casting a baleful eye at Stone, "it would be nice to name one Oliver. That was my daughter-in-law's maiden name."

"I know," Ash said. "They were so brave to go to Mississippi that summer."

Gran nodded. "When my son said he wanted to do civil rights work that summer, I was proud. Idealistic at the time. I wanted to see Dr. Martin Luther King's dream realized. I'd listen to the church choir, think about his words, and it seemed like the whole universe was singing. The waves beating on the shore, the wind moving in the trees, and the sounds of streams and brooks. I thought life was like church, where you have to sing with a full voice. I encouraged my son to answer the call, to help people register to vote. I encouraged him. It was a terrible mistake."

Ashton reached for her hand.

"I remember the last lynching here in Miami, in Ojus, in 1937," Gran said. "I was just a child then. Later I was teargassed once, at a peaceful protest here in town. I still remember the screams when the tear-gas bombs were thrown. All I could think of was, *Change this.*"

"I didn't know about that," Stone said.

"A lot you don't know," she said. "Your daddy and your momma, they got sprayed with water hoses and had police dogs set on 'em. They were shell-shocked that summer. When your daddy came home two weeks early, he looked like he'd aged ten years. He brought her with him. First time I met the girl.

"She was a precious daughter-in-law, but Lord-amercy, up till that summer, she hadn't seen the bad in people. Took some time before they told me all they saw. My son said, 'Mama, there are smiling people out there with devils' faces.' We never talked about it again.

"Then, all those years later, a man from Mississippi called to tell my son they wanted justice for that young man who was killed. We talked and talked about it and, God forgive me, I made my second terrible mistake. I said they should stand up for justice. You can be a quiet soldier, I told him, an unarmed soldier. Education and knowledge are weapons. History is a weapon. So is the law. And the best way to help yourself is to help others.

"But evil never changes," she said, her voice small, hands clasped in her lap. "It was my fault. If I'da argued against it, hard, they wouldn't have been taken from me and Sonny."

Stone sat listening. "It wasn't your fault, Gran."

"So you always believed that their murders were connected to what they saw in Mississippi?"

"Yes, ma'am, I did."

"Call me Ash, please. Did you tell the homicide detectives that?"

She shook her head. "They were white policemen. I

didn't know if I could trust them. Or if they'd believe me. It wasn't so much that I was scared for myself, it was that I had to take care of Sonny. What if something happened to me? I had to be here to raise him right. If I didn't, who would?"

"You made the right decision under the circumstances. Obviously you did a wonderful job. Just look at him." Ash paused and smiled warmly at them both.

"What about Officer Glover?" Stone asked.

"He was different," Gran said. "He knew your momma and daddy. He'd go by almost every day for lunch or for a meal to take home. He always insisted on paying, not like those police who always expected everything free.

"That's how he happened to find 'em that night. Ran out of his patrol car in the rain to pick up some barbecue. Had to be right after it happened. Said he could still smell the gunpowder in the air when he walked in. It tore him up. He was a good man. Remember how kind he was that night, Sonny? Even came to the funeral to pay his respects.

"He came by to see me later, Sonny. He wanted to get ahead, thought maybe he could work on the case hisself. The homicide detectives weren't too smart, to blame robbers, he said. He thought they were wrong. But they didn't want his help, resented anything he tried to do.

"After we talked a few times, I told him about what happened that summer in Mississippi. I didn't know the name of the man who had called, but I knew he said he was from the Justice Department. Ray Glover and me both wondered if it was true or if he was one of the policemen who did the killing, still stalking the witnesses years later. Officer Glover was real excited, said he'd find out. But somethin' went wrong. He said he'd been warned. People didn't believe him and he had to get out of Miami. Said he was gonna stay on the case. Said if he could just solve it, he'd get his badge back, be able to work anyplace he wanted.

"He moved a lot but always let me know where. Then he stopped calling. I had a bad feeling after a while and called him. Katie, his girlfriend, cried like a baby. Tol' me he was dead. Poor thing said she didn't know what to do. Do nothing, I told her. Just mind your business and stay alive. Life is always the best choice. That's what I learned from it all. I learned it the hard way."

"You should have told me all this before, Gran."

"It wouldn't have helped you. It would only have made you hate."

"She's right," Ash said. "The time was never right. But it is now. What goes around comes around."

CHAPTER 21

"The mother pushed her off that roof. She just didn't do it physically," Burch told K. C. Riley. "If you could file murder charges for driving another person to suicide, I'd arrest her myself."

"How many victims will this case claim in the end?" Arms folded, Riley paced her office where the team had gathered.

Burch and Nazario had gone straight from the airport to the station. Riley told them that while they were gone Stokoe had passed the polygraph with flying colors.

"We know now who those babies weren't," she said. "They were unrelated to the Nolans. They were apparently full term and healthy, umbilical cords gone, their little navels healed or healing. They were well fed and ranged in age from newborn to nearly a month old.

"That means seven sets of parents out there somewhere. Fourteen people, to say nothing of grandparents, cousins, aunts, uncles, brothers, sisters, neighbors, and obstetricians. One infant might be lost and forgotten—not seven." She stopped pacing, sat down at her desk, and stared at the detectives.

"The fault lies with us. We're missing something. I

want to send you guys away again, back to Miami, 1961. What was happening in this city? In the world around it? There has to be something obvious that we haven't put together."

"Sure, a time machine would come in handy," Burch said, "but we don't have one."

"Yes, we do," Riley said. "It's sitting right over there on the bay. They call it a newspaper. Today's newspaper is tomorrow's history.

"Burch and Nazario, go over there first thing in the morning. Start reading the *Miami News* for the summer of 'sixty-one—on microfilm, microfiche, in a computer database, or whatever the hell other way you can access it. Read the stories, the ads, the features, the editorials, even the goddamned letters to the editor! Learn about the mayor, the crime trends, the movers and shakers, who was in trouble, who wasn't. Total immersion. I want you to come back knowing more about 1961 than you do about last year."

"We already checked the logs for that year, looking for an MO or a pattern," Burch protested. "Nothing looked related."

"Something was," she said. "Those infants didn't fall out of a spaceship. Miami was so much smaller then. Take notes, use your imagination. Sweet-talk somebody at the paper into letting you into their files. You all have reporters you whisper secrets to once in a while. Call in your favors. Didn't you have a reporter friend, Stone?"

"No way. I don't talk to that woman."

"Swell," Burch said, jet-lagged and annoyed. "You

stonewall the press every chance you get, kick reporters to the curb, alienate them and their bosses, and now you want *us* to ask *them* for favors?"

"Yeah," Riley said. "Ain't life a bitch?

"We could subscribe to their online service, but I don't think it goes back that far, and it would cost us. Unfortunately, we already blew our budget on your little cross-country sightseeing trip. Airfare, hotels, meals, and your little jaunt to the Alamo. So go make nice with the press, tell them I'm an evil bitch and forced you into it, tell them I'm a pain in your ass, too."

"That ain't no lie." Corso grinned.

•   •   •

"Dammit," Burch said later. "The son of a bitch did it again. Corso hears us mention seeing the Alamo and runs back to tell Riley. Son of a bitch. Like we didn't do nothing but sightsee out there."

"I hear you," Stone said.

"Does it all the time. She asked me how I liked Feng Shui the other day. He blabbed to her about that, too. What's your beef with Corso?" Burch asked. "I been seeing how you two don't hit it off either."

"How can I respect a white guy who calls me dawg or homie?" Stone said. "Who greets me with 'Wazup'? And calls my apartment a crib? Is he trying to be black? Is he having an identity crisis or what? The man's a weak genetic link."

"Damn straight," Burch fumed. "I'd like to muzzle that son of a bitch. He's a spy. That's what he's always doing in Riley's office, spilling his guts, gossiping. She loves it; it's a way to keep tabs on us.

"At least you're making excellent progress," he told Stone. "Keep doing what you're doing in your case and yell if you need help. First thing tomorrow, me and Nazario take a ride in the time machine."

•   •   •

Before heading home, Nazario called Kiki to say she was right about Captain Cliff Nolan, and to make a dinner date for the following night.

"I often do research at the *News,*" she told him when he mentioned their mission. "My friend Onnie works in the library and I sometimes help reporters with historic background. Maybe I can help."

•   •   •

The first sign of trouble Nazario saw when he pulled into the driveway at Casa de Luna was the lights ablaze in his small upstairs apartment as well as in the big house.

He let himself in and surprised Fleur, who was applying makeup from lots of little pots, vials, tubes, and bottles she had spread out across his bathroom counter.

Women's dresses, most of them shiny, metallic, or glittery, crammed his closet, along with sparkly stiletto heels.

"Hi, honey," she chirped. "You're back."

"Yeah." He put down his overnight bag. "I thought you'd have your own place by now."

"What do you think?" She spun around, the light reflecting off the paillettes on her shimmery dress.

"Nice." She did look beautiful.

"Or do you like this one better?" She held a silky red dress up in front of her.

"You've been shopping?" he said hopefully.

She regarded him fondly, then picked up a lip brush. "Not exactly. I have to work for a while before I do that."

"So where did all this girly stuff come from?" he asked, as though he didn't know.

"I had to borrow some of Shelly's clothes," she said.

"That's not good," he said.

"We always shared clothes when we were roommates."

"Yeah, but she's your father's roommate now."

"If she's got my father, I'm entitled to wear her Versaces and Guccis."

"Are they dry-cleanable?" he asked mournfully. "They sound expensive."

"She's got so many, she'll never miss them," she assured him.

"You promised me, Fleur. You said you'd have another place to stay by now."

"It's not like I haven't been trying. It's just taking a little bit longer than I thought. I've got a job, I'm working tonight. You should have called, sweetie. I would have had dinner ready."

He frowned. "You don't have to do that."

"I want to. Why don't you sit down and relax?" She put her hands on his shoulders. He smelled liquor on her breath.

She turned to the stove, a bit wobbly on her high heels.

"If you're gonna cook, wouldn't it be safer to take off that dress?" He wondered how much it cost.

"Okay," she sang out. "Unzip me." She backed up to him, hips thrust to one side.

He fumbled with the zipper. When it was partway down, the label was exposed. The word *Paris* confirmed his worst fears.

As he gently eased the zipper down the rest of the way, she reached back, took his hands, and guided them to her breasts.

"Fleur, don't do this to me," he pleaded. "I'm tired, frustrated, and horny. Just don't."

She giggled. "You know you want to."

He stepped away. "I'm serious."

She reached back and unfastened her lacy push-up bra.

"No way," he said.

She pouted, rehooked it, and zipped up her dress. "Okay, I'll just make you dinner. I still have time before I have to go to work."

She insisted, stirring something in a huge steaming pot on the stove as he tried to find room to unpack his toiletries among all her things in the bathroom.

She offered him an appetizer.

Carrots, broccoli, and cauliflower arranged around a puddle of sauce on a silver tray that looked like the real thing and he did not recognize as belonging in his apartment.

He dipped a carrot in the sauce and nearly broke a tooth.

"What is this?" he asked, then saw the empty frozen-food cartons in the sink.

"This is nice, Fleur. But I don't think frozen vegetables are . . ."

She was slapping the bottom of a Heinz ketchup bottle, pouring it over a bowl of undercooked pasta.

"Spaghetti?" she offered proudly.

Relieved when she left for work, he cleaned up the mess, threw the pasta in the garbage, and went to bed.

CHAPTER 22

Ray Glover was murdered. Every expert who saw the file agreed. The driver who hit him had backed over his body more than once.

"No surprise," Ashton Banks said. Stone had taken the reports to Riley's office, where the two women were meeting with Assistant State Attorney Jo Salazar.

"Our experts concur, as well. We subpoenaed personnel records for the suspects. They were all still on the job at the Bigby Police Department but didn't work the day Glover was killed, the day before, or the day after.

"Officers Ron John Cooper, Ernest Lee Evans, and his son, Wesley, who had joined his father on the department by then, all took vacation days. To go hunting, they said."

"What about—" Stone said.

"We checked that, too," she said, eyes soft. "They were also missing from work the week your parents were killed. Took vacation days, to go hunting."

"Son of a bitch," Stone said, his voice hollow. "It's true. They did it. I kind of hoped it wouldn't be cops."

"We'll get them this time," Banks said.

"Damn straight," Riley said.

•   •   •

Ashton Banks wanted to taste Miami's famous Cuban food. Stone took her to Versailles in Little Havana. They drank *mojitos* and ate *arroz con pollo*.

"I know why you like these." She grinned, swirling the mint in her mojito.

He ordered smooth, custardlike flan for dessert, with Cuban coffee.

"Now, wait a minute." She studied the menu and the cups on neighboring tables. "How many kinds of Cuban coffee are there? Does it come in different octanes? Do they use different beans?"

"It's not the beans," he said, "it's how it's prepared. The sugar is mixed in right after the espresso is brewed. *Colada* is extra-thick espresso with no milk. It comes in tiny plastic cups for quick, nearly lethal caffeine jolts.

"A *cortadito* is half espresso and half milk in a small cup. And then you have *café con leche*, warm milk and espresso in a big cup, more milk than coffee. Probably the safest for a beginner."

"Let's try one of each," she said. "I want to experience them all."

"Okay, Cold Case Girl, don't come crying to me if you don't sleep for a week."

Maybe it was the mojitos, the coffee, or the company. They talked nonstop. About everything, not just the case. Eventually Stone stopped talking and just watched her.

"What are you thinking?"

He shrugged.

"Come on," she coaxed.

"That you're really something."

"So are you."

She kissed his cheek at the hotel.

"Is that an invitation?"

"It's good night." She left him standing in the lobby.

●   ●   ●

Stone returned to the station on a caffeine high, too hyper to go home. It was late and the public lot out front was nearly empty, so he parked there instead of in the police garage.

The desk sergeant looked up from a report he was writing. "Stone! Somebody was just looking for you. A minute ago." He glanced around the lobby. "He catch you on the way in?"

"No, he leave a name?"

"Nah. Just wanted to know if you were here, then asked what your hours were. Funny, because that's when I looked up and saw you gettin' outta your car in the parking lot. 'You're in luck,' I told the guy. 'Here he comes now.' Went back to what I was doing. Where'd he go?"

The lobby was empty. So was the parking lot.

Stone shrugged. "If it's important, he'll be back."

He went to the fifth-floor homicide office. Most midnight-shift detectives were out at this hour. He liked being alone where he could think.

The copy of Glover's police identification photograph he had requested from Personnel was in his mail-box. Glover smiled confidently from his ID picture, proudly wearing the badge, the creases in his dark blue uniform pressed so sharp they could cut your eyes, try-ing the best he knew how to do the right thing. Stone smiled back.

He clipped the photo to the front page of the Collier County accident file retrieved from the medical exam-iner. He had wanted to attach a photo of Glover as he remembered him to the front, to be seen before the pic-tures of a grotesquely crumpled corpse in the road and the grisly morgue shots that followed.

He left a short time later, waved to the front desk ser-geant, and headed to the parking lot. As he strode down the wide ramp to the pavement, a corner of the four-foot-high brick barrier wall disintegrated in front of him. He saw it explode before he heard the shot and saw the muzzle flash.

Somebody was shooting at him. Stunned, he hit the ground and drew his own gun. Sprawled on the tiled floor of the ramp, he was showered by a rain of brick fragments. The muzzle flashes came from the overpass, a section of I-95 just before the off ramp. He had stashed his radio in his briefcase and fumbled to open it, keeping his head down as a slug slammed into the bulletproof glass door and ricocheted crazily.

He fired back, in the direction of the flash. The desk sergeant ran out the front door, gun drawn.

"Are you hit?"

"No! Get down!" Stone shouted. "It's from the over-pass."

The sergeant was already on the radio.

A final barrage, two, three, four shots, came as the few police officers in the station burst out of stairwells into the lobby and sirens converged.

Then the unseen shooter was gone with the high-powered whine of an engine, merging into northbound traffic.

"Shit, did anybody see him?" Stone sat on the tiled floor of the ramp, breathing hard, shattered bricks around him, his gun in his hands.

Nobody had.

CHAPTER 23

"Do you want us to come in?" Burch said.

"No, go work the time machine." There was nothing they could do for Stone at the moment, Riley said. He was uninjured and the gunman had vanished like a puff of smoke.

"Christ. Think it's related to his case?"

"Wouldn't surprise me," she said. "Something's not kosher in Mississippi. I hate it when other agencies get involved. You don't know who to trust."

• • • •

Onnie in the *News* library set Burch and Nazario up to view old newspapers on microfilm and showed them how to access stories in the system.

"Fleur didn't come back before I left this morning, a good sign," Nazario hopefully assured Burch. "She must be out looking for a place or hooking up with a new roommate."

The two plunged into old news on microfilm. Miami Beach was still a sleepy Southern resort city when

Pierce Nolan was murdered. South Beach was populated almost entirely by senior citizens. Arthur Godfrey was broadcasting his radio show from the Kenilworth Hotel in Bal Harbour. The times, though about to change, seemed so innocent. JFK was president and many believed that RFK might succeed him one day. Martin Luther King Jr. was still alive and preaching. The future seemed limitless. Yuri Gagarin had kicked off the traces of gravity and become the first man to venture into space, followed closely by Alan Shepard, the first American, in his *Freedom 7* spacecraft.

Shadows of war hovered on the horizon. Young men were being drafted and sent to Vietnam. The Bay of Pigs invasion had failed that spring and the captured invaders remained Castro's prisoners in Cuba.

Miami housing was cheap, traffic was nil, and the land west of 57th Avenue and north of Flagler Street was sparsely populated and considered to be the swampy fringe of the Everglades.

"Man," Nazario said. "Look at these ads! In 1961 you could buy a house on the water for thirty thousand bucks."

During a break for a cup of coffee, Craig Burch used two fingers to idly type the key words *Miami* and *babies* into a computer terminal in the *News* library. The system held stories dating back only as far as 1980, the year the newspaper began using computers. But the response was instantaneous. More than six hundred stories contained the words *Miami* and *babies*.

He disregarded those involving medical break-throughs, then began to scroll through the long list containing the first line or two of each story. Many mentioned an Elizabeth Wentworth.

He leaned back in his chair, sipped his lukewarm coffee, and frowned.

"Elizabeth Wentworth," he muttered, thinking aloud. "Why do I know her name?"

Without looking up from his viewfinder, Nazario, who was reading a forty-four-year-old newspaper on microfilm, replied: "Homicide victim, that August. The day before Pierce Nolan. Beaten to death, I think. Why?"

"Holy shit," Burch said.

•   •   •

Elizabeth Wentworth, N.D., a licensed naturopath, had had *everything* to do with babies. Early in her career she illegally aborted them. Later she delivered them and arranged their black-market adoptions.

The full scope and breadth of what she did had not become fully known or widely investigated until the early eighties, decades after her death. The story began to surface when young adults who had been born in her clinic and adopted as infants began the trek to Miami, one by one, in search of their birth mothers. Unlike other adoptees, able to legally access their birth and adoption records, they had no luck.

No such records existed. Elizabeth Wentworth had erased their pasts by simply listing the adoptive parents' names on their birth certificates as the natural parents. That left no paper trail, no written history to trace.

Her guarantee of privacy to unwed mothers and

adoptive parents was the key to her success. Young unwed mothers didn't want the world to know what was a shameful secret in the fifties and sixties.

Adoptive parents appreciated knowing that there would be no interference from pesky social workers or mothers who might change their minds and demand their babies back.

Word spread like wildfire and Wentworth's practice grew into one of the largest illegal adoption operations in the nation.

Parents from all over the country sent their pregnant teenagers on "vacations" to Miami. The girls later reappeared, suntanned and slim. Childless couples returned home from Miami "vacations" as families, their own names listed on their new babies' birth certificates.

Decades later, a trickle of adoptees in search of their birth parents eventually become a flood. Wentworth, it was learned, had arranged hundreds of black-market, backdoor adoptions.

Frustrated adoptees had even formed a loose-knit support group seeking clues to their origins, but never succeeded despite their relentless search for Dr. Wentworth's records.

Apparently, she kept none.

Scandalous investigative news stories broke in the eighties after the adoptees sought help from the press. Dr. Wentworth had paid Miami police to protect her illegal adoption industry—and even more. Should a new mother at her clinic waver when it came time to give up her baby, police would put her on a bus out of town.

The state license board later decreed that no new naturopaths would be licensed in Florida.

Dr. Wentworth's spotty history of arrests and investigations for performing illegal abortions came years before *Roe versus Wade*. She later converted the second floor of her large home into a shelter for pregnant girls about to give birth. The first floor was her office and clinic.

That was where she was found brutally beaten to death at age thirty-nine. Her secrets died with her.

"This could be it," Burch said, "if there's a link between her and Nolan."

"They were about the same age," Nazario said. "Miami was a small town. They must have known each other."

Wentworth's obituary said she'd been divorced, that her maiden name was Rahming. She was a Miami High graduate.

So was Pierce Nolan. The *News* library kept a collection of old yearbooks.

"*¡Aquí está!*" Nazario said. "Here it is!"

Elizabeth Rahming and Pierce Nolan were two of four hundred students in the same senior class.

Nolan, rugged and handsome, played football. Elizabeth Rahming was a majorette, a baton held high in one photo.

In a page of prom photos, one shot had captured them together amid balloons, streamers, and other dancers.

Pierce Nolan later went off to college and to war, met a beautiful New York socialite, brought her back to Miami as his bride, and raised a family.

Elizabeth Rahming became a naturopath, opened a practice, married, and later divorced, a man named Donald Wentworth.

And in Miami, in August 1961, the boy and girl who danced at the prom together twenty-two years earlier were murdered, just a day apart.

CHAPTER 24

"Did you go out to play after you dropped me off?" Ashton Banks looked puzzled.

"Not exactly," Stone rubbed reddened eyes. "I stayed here late writing reports."

She had rented a car, stopped by the U.S. Attorney's office, and conferred again with Miami-Dade prosecutor Jo Salazar.

"I've found a court reporter, somebody really good, to take your grandmother's statement," she said.

Ash returned to confront him at his desk after being briefed by Riley. The lieutenant, pale and grim, had come in after the shooting and remained the rest of the night, throughout the fruitless search for the gunman.

"Excuse me," Ash said. "You neglected to mention you were shot at last night."

"You didn't ask," Stone said. "No big deal. Nobody got hurt."

"Does this mean that every day for the rest of our lives I have to ask if you were shot at last night? You complained that Gran is closemouthed. No mystery who you take after. What do you think?" she asked gravely.

"Could be anything. Gang initiation, mistaken identity, somebody I once arrested paroled and pissed off, or just some wacko with a new high-powered toy and a dislike for cops."

"You weren't in uniform." Her big eyes were serious.

"This is Miami." He shrugged. "The media got ahold of it, but since nobody was hit and it happened after the morning paper went to press, it won't be much of a story and PIO promised not to release my name. Don't mention it to Gran. Okay?"

"'Kay." She frowned, her voice hesitant. "Your lieutenant thinks it might be related to our investigation. You don't think . . ."

"You tell me."

They stared at each other.

"Can your grandmother give her statement today? I planned to take it at the U.S. Attorney's office downtown. But if she'd be more comfortable at home, we can arrange to do it there."

"I'll ask 'er." He reached for his phone, which rang before he could pick it up.

He answered and winked at Ashton Brooks.

"It's your buddy Asa Anderson."

Stone's smile faded as he listened. He motioned for her to pick up an extension.

"Glad I got you both," Anderson said urgently. "Wanted to give you a heads-up. For safety's sake I assigned a loose surveillance on the suspects. They're gone. All three. Ron John Cooper, Ernest Lee Evans, and his son, Wesley Evans, a police sergeant up here."

Ashton Banks's eyes widened. "Since when?"

"They were last seen shortly before you took off for Miami. Wes Evans took a vacation week. His dad and Cooper disappeared from home and all their usual haunts about the same time.

"We're trying to track their credit card use. But these guys are cops. The only charge we have so far was when Wes gassed up his vehicle more than forty-eight hours ago. His dad was with him. Told the gas station attendant he was going hunting.

"Watch yourself. They could be on your turf by now."

"I think they are." Ash made eye contact with Stone.

"They're here," Stone said flatly. "Somebody showed up at the station last night, asked for me, then disappeared. A short while later I was shot at from ambush. The desk sergeant is working with a police sketch artist right now."

●   ●   ●

"I want the suspects' pictures down here now," Riley said. "Betcha diamonds to doughnuts that one of 'em's a good match for the police sketch we come up with.

"Look, lady," she told Ash. "There's no doubt in my mind that you people have a serious leak in your office. It's already been responsible for several deaths. Now it's compromised the safety of one of my detectives. If you want us to continue to cooperate with you and your agency, stop sharing information with anyone in your office. And I mean anyone, until the leak is identified and arrested along with the suspects.

"You'd be stupid to go back to your hotel. Check in someplace else, over on the Beach. Blend in with the tourists. Don't tell your office where you're staying."

She turned to Stone. "Put on a vest, take Corso and a uniform backup and go get your grandmother out of that house."

"I was just about to suggest that," Ashton Brooks said.

• • •

"Jesus, these guys are old men now," Corso said in the car.

"That doesn't make them any less dangerous," Ash said, her expression grim. "Men that age don't last long behind bars, especially former cops. Any sentence of significance is a death sentence. They know that."

"Yeah, but what are the chances they'd really come here? They wouldn't dare come after a cop."

"What about Glover?" Stone asked.

"What about last night?" Ash said.

"That shooter knew what he was doing. That first round missed me by inches."

"Shit, now you're spooking me," Corso said, reluctantly putting on his Kevlar vest.

"Of course, cops know that high-powered, armor-piercing bullets will cut through our vests like butter," Stone said. "Only cops have legal access to that ammo, and ballistics confirmed an hour ago that that's what the shooter used last night."

"Thanks for sharing," Corso said. "Times like this

I realize I coulda been a fireman, or sold insurance."

"Or used cars," Stone said.

"Or time shares," Ashton Banks said.

Stone did a double take and grinned at her. She'd pegged Corso pretty fast.

"Gran will never leave her house," he warned. "She's really stubborn. I've been through this with her before."

"We'll see," Ash said.

"She's small," Corso said. "She don't wanna go, we just pick 'er up and carry 'er out. What's she gonna do?"

•　　•　　•

Gran looked perky when she opened the door. It wasn't Sunday but she wore her Sunday best, a white dress with navy blue trim.

"Cold Case Girl!" She beamed. "I thought you'd come by today."

"Hi, Gran," Ash said. "We're arranging for a court stenographer to take your statement, but right now we think it's best to relocate you. For everyone's safety, until we pick up the suspects."

"Relocate?" Gran put down the dish towel she was holding.

"Yes." Ash flashed her megawatt smile. "Isn't it great? To a nice, comfortable Miami Beach hotel, with a big pool, room service, and a minibar. You won't have to cook, clean, make your own bed, or pick up a thing. It'll be a vacation."

"But I volunteer at the outreach center every

Saturday," she said. "Somebody has to be there, to stand up to the people who try to stampede into the food bank and grab everything. You have to stop 'em, or there's not enough to go round."

"They'll appreciate you more when you come back. Besides, we'll have fun. I'm coming with you. In fact, I'll help you pack."

"Whatever you say," Gran said docilely.

"Come on, sweetheart." Ashton put her arm around Gran and they headed for the bedroom. "Where's your bathing suit? You have to bring a bathing suit." She flashed a sweet smile over her shoulder at Stone, who stood stunned.

"Never think you can understand a woman, no matter how old they are," Corso said.

•　•　•

Ash and Gran sat in the back, Stone and Corso in the front with a shotgun. A marked patrol car trailed behind them.

"I don't think I'll need the minibar," Gran said as they drove to the Barcelona Hotel on Miami Beach's Collins Avenue. "I don't drink much, just a little glass of cherry cordial at Christmas."

"You don't have to drink to love a minibar," Ash said. "They've got juice, bottled water, cheese, chips, cookies, chocolate, every kind of snack. Once, in Portland, Oregon, I stayed at a hotel that had a whole smoked fish in the minibar. Had to be a foot and a half long."

"You're joking with me."

"No way, I swear. Wait till you see what we find in

ours. Open the door and it's like Christmas morning," Ash said, her big dark eyes scanning the street as she spoke.

"How much does it cost?"

"That's the beauty of it," Ash said lightly. "They just add it to the bill, which the Southern District of Mississippi will pay."

"'Bout time Mississippi paid for somethin'," Gran said.

Stone got them checked into the hotel and promised to meet them at five for an early dinner at a nearby restaurant.

●   ●   ●

Back at the station, he found Asa Anderson had transmitted the suspects' photos, which he had copied to distribute at roll call. A short time later Anderson called with a description of the vehicle the suspects might be driving.

"It's probably a white 2003 Ford F250 pickup. The two older suspects' vehicles are here, haven't been driven in days. Wesley's got three registered. This is what he was last seen driving, the only one we can't locate. It's got a king cab and a topper on the back, fully loaded. Bucket seats in front, a foldaway bench seat in the back. Where's Ash?"

"At her hotel."

"The Hyatt?"

"We're not saying."

"Not even to me?" he bellowed indignantly. "The guy who wants to make this case the most?!" He paused, then sighed. "I understand, Detective. Good thinking. At this point, trust no one.

"We've got us an internal investigation under way, trying to find out how the suspects got so much inside information so fast. By the way, who'd you talk to first in this office?"

"Didn't get a name from the original receptionist. Female, sounded young, said she'd been there a year. Didn't recognize your name and couldn't find it on a personnel roster."

"That would be Gloria."

"Asked her to connect me to whoever'd worked there the longest. She transferred me to a woman she said had been there about a hundred years but warned me not to say she'd said that."

"Yep, that's Gloria all right."

"The woman's name was Mildred."

"Mildred Johnson." He paused. "You say why you were calling?"

"I didn't go into detail but gave her my name and where I'm from. She was talkative at first but wouldn't give me your number. I called back and got it from a guy named Warren in Human Resources. Didn't go into specifics with him, either."

"He's a relatively new hire," Anderson said thoughtfully. "We're on it."

∙   ∙   ∙

"Look at this, Famous Amos chocolate chip cookies!" Ash giggled as they explored the minibar. "Let's eat them now."

"Before dinner?" Gran looked shocked.

"Somebody has to do it to make room in there for your medication. The minibar is the best place to keep it."

Gran rummaged in her suitcase, opened her purse, then closed it.

"Have you got it?" Ash asked, smile fading.

Gran shook her head. "I took it out and set it on the kitchen counter. Musta forgot to put it in my bag. But that's all right, I can do without it."

"When are you supposed to take your pills again?"

Gran shrugged. "'Bout three o'clock, I guess."

"Well, we'll just call your tall, good-looking grandson. He'll have somebody bring it over. If we're lucky," she whispered, "he'll bring it himself. I wouldn't mind seeing some more of him."

"Sorry for the trouble."

"No problem. At all. It's our fault for rushing you out of there so fast. We should have seen to it that we didn't forget anything."

Stone was at roll call, the secretary said, distributing the suspects' photos to the troops.

"All right," Ashton said. "Just give me your front-door key. I'll hop in a cab downstairs and run out to your house to get it for you. Let's order tea from room service now and I'll be back in time to drink it with you."

She insisted it wasn't too much trouble.

●   ●   ●

Traffic was heavier than she'd hoped, but Ash was back in forty-five minutes. "See?" she said cheerfully. "Told you I'd be back in the blink of an eye."

"Took a little nap while you were gone." Gran yawned, her eyes shiny. "Dreamed I was floatin' in warm water. I been dreamin' that a lot lately. Think that's what dying is like?"

"I think that's what swimming in the ocean off Miami Beach in August is like. We'll find out before we leave here, I promise."

They had just enough time to freshen up for dinner. The restaurant was five blocks away and Gran wanted to walk, so they had to leave early.

• • •

Stone scooped up the ringing phone on his desk. It was a neighbor he'd asked to keep an eye on Gran's place.

"Sammy? Thought you might wanna know. One of those big ol' pickup trucks, a white one I never seen before with fancy wheels. It drove past your granny's house, two, three times, real slow. Then it parked down the street."

"How many people inside?"

"Couldn't tell. Had real dark-tinted windows."

"Is it still there?"

"No, it left. After the taxicab did—one a those Beach taxis stopped at your granny's. That good-looking gal, dressed to go to business, went in, came right out."

Ash? he wondered.

"Ever see her before?"

"Yeah, I think she was out here this mornin' with you."

"Thanks, Will. Call me if you see anything else."

He issued a BOLO to uniform patrol that the suspect vehicle might have been spotted, then called Ash's cell phone from his unmarked.

No answer.

Ash stepped out of the bathroom, lipstick in hand.

"Something's ringin', but I can't see where it is," Gran said.

"My cell phone, in my jacket pocket." Ash went to the closet as it stopped ringing. "Darn." She frowned. "The battery's low. Ready?"

They stepped out into the hallway to board the elevator.

Stone called the hotel; their room didn't answer. He was already crossing the causeway, Miami Beach spread out before him, a fairy-tale kingdom of pastel towers and swirling clouds against an unforgivingly bright backdrop of brittle blue sky.

•   •   •

"Sure you wouldn't rather take a cab?" Ashton said as they stepped out of the mirrored elevator into the hotel lobby.

"No, I like walkin'. Exercise is good for me and I like to smell that ocean breeze. Used to bring Sonny over here to the beach when he was jus a little boy—taught him to swim myself. Had to learn it first. Did it by watching old Esther Williams and Johnny Weissmuller movies on TV. Most Overtown children never do learn to swim. Can't tell you how many little ones we lost, drowned in canals and pools over the years. Sonny learned real fast."

The afternoon sun was radiant. "How beautiful those big palm trees look silhouetted against the sky," Ash said. "Their trunks look like poured concrete, too perfect to be real."

"Royal palms," Gran said. "Have to be careful what you plant under 'em. When those big, heavy fronds drop off, they flatten everything underneath—people, too. Did you see that live oak in my backyard? Couldn't keep Sonny out of it when he was a boy. Used to be his favorite spot. Sittin' up in those branches was like flying, he said. The branches would sway in the wind and he could hear the birds and the leaves. Thought he might grow up to be a pilot."

"What was he like as a little boy, Gran? And growing up, did he play sports in high school? Who did he take to the prom?"

"Where should I start?" Gran said. "Is that your phone?"

Ash answered.

"Yes, hello? Hello?" She sighed. "Darn, it cut out. This worthless piece of junk."

"Never liked 'em myself," Gran said.

"I think that was Sonny," Ash said.

"I'm the only one who calls him that," Gran said.

"Whoops. Would it make him mad if I did?"

"He might like it."

"Would it make you mad?"

"I like it."

Arms linked, they walked across the street, headed south.

• • •

Stone pulled into the hotel's porte cochere.

"You can't leave your car there, sir," a uniformed valet barked.

"Police business." Stone flashed his badge, strode into the lobby, and picked up the house phone. No answer in the room. He went up there anyway and banged on the door. Nothing. He took the stairs back down.

"I don't know, sir," the front-desk clerk said. "I just came on duty. Maybe the doorman . . ."

"Yeah." A big grin creased the doorman's weathered face. "The pretty girl with the elderly lady—her grandmother, I think."

"Did they take a taxi?"

"No, they were walking."

He drove south, toward the restaurant, scanning the street. To his relief, he spotted them on the far side of Collins Avenue. Ashton in her dark suit, Gran in her white dress, strolling amid sunburned tourists, tattooed locals, and conventioneers wearing name tags. Arm in arm, they were chatting as though they'd known each other forever. He smiled, enjoying the sight, and drove on, planning to intercept them at the next corner.

That's when he saw it, a big white pickup, headed north. It slowed down, changed lanes, moved closer to them. A dark-tinted window rolled down. He saw the gun barrel protrude.

Stone hit the brakes and leaned on the horn.

He saw Ashton's graceful neck as she turned, eyes wide, taking in the scenario instantly. She pushed Gran to the sidewalk just as the first shots were fired. Ash covered her with her own body, shouting for everyone to get down. People scattered and screamed.

Stone bailed out of the car, gun in hand, and sprinted across four lanes of traffic. Cars swerved and brakes squealed. He scaled a hedge in the landscaped median as two vehicles collided with the grinding sound of metal on metal.

A final shot was fired from the pickup as it roared north with the familiar high-pitched whine of its powerful engine.

Breathless, Stone assumed a shooter's stance and fired a single round. The back window shattered, but the Ford never slowed down, weaving and swerving through traffic too dense for him to safely fire again.

He ran toward the bright-red blood that stained Gran's white dress and spilled over onto the sidewalk.

He radioed for backup, for rescue, for an ambulance, and Miami Beach Police, rattling off the suspects' direction and vehicle description. Ashton, her own gun in hand, got to her knees.

"You okay?" he asked.

"Sure," she said. "Take care of your grandmother. . . ."

"Gran, Gran!" He looked into her frightened eyes as he searched for wounds, the source of all the blood.

"Please, Sonny," she begged. "Call an ambulance. For her."

He followed her eyes and looked up as Ash sagged back to the ground. "I'm okay," she said, and spit up blood.

The crowd pressed in as police and rescue arrived. "We've got a federal officer down!" he told the first medic.

"Don't let her die, Sonny." Gran's voice was shaky.

"They killed her!" wailed a voice from the crowd.

"It was him!" a woman screamed, and pointed at Stone. "He had a gun. He was running through traffic, shooting."

"Don't move!" a pudgy Miami Beach policeman told him. "Put your hands on the car."

"You're wasting time!" Stone shouted. "I'm a Miami police officer, that's my city car over there. The shooters are northbound on Collins, in a white 2003 Ford pickup with Mississippi tags! I can give you the license number."

"Take it easy," the cop said slowly. "Hand over your gun and let's sort all this out."

"You've got to cover the causeways. Stop them before they make it back to I-95!"

"Hold your horses," the cop said placidly. "What did you say your name was?"

"You stupid son of a bitch! Where's your supervisor!"

●   ●   ●

Miami Beach police officers sighted the fleeing pickup speeding westbound on the 79th Street Causeway. When they tried to stop it, the two pursuing squad cars collided. One spun off the other and slammed into a fully loaded North Bay Village garbage truck. Both patrol cars were totaled.

Ash was airlifted to the trauma center.

Stone drove there with Gran.

"Every cop in the county is looking for them," Riley assured him by radio. "You'll be the first to know when we spot them."

Ash was unconscious, suffering from a chest wound, en route to surgery by the time they arrived.

Full of grief and rage, Stone punched the wall. They had killed his parents, Ray Glover, and a young civil rights worker. They shot Ashton and tried to kill him and his grandmother. And they were still out on the street.

"She's in good hands, Sonny." Gran tried to comfort him. "She's a strong girl, with youth on her side. We have to pray."

"You were right," he said, eyes wet. "I should have stayed out of it.

"Oh shit," he said, looking up. "Just what I need."

Corso was striding down the hall toward them.

"Stone! Stone!" He panted, puffing and out of breath. "You won't believe this!" He lowered his voice. "They're here."

"Who?" Stone felt numb and weary.

"The fucking suspects!" he said under his breath. "The lieutenant sent me over in case you need anything. I come up to the ER, and there's the white Ford, Mississippi plates, your bullet hole in the back window."

"Where?" Stone got to his feet.

"Outside the goddamn ER. One a the suspects either stroked out or had a fucking heart attack. His son hauled his ass in here."

"They're in custody?"

"Hell, no," Corso said, sotto voce. "Wanted to tip you first, ya know, in case you want to get your licks in."

"Are you crazy? What if they walk out!"

"Ain't going nowhere. Old guy's white as a sheet, flat on his back, gasping like a fish outta water."

"Put it on the air and let's get down there. Wait here," he told Gran.

"Okay." Corso shrugged. "The collar is mine."

•   •   •

Former Bigby, Mississippi, sheriff's deputy Ron John Cooper, sixty-one, was apprehended outside the ER as he walked toward the Ford pickup. Ernest Lee Evans, sixty-four, went to cardiac intensive care, where he was handcuffed to his bed.

His son, Wesley, forty, a belligerent, overweight deputy sergeant, identified by witnesses as the man who shot Ashton Banks, was handcuffed and jailed.

"You'da done the same thing if it was your father," he muttered sullenly as Stone handcuffed him.

"It *was* my father," Stone said. He had thought he would want to kill them. Instead, the sight of them made him sick.

CHAPTER 25

"Tonight is just for us," Nazario promised Kiki when he picked her up. "I won't mention work or any member of the Nolan family, not even a distant cousin. It's just me and you, getting to know each other."

"A real date!" she said as Fergie and Di scampered around her feet. "Sounds good to me."

As they arrived at Caffe Abbracci, a popular Coral Gables restaurant, Nazario's beeper sounded. He had turned off his cell phone.

He called the station as the maître d' checked their reservation.

"No! He okay? She gonna make it? *¡Dios mío!* Glad they got them. You did? Hot damn! Great, Sarge. Things are going our way. *Mañana.*"

Lips pressed tightly together, he took Kiki's elbow and suavely steered her toward their table.

"Something you'd like to share?" She placed her napkin in her lap. There were fresh flowers, crystal, and fine china.

His eyes glittered. "The job. I know I said I'd keep it out of our evening, but it's been one of those days. A member of our squad—you know him, Stone—was involved in a shooting over on the Beach. He's okay. They got the suspects, but somebody else was hit and it's touch and go. And it looks like we finally have a *good* lead in the Nolan case. Nothing solid, but one that may take us somewhere. *Me siento* super *bien acerca caso*. I have a good feeling about it."

"I hope you have a good feeling about tonight."

They smiled across their menus.

The busboy lit the candles.

"The only time I've seen you this excited and happy," Kiki said, "is when you're discussing your job. I don't mind. It's stimulating, contagious. I love to be with passionate people who care about what they do. I know just how you feel. I located the casualty list from the battle at the Jarama River. Guess what? Captain Clifford Nolan was on it! It confirms everything Summer told you. I'm so excited, Pete.

"Whoops." She clapped her hand over her mouth. "I mentioned a Nolan. That's the last time tonight. I promise."

They ordered wine and appetizers. Drank a toast, and just as the stuffed mushrooms arrived, his beeper chirped again.

"Sorry, I shoulda turned it off," he muttered. He squinted at the number, then dialed it.

"You called me?" he demanded after identifying himself.

His face changed. "When? Give me a description. What hospital? I'll be right there."

Kiki lifted her eyebrows and put down her breadstick.

"I will make it up to you, *mi amor, te prometo*. I swear," he told her. "I am so sorry. I have to leave. Here's my credit card. Order anything. . . ."

Her mouth dropped open. "No way. I'm not staying here without you. It can't wait?"

"No." He signaled the waiter.

"Okay." She snatched up her purse. "Let's go."

He looked longingly at the crunchy salads the waiter had just brought, pushed back his chair, and asked for the check.

"Sorry, I'll have to put you in a cab," he said as they hurried out to the valet.

"What's wrong?" She looked bewildered.

"A friend in trouble."

She cut her eyes at him. "How serious?"

"Don't know yet."

Nazario dug in his pocket and came up with some crumpled bills. Some he shoved at the valet who brought the car, the rest he gave to Kiki. "Here, for cab fare."

"No thank you. You invited me out for the evening."

"*Sí.*"

"So we are out for the evening. That means I go where you go. Maybe I can help." Before he could protest, she opened the passenger-side door and slid into his car.

He didn't want to waste time arguing.

"Where are we going?" she asked as he swung out onto LeJeune Road.

"South Shore Hospital, the ER."

His attempt to explain sounded lame, even to him.

Kiki was game, and kept up with him, into the ER,

still at his elbow as they directed him to the patient.

A young woman, her skin unearthly pale, lay semi-conscious on a gurney, body limp, eyes glassy.

"Her name is Fleur Adair." He spelled it for the nurse.

He took the patient's cold hand. "*¿Qué pasó?* What happened?"

"Pete. I dunno," she mumbled. "I was working at a party. Las' thing I 'member . . ." Her voice trailed off.

"How did you get my name?" he asked the head nurse.

"She had your business card on her. She's still very groggy."

"Who brought her in?" he asked.

"Fire Rescue." The nurse consulted a chart. "Found unconscious on the beach behind the Regent Hotel. Looks like it may have been a date rape drug, probably Rohypnol."

"A roofie. Did you do a rape kit?"

"She refused when she came around, didn't want anyone to touch her."

"Where are her clothes?"

The shimmery dress was there, and one stiletto high heel.

"Where's her other shoe?" Nazario asked.

"Probably in the same place she left her underwear. That didn't come in with her, either."

He sighed. "Goddammit. I can tell you her next of kin. I don't know her exact DOB, but she's twenty-four."

"Insurance information?"

He became aware of Kiki's sidelong stare. "No. I hardly know the girl."

"The doctor will be in to check her shortly. When she perks up a little more, you can probably take her home, as long as somebody will be with her."

"She doesn't have a place to go at the moment."

"Then she'll have to stay here for a day or two. Here's the doctor now," she said. "You two can wait outside."

They sat in the waiting room in silence.

"She looks terrible," Kiki finally said. "The poor thing. You think somebody slipped drugs into her drink?"

"Probably," he said.

"Do you have to be involved?"

He nodded.

"But why, if you hardly know her?"

"She doesn't have anybody."

"It's so sordid." She shuddered. "Why not walk away, Pete? You're better than this."

"You don't understand."

"Try me."

He shook his head.

"Pete, tell me about your most recent relationships with women."

He turned to look at her, puzzled. "Who are you? My shrink?"

"I'm curious." She toyed absently with the gold bracelet on her slim wrist. "I might understand you better."

"Relationships." He thought about it for a long moment, then sighed. "There was one that was real. Pretty serious, I thought. An artist. She'll be famous someday. The girl is driven. A huge talent. She's wonderful."

"How did you meet?"

He wasn't sure how much to reveal, but it was certainly better than talking about Fleur. He definitely did not want to explain how they had met.

"Work related," he said vaguely.

"How?"

Somebody had told him—was it Corso?—to never, *ever* discuss other women with a female you had designs on. The best course of action is to pretend that you never knew another woman before she walked into your life. Otherwise, it always comes back to bite you and will forever be used against you, and you are screwed.

"How did you meet her?" Kiki persisted.

"She was a victim when she was sixteen. Raped on her first date, shot in the head, and left for dead. The boy she was with was shot, too. He died."

"Oh my God." Kiki shuddered.

"It stayed unsolved until Craig Burch, the original detective, stumbled onto something at the morgue twelve years later. We took it on and that's how I met her. After a lot of twists and turns, we solved the case."

"You still see her?"

"No. I think after it was over, she didn't want to see somebody who'd remind her of what happened every time she looked at him. *Naturaleza humana.*" Human nature. He shrugged wistfully. "Makes sense."

She nodded. "Who else?"

"What, are you writing a book?"

"I just like to know what I'm up against."

"Kiki, the only thing I want you up against is me. I'm single, solo, *sin problemas.*"

"Who else?"

He caved. "There was a girl I met working undercover. A dancer, a stripper. Sweet, beautiful, *tremenda mujer,* but she's got some bad habits she won't break. I didn't want to hang around and watch her self-destruct."

"Did you ever date a normal person?"

He thought for a moment. "How do you define normal? My sergeant, *es un buen hombre,* a good man, even though you two maybe got off on the wrong foot, he always says, 'Everybody looks normal, till you get to know them.'"

"True, I guess."

"Maybe I don't meet many of what you might call normal people on the job. But the job is my life. I don't meet many people any other way. But that's how I met you and that was a good thing.

"Maybe"—he dragged his palm through his hair to the nape of his neck—"maybe I just don't know how to act around normal people."

She took his hand.

• • •

The doctor said Fleur would be all right, would probably sleep for some time, but shouldn't be home alone. She had again refused a rape exam. Nazario tried to talk her into it.

"No, I don't wanna be examined. I don't wanna police report. It's not like it never happened before," she said, slurring her words. She refused to stay in the hospital.

Nazario called Sonya Whitaker, Adair's secretary.

"The poor kid," she said.

"I can't stay home with her, I'm working on a case. What should we do?"

"I'll go ahead and authorize payment for a nurse to stay there with her for a few days. My God, the kid's in the hospital. If Shelly has me canned for this, so be it."

"Thanks, Sonya. I'll take her back to the house."

He and Kiki took Fleur back to Casa de Luna.

"You both live here?" Kiki asked, wide-eyed, as the Mustang swept into the huge circular driveway.

"Actually neither of us do, technically. I stay in the apartment over the garage, in exchange for security."

They helped Fleur, still groggy and wearing paper hospital scuffs, up the stairs. "Who are you?" she mumbled, halfway up, noticing Kiki for the first time.

She was asleep before her head hit the pillow.

"Are you always this way?" Kiki asked as they waited for the nurse.

"What way?"

"The knight on the white horse, compelled to rescue women in distress."

"I don't think that's me."

"It's sad, if it is," she said.

He was almost afraid to ask why, but he did.

"Because I don't need rescuing."

She left him waiting for the nurse and took a cab home.

"Do I get another chance?" he asked as the cabbie honked the horn downstairs.

"I don't know," she said sadly, kissed his cheek, and left.

CHAPTER 26

"The woman played God, handing out babies like puppies, without home studies or references," Burch told Riley at an early morning squad meeting. Only Nazario was present. Stone and Corso were still at the hospital.

"She even adopted out three unrelated infants as triplets, according to news stories from the eighties. One had surgery at age nineteen and needed blood. That's when they found out they weren't related. Not to their parents or each other. Up to then they didn't even know they were adopted. When they tried to locate their birth mothers, they discovered they had no traceable past.

"Either the doctor kept all her records in her head, or they disappeared after her murder. Nobody complained at the time of the adoptions. Being an unwed mother wasn't a badge of honor like it is today. It was a scandal back in the fifties and sixties."

"So where do we stand?" Riley asked.

"We know Wentworth and Pierce Nolan knew each other—maybe were even boyfriend and girlfriend for a time in high school. Our best lead to a possible relative of one of our Baby Does is a Miami kid who filed a police complaint against the doctor a week before her murder. The hard copy was cross-filed in Records, under her name.

"Teenage kid walks into the station to report that Dr. Wentworth is arranging the adoption of his girl-friend's baby without his consent. Claims to be the father. The girl's underage. The officer writes a report and notes that the kid himself can be charged with statutory rape if her parents want to prosecute.

"Don't know if anybody looked into it. Wentworth is killed a few days later. The kid's name surfaces that first day as one of many suspects. His parents claim he was home with them at the time of the murder. Pierce Nolan is killed the next night. And that's all she wrote. His case is so high profile that all available manpower is assigned to it and the Wentworth investigation winds up on a back burner.

"Nobody ever seems to connect the two. The victims and the methods are totally different. She's a shady lady doctor with past abortion arrests and a thriving black-market adoption practice. She's savagely beaten in what looks like a crime of passion. He's a highly respected pillar of the community, shot in a cold, calculated ambush by a killer lying in wait.

"We didn't connect them either, at first. We checked the old homicide logs for similar cases, but all Wentworth's entry said was 'middle-aged white female beaten to death in her home.' Had it mentioned that the crime scene was also an adoption clinic and a home for unwed mothers, it would have caught our attention.

"Donald Wentworth, the ex-husband, is still alive.

He and the doctor had been divorced for years at the time of her murder. He'd remarried and said he didn't know much about what she was doing. A niece of hers, Pauline Rahming, nineteen, also lived and worked at the clinic. She discovered her aunt's body. She's still around as well. So is Ralph Plummer, the kid who filed the police complaint. Owns that Ford dealership up in the north end, near Aventura."

"Talk to him first," Riley said. "See if he'll give us a DNA sample. Then look up the niece. See what she knows. What did Wentworth's scene look like?"

"Bloody. Nobody else there when her body was found. No unwed mothers upstairs. No babies in the clinic. No prospective parents waiting in her office, which is where she was killed. Looked like the killer didn't bring a weapon, just used whatever was handy at the scene. She was kicked, stomped, bludgeoned with everything but the kitchen sink. Even slammed over the head with a manual typewriter.

"Funny, the crime scene photos show an empty bird-cage broken on the floor. No bird. Just a cage."

"The fact that the doctor paid off cops for protection might account for the lack of follow-up," Riley said. "An in-depth investigation might have turned the spotlight on things the department didn't want the public or the press to know.

"Hey, look who's here!"

Stone and Corso had stepped off the elevator. Both looked exhausted.

"How's Ashton?" Riley said.

"If there are no complications, it looks like she'll

make it," Stone said. "The doctors say she was lucky, the bullet slid right between her ribs. Otherwise chunks of broken bone would have pierced her lungs. She lost a lot of blood."

"And your grandmother?"

"Shaken up, worried about Ash, glad it's over. Talked to her a little while ago. She's back in her kitchen, making soup to take to the hospital."

"What about the suspects?"

"Remember, I'm the guy who spotted 'em." Corso beamed.

"Did they cop? How are the interviews coming?" Burch asked.

"Good." Stone poured himself a cup of coffee, then sank wearily into a chair. "Ernest Lee Evans opened his eyes in cardiac intensive care, thought he was about to meet Jesus, and confessed. He threw the others under the bus."

"Joke's on him," Corso said. "Dumb son of a bitch didn't die. He's already out of ICU, handcuffed to a bed in the jail ward.

"His statement'll stand the hair up on the back of your neck. Said they read in the paper that morning about a rash a armed robberies at small businesses, so they decided to kill the victims at work, make it look like a robbery.

"The night they did the killings at Stone's Barbecue, Evans and his partner planned to go over to Stone's house and kill the whole family. What spooked 'em and made 'em think better of it was Officer Ray Glover. Right after they leave, guns smoking, they see his patrol car whip around the corner in the rain and pull up in front of Stone's.

"Shocked to see anybody arrive so fast, they figure a witness musta seen 'em and called the police, so they panic and beat feet back to Mississippi.

"When they heard recently that Sam Stone tried to contact Asa Anderson at the federal prosecutor's office in Mississippi, they regretted not going to the house to finish the job that night.

"They assumed Stone here was the witness, that he'd been at the Barbecue that night, a little kid in the back room, or hiding under a counter, that he mighta seen 'em and that his grandmother hadda know everything."

"Did they kill Glover?" Riley asked.

"Yeah. He was working it, even showed up in Mississippi trying to solve the case on his own, so he hadda go. They went to Immokalee, ran him down, backed over 'im, even kicked 'im a few times to make sure he was dead."

"And the leak?" Riley asked. "How did they know . . ."

"Evans confirmed what Asa Anderson already suspected," Stone said.

"Yeah," Corso said. "One Mildred Johnson, the nice, motherly, talkative, longtime legal secretary and office manager in the criminal division of the U.S. Justice Department's Southern District of Mississippi, talks to her younger sister, Sheila, every day. Sheila Evans. Married to Ernest Lee Evans's brother, Earl, a Bigby, Mississippi, fireman."

"I *knew* it," Riley said, squeezing the hand grenade. "Son of a bitch."

"The suspects had an open pipeline. Every time a word about the case came up in that office, she hit the horn to her sister. She's in custody, being interviewed as we speak. The federal magistrate here has ordered these guys held without bond until a hearing next week."

"Nice work," Riley said. "Now let's close the other one and make it two for two."

"Never satisfied," Corso muttered indignantly, "no matter how hard you work, no matter how much you give 'em."

CHAPTER 27

"So let me get this straight," Burch said as he drove north on Biscayne Boulevard. "You had Fleur, Kiki, *and* a nurse up there? Ain't it getting a little crowded?"

"Kiki left," Nazario said morosely, "before the nurse arrived."

"Oh, so what's nursie like?"

"Hefty black lady in her fifties."

"Thank God for small favors. What'd I tell you when the Adair girl first showed up?"

"I know, I tried. But she's on a downward spiral. The kid needs therapy, rest, and some self-esteem."

"None a that is your responsibility."

"How can you turn your back on a slow-motion train wreck? That's what watching her is like."

"Humph. Hear Corso claim credit after all Stone's work?"

"Yeah, typical. Riley knows better. But Corso made a good catch. Hears the description and there's the car right in front of 'im."

"Strictly coincidence, always in his favor. Guy leads a charmed life."

• • •

A huge two-story-high American flag hung limp in the airless humidity, signaling Ralph Plummer's Bayside Ford.

Sleek, shiny machines, including a new low-slung Thunderbird, gleamed on the showroom floor. Heady new-car aromas from SUVs, pickups, convertibles, and sedans permeated the air. Plummer's office was on a second-floor level, overseeing the showroom below.

His attractive, well-groomed secretary spoke with a British accent. His office was immaculate.

So was he. A tall and muscular, still-handsome man, Ralph Plummer wore a short, neat beard. His piercing dark eyes remained clear and intense at age sixty-one.

He held the business card Burch had given his secretary. "I was almost expecting you," he said gravely. Despite his sad demeanor, Plummer's handshake was firm, his attitude friendly.

"We're not here to buy a car."

"I know." He nodded. "I planned to call you." He sighed and sat down behind his desk. "I read the newspapers. Those dead infants found at the Shadows." His well-manicured fingertips formed a pyramid and he stared at the floor. "I hate to say it, but there's a possibility, a good one, that one of those children, one of those babies, might be my son."

He raised his eyes and stared at them bleakly.

"Tell us what brings you to that conclusion, Mr. Plummer," Burch said.

"Call me R.J." Plummer lined up three identical pencils in a precise row on his desk as he chose his words. "It's difficult to accept, but the time frame is accurate. I've agonized about their discovery since the first news story. It would explain a lot. The minute I heard about it . . ." He paused to press an intercom and asked his secretary to hold all calls.

"To put it bluntly, it would explain why I never found my boy. Over the years I've spent a fortune on private investigators. I've listed his place and date of birth on every Web site that helps to reunite adoptees with their natural parents. Nothing. Now I suspect that the reason I never found him was because he was no longer in this world to find. That he's been dead from the start. A bitter pill to swallow."

"Would you be willing to give us a DNA sample? Then you'll know for sure," Burch said.

"Of course," he said. "Thank God for the technology. It will either give me closure or the impetus to keep on searching."

"The child's mother was a Lorraine Conrad?" Burch asked.

Plummer smiled ruefully. "Sweet Lorraine. The first girl I ever loved. The love of my life. Nothing, nobody, ever affects you as much as your first love. I was sixteen when we had sex. She was fifteen. I remember that first time like it was yesterday."

"Teenage hormones," Burch said. "Passions run high." His heart sank as he thought of his daughters, Jennifer and Annie, and his boy, Craig Jr.

Plummer reminisced from behind his desk. "It was summer."

Damn, Burch thought. Coulda told you that.

"I loved that little girl. The sweetest thing. Long golden brown hair all the way down her back, soft and silky with all kinds of highlights from the sun. Still young enough not to know how beautiful she was.

"It was the first time for us both. We'd been going steady for six months. I knew we would do it. Not if, just a question of when and where. I'd been reading everything I could find on the subject. Some neighbors had pitched a tent in their backyard. I don't even remember why now. But they weren't home.

"It was dark. It was late. We were lying in there on a blanket. She let me take off her clothes. I could feel the heat rise off her body. After that, we did it every chance we got.

"We stayed lucky for about a year. Had our ups and downs, little spats and scares, but then she got knocked up right around her sixteenth birthday. I was seventeen then. Her parents had an absolute fit."

"Let me ask you something," Burch said, arms folded. "You'd been having sex with their teenage daughter for a year and her parents had no clue? How'd you pull that off?"

"You know how it is." Plummer smiled and hitched his shoulders. "They trusted us, and when there's a will, there's always a way.

"My parents were upset, too, just furious, but once they calmed down, they agreed to sign for us to get married. Said we could have the baby and live with them until we finished school and got on our feet. But her parents would have none of it. Took her out of school and wouldn't even let me see her.

"Abortion was still illegal back then. They persuaded her to give up the baby for adoption. That was my child. My firstborn. There was no way they could take that baby away from me, I thought. But I was wrong. I was a minor, I had no rights. I'd always been able to talk my mom and dad into anything. But they wouldn't listen this time. Both sets of parents got together and agreed. Mine told me her parents had the legal authority and there was nothing we could do. They were probably secretly relieved. They said it would give us better starts in life, better futures. But what about my child's future? I never forgave them.

"When I heard they'd sent Lorri to Dr. Wentworth's clinic, I went there and tried to see her. The doctor said Lorri didn't want to see me. I knew that was a lie, but she called the police. A couple of officers ran me out of there, warned if I came back I'd go to jail. Hell, I was hoping to get into a good college, maybe get a draft deferment and stay outta Vietnam.

"It didn't surprise me to read years later that those cops were on the doctor's payroll.

"I never even saw my son. Not once. Tried for years to find him. But the goddamn doctor was dead and didn't keep any fucking records. I hired private detectives. Even took blood tests a couple of times to see if maybe they had found my son. They never did.

"I always looked for him among young people on the street. Wondered if I would spot him in a crowd. I'd look in the mirror and wonder if he was wondering, looking in a mirror somewhere, too. Does he have my eyes? Is his smile like mine? Does he have Lorraine's golden brown hair?

"She was beautiful. We were like Romeo and Juliet. Star-crossed lovers. They shouldn't have kept us apart."

"Did you ever see her again?" Nazario asked.

"Hell, yeah." Plummer tossed it off like an after-thought. "We got married as soon as she was eighteen. But it was never the same. The moment had passed. We had three other kids, two girls and a boy, stayed together nine or ten years, then divorced. Bitch took me for a lotta money.

"It would have been different," he said, "if we'd been allowed to stay together from the start, when the magic was still alive."

"Where's your ex-wife now?" Burch said.

He shrugged. "Living up in Boca Raton, working as a bookkeeper."

"Do you have any idea who killed Dr. Wentworth?"

"No. The morning after it happened, a detective came to our house. My folks nearly had heart attacks. But they confirmed that I was home when it happened.

"Had the doctor lived, I mighta found my son. What about the babies, Detectives? Lorraine only saw our son once, but she swore to me on the Bible that he was beautiful, perfect, and healthy. How did he die? Did Wentworth kill them?"

"We're not sure yet. They're still doing tests," Burch said.

"I don't understand." Plummer rose from his desk, walked to a window, and stared out at passing traffic. "Why would she kill them? Babies were her bread and butter, her source of income. She profited from their adoptions. Why would she hurt them?"

"All I know is that crib death ain't contagious," Burch said. "Did you know Pierce Nolan?"

He turned to look directly at them. "I knew of him. He was a prominent, big-time man about town, but I never met him. His murder was the talk of Miami, stayed on the front pages for a long time. If one of those infants is my son, I'd like to know how the hell they wound up at his place."

"Good question."

CHAPTER 28

"He lied," Nazario said as they walked to the car.

"Sure he did," Burch said. "He's a car salesman."

"Hard to read him." Nazario scowled. "It's like he has something wrong with him. But he definitely lied when he said he never met Pierce Nolan."

"I hear you. See his desk? How neat it was? Guy runs a big operation like that, tons a paperwork, yet not a pencil outta place."

On the way back to the expressway, a homeless man under the I-95 overpass waved and held up a crudely lettered cardboard sign:

VIETNAM VET. LOST JOB. BABY DIED. WIFE LEFT. PLEASE HELP.

"Guy looks way too young to be a Viet vet," Nazario said.

"Able-bodied, too," Burch commented.

A hundred yards later, at the on-ramp, stood another tattered wraith, holding up his own hand-lettered sign:

WHY LIE? I NEED A BEER.

"My kinda guy." Burch slowed down. "Let's give 'im a five. I'm so goddamned sick a liars."

• • •

"Look at this." Nazario had checked records back at headquarters. "Sweet Lorraine, the love of his life, took out multiple restraining orders against Plummer over the years. Had him arrested twice for domestic abuse."

"I'm starting to lose patience with all these self-absorbed people playing fast and loose with the past." Burch jabbed at his phone, punching in the number of Plummer's ex-wife, Lorraine, in Boca.

"I'm sorry, I don't think I should talk to you," she said.

"I'm sorry, but I think you should. We'll be up there in an hour."

"No, no, not here!"

"Then we can arrange to bring you here," he said.

"Wait! Wait. I'm driving down to visit my grand-children in North Miami tomorrow."

She agreed to talk to them then.

• • •

They found Pauline Rahming working as a part-time assistant in a day-care center.

A small woman with a curly gray perm, she had dark, darting eyes and a crusty manner.

"I saw the stories in the paper," she said.

"Good," Burch said. "Then we don't have to explain."

Her eyes followed the children as they frolicked in the center's backyard playground.

"Go tell your boss you're taking a time-out to talk to us," Burch said.

"I can watch the children and talk to you at the same time," she snapped. "It's called multitasking."

"I don't *like* multitasking," Burch said. "In fact, it's one of my pet peeves. I find that people who multitask are invariably the ones who absentmindedly leave toddlers to die in closed cars parked in the sun in hundred-degree-plus temperatures because they are trying to do too many things at once. When I talk to people I want their full attention. We can make that happen by taking you downtown with us. You can focus there. You won't have children, or anything else to worry about. Only us."

• • •

They took a back booth at a nearby diner, where they could drink coffee, bask in the air-conditioning, and talk uninterrupted.

"My aunt Elizabeth was an early feminist," Pauline Rahming said defensively. "One of the first, before her time. A hero. All she cared about in this world was what was best for those babies. Those ungrateful adopted children who showed up in the eighties didn't appreciate what she gave them. Life. She gave them life. They slandered her, denigrated her memory, and impugned her motives, when most of them wouldn't be walking this earth without her. She was brave enough to offer an alternative to abortion."

"Her motives weren't entirely unselfish," Burch said. "I understand she lived pretty well."

"True, she drove a big car, wore nice jewelry and fine clothes, but that was all part of the image she had to maintain. People need to have confidence in their doctor. And her expenses were staggering. A parade of police officers marched through the clinic like clockwork every Friday to pick up their envelopes. If she didn't pay, they'd make trouble. She fed and sheltered the mothers, delivered the babies, arranged the adoptions. She worked like a dog. We both did. She took me in and raised me. Elizabeth Wentworth was a saint."

"She was no saint," Burch said. "She murdered those babies."

Pauline Rahming's jaw dropped. "She didn't! She'd never harm an infant, or anyone. Never! Never! Never!"

"Somebody did," Burch said mildly. "Weren't you the only other person there at the time?"

Her eyes widened. "I *love* children. I've devoted my life to them. My only regret is that I never had any of my own."

"Did Aunt Liz keep records?"

"The records!" She fiercely pounded a small fist on the Formica tabletop. "The records, the records, everybody harps on the records! She had a little journal. More like an engagement calendar. That's all. There were no filing cabinets stuffed full of records, there never was. That was the entire point, to protect the privacy of everyone concerned."

"Did you know Pierce Nolan?"

Her eyes darted between them as if she were a defenseless creature cornered by predators.

"We know your aunt knew him," Nazario said gently.

"Who told you that?" Her eyes never stopped moving.

"Nolan was her prom date at Miami High. They'd known each other since high school."

She shrank back in her seat, shriveling up as though cold, shaking her head.

"No," she said. "It was elementary school. But they hadn't spoken, or even seen each other in decades."

"So what finally brought them back together in August 1961?" Burch asked.

She rocked back and forward, eyes distant.

"We were in trouble," she whispered, "terrible trouble. She had nobody else to trust or to turn to, and Pierce Nolan was a brilliant, influential man. Aunt Liz said he'd know what to do, how to help us."

"Did you kill the babies?"

"No! Nobody killed them. It was an accident." She dug a tissue out of her bag and blew her nose.

"How did this accident happen?"

"We were already under stress." Sniffling, she crumpled the tissue in her hand. "The police wanted more money. A young man had gone to them, filed a complaint. He'd come to the clinic trying to see his girlfriend. Her parents had made it clear there was to be no contact between them.

"But the pressure on us was nearly over. We could see the light at the end of the tunnel. We had seven babies in the clinic. The mothers had all been released and adoptive parents from all over the country were due to arrive over the next ten days to take their babies home. They'd already paid half the adoption fee, the balance would be paid then.

"Aunt Liz had been under so much stress, she needed to get out, and when the mothers had gone, she felt free to do so. The babies were beautiful, healthy, about to go to their new lives, and we'd have cash coming in.

"She went shopping that afternoon, met a few friends for dinner, and they went out to a club afterward.

"I didn't feel well, so I went to bed earlier than usual. I felt queasy, as though I was coming down with something. It had started that afternoon.

"My room was at the far side of the house, next to her office, but I knew I'd hear the babies. They'd wake me. When one cried, they'd all wake up to join in, and I'd have to get up to go feed them.

"But they never cried. My aunt came in at about three A.M. and stopped at my room first to ask how they were, if they'd all been fed.

"All I remembered was her shouting and shaking me. I couldn't answer. I was slurring my words. She slapped me, furious. She thought I'd been drinking. That I was drunk. Then she saw the canary dead in its cage.

"She started to scream, 'Oh no! The babies! Oh no!'

"She ran to the nursery. But she was too late. They were all dead in their cribs. She dragged me out of bed, out into the backyard, then ran back inside to open all the windows."

"Carbon monoxide?" Nazario said. "Was a car running in the garage?"

"No," Pauline said mournfully. "It was the gas company. They'd been changing the lines to natural gas. A crew from the gas company had come earlier in the day.

They did some work, changed the lines to the refrigerator. We had a gas-operated refrigerator then. Somehow the fittings weren't right. I don't know the specific details, but it killed them all. Would have killed me, too, if she hadn't come home in time. She unplugged the refrigerator, turned on fans, opened all the windows.

"I couldn't even put my own shoes on. Couldn't keep any food down, had a headache for three days.

"Aunt Liz didn't know what to do. The new babies that the parents were coming to take home were all dead. The police were demanding more money. That young man kept coming, banging on the doors shouting that he wanted to see his infant son. We were in terrible trouble."

"You might have called the police," Burch said.

"My aunt would've gone to jail, there would've been terrible publicity. Her life would have been ruined. She said we couldn't tell anyone. She wrapped them all up. Put them in a box. It was the heat of the summer." She shuddered, eyes wet.

"She was desperate, out of her mind. She finally decided to call Pierce Nolan. Old friends were the best, she said. She told him we needed his help, begged him to come. Said he was the only one she could trust, pleaded with him, for old times' sake.

"He came. He was horrified when he saw what had happened. He agreed that it would ruin my aunt and all the young women who had given those babies up for what they believed would be better lives.

"The world was closing in on us. The next knock on the door could be the police or the parents. We had to get the bodies out of there. Pierce Nolan put the box in the trunk of his car. He said he would find a temporary place to keep them until he could take them out on his boat and bury them at sea.

"He said we were to never talk of it, or call him, again.

"We were so grateful, we were both crying. Aunt Liz was still in financial trouble, still had to deal with the adoptive parents, but she thought she could talk her way out of it without having to return any money. She decided to tell each couple that the child they'd been promised had died unexpectedly. Then she'd promise them a healthy baby within the next few months. Naturally they'd be upset and disappointed, but she thought they'd wait.

"The first couple arrived the next day. The woman cried, the husband was furious. He demanded their money back and threatened to call the police and the newspapers. He accused her of operating a racket, of selling their baby to another couple who offered more money. She tried to calm him down for more than an hour. I thought she had.

"There wasn't that much for me to do with the babies gone and no pregnant girls upstairs, so I went to a movie the next day. I was upset and depressed. I cried every time I went into the nursery. So I went to a matinee, saw a John Wayne Western.

"I couldn't remember anything about the show later. What I saw when I came home erased it from my memory. I found my aunt Elizabeth dead, blood everywhere. It was horrible. Somebody had killed her. I didn't know if it was the parents who had been there, some other set of parents, the police, that angry young man, or a robbery. She was always paid in cash, and kept money on hand to pay the police. Someone may have known that at times there was quite a bit in the office, but there wasn't then. Nothing seemed to be taken. Except her little book, but the police might have taken that during their investigation."

"Who do you think killed Pierce Nolan?"

"I don't know." She sounded weary. "He was a decent man."

"You've had all these years to ponder it," Burch said. "Who do you think killed your aunt?"

"I don't know. All I know is who killed those babies. Me." Her features collapsed. "It was me. I should have known something was wrong when I began to feel sick. It was my fault. All of it was my fault," she whispered.

"No," Burch said. "It wasn't."

CHAPTER 29

The detectives took Pauline Rahming's sworn statement at the station and went home early.

Riley felt jubilant. Burch was troubled.

He stepped into his foyer, turned right, stumbled, and heard a gonglike sound as a sharp pain shot up his shin.

"What the hell is that thing?" he asked as he hopped on one foot.

"A Ming dog." Connie gave him a smooch on the lips.

"Ain't the sheepdog enough? What's this one made of, cast iron?"

"I think so. It's for protection."

"It sure didn't protect me." He rubbed his shin and winced as Jennifer breezed by and kissed his cheek.

"Hi, Daddy. Bye, Daddy." And she was gone.

"Hey, where'd she go? What's that she's wearing? That looked like a bathing suit top and shorts."

"To the municipal pool," Connie said. "There's something going on."

Burch looked out the front window. "There's something going on all right. She just jumped in a car with a strange boy. Looks like an old Volvo."

She joined him at the window. "He's not strange, that's Zell."

"How old is he?" He peered out, trying to see the tag number, but the car had already pulled away.

"Seventeen, I think."

"What do we know about him?"

"He's a nice kid. Nothing to worry about. She'll be home in time for dinner."

"Where there's a will, there's a way."

"Not Will, Zell."

Burch sighed and followed Connie into the kitchen. He'd planned to offer help with dinner. His heart wasn't in it.

"Where are you going, honey?"

"Have to check something out. I'll be right back."

The municipal pool was only eight suburban blocks away. He was almost surprised to see the old Volvo actually parked outside. No sign of Jennifer.

He strode past the rest rooms and cabanas toward the sparkling Olympic-sized pool. He didn't see them. Seething, he whirled around to go back and check the car. That's when he saw them. Splashing in the kiddie pool, surrounded by tots. He stared at the children, stepped closer, and felt a painful catch in his heart. The palm of Jennifer's hand supported the stomach of a little one who was attempting to swim but couldn't seem to kick or turn her head from side to side.

A friendly middle-aged woman greeted him as he watched. "Are you the parent of a special-needs child?"

He swallowed, then spit out the truth. "No. I'm a special-needs parent."

"I beg your pardon?"

"Because of my job, I can't seem to trust my own children."

•　•　•

"She's watching TV," the nurse told Nazario cheerfully. She sat knitting at the kitchen table.

Nazario found Fleur curled up in bed, watching a tape.

"How you feeling?" he asked.

She didn't answer, eyes glued to the television screen.

"Whatcha watching?" Following her gaze, he did a double take.

She was watching graphic hard-core porn.

"Hey." He gaped at the images. "Where'd that come from?"

"It was delivered this afternoon," she said, her voice a dull monotone.

"Dios mío." Upon second look, there was no mistaking the half-moon tattoo on the female star's ankle.

"You?"

She nodded, still watching, biting her lower lip.

He sighed. "What does he want?"

"Fifty thousand dollars," she said slowly.

"Who is he?"

"I . . . I knew him in high school. I was happy to see him at the party. I trusted him."

Nazario watched a few more moments of the tape, arms crossed. "You were unconscious, Fleur. Look. You were totally out of it. *Ese hijo de puta.*" That sick son of a bitch. "You were raped."

"I don't remember it." She sounded numb. "I knew something happened because I had my dress . . . Shelly's dress . . . but no underwear."

"What is he threatening?"

"To send it to my father and show it on the Internet."

"We'll take it to the Sex Crimes Unit. This pervert has to go to jail. For a long time. They have a special prosecutor—"

"I can't!" The raw pain in her cry stopped him. "I won't." She pulled the sheet over her face.

He patted her shoulder. "It's not your fault, Fleur."

"I want it to go away."

"Do you have the money?"

"No, it might as well be fifty million. He thinks I have money because my dad does. He doesn't believe me."

"You talked to him?"

"His phone number came with the tape."

"Address, too?"

"His apartment. He said to bring the money there."

"I'm a cop." He sighed. "I can't raise that much, either."

"I know. Can you talk to him?"

"What's his name?"

"Larry Malek. Lives in an apartment on West Avenue. Pete, I can't, I won't, live with the thought of my dad . . ."

He turned off the tape. "Get some rest, *mi amor.* Don't worry. We'll work something out."

"Don't tell anybody, Pete. Anybody. Promise?"

"I promise."

● ● ●

The apartment was low rent for Miami Beach. Garden style, three-story. Larry Malek was three flights up.

"Fleur sent me," Nazario told the eye behind the peephole.

"I don't want any trouble." Malek opened the door. "This is a simple business deal. No muss, no fuss. No complications."

Malek was a South Beach pretty boy, a baby-faced fellow with a shock of curly dark hair hanging low over his forehead and a cigarette in his mouth. "I don't like the idea of her sending a guy," he said as Nazario stepped inside and looked around.

The apartment smelled stale and was such a mess that it looked like a crime scene. A sweating can of beer and a couple of empties stood among the scattered porn magazines on the coffee table. The TV was on, the tape rolling. Nazario tried not to look at it. He glanced into the bedroom. The bed was unmade. A video camera sat on a dresser, but the room didn't look like the setting for the sex tape.

"You don't think I'd shoot it here, do you? I'm not that stupid." Malek turned off the TV. "You're probably that cop she mentioned. But if you're any friend of hers, you and I both know she can't take the heat. She's not gonna report anything. So don't try to be a hero and do something stupid. All you'll wind up doing is losing your job and reputation for some poor little rich girl who couldn't care less what happens to anybody but herself."

Nazario tried to reason with him, explained at length that Fleur was on the outs with her dad and had no resources of her own.

"She doesn't even have a place to stay. She's a sick chick. She needs help. Not this. You can't squeeze blood out of a stone," Nazario said.

"Don't give me that," Malek said irritably. "People who grow up in her shoes are never totally tapped out. They have all kinds of assets. The stock Grandma gave them. The jewelry from Mom. The trust fund from Dad. All the damn antiques, silver, and art in that great big house? I bet Dad even left a checkbook or a credit card or two in there somewhere, even if he is out of the country. The son of a bitch won't miss it. Fleur has a hundred and one ways to raise that money. This is starting to piss me off. I should have asked for more. This tape could bring big bucks on the Internet. I guess that's the route I have to take. I thought I'd do her a favor. But fine."

"Fleur is no Paris Hilton," Nazario said. "She's bruised, broke, and not responsible for her actions. I'd be careful if I were you, buddy."

"Is that a threat?"

"Hell, no. If she was stronger and in her right mind, you'd already be in jail on rape, drug, and extortion charges. I'm just warning you that some people, especially depressed women, can only be pushed so far. You don't want to be responsible for what she might do. Think it over, be a decent guy. It might feel good for a change."

"Don't gimme that," Malek said, disgusted. "A guy's gotta make a living. It's every man for himself. Think I like this dump? Know how high the rents are in South Beach? I'm just looking for a modest payday, a little down payment on a decent condo, nothing fancy. As for Fleur, she's not gonna hurt herself. This could be the best thing that ever happened to her. Maybe it'll wise her up and she'll get her act together once she realizes how much worse it coulda been." He glanced at the TV screen. "See the quality on that tape? Top-notch. I did a good job, if I must say so myself. It's hot stuff."

"How can you live with yourself? *Esto no lo hace un hombre,*" Nazario said. "The girl was unconscious. That had to be like having sex with a corpse. That must be how you like it, a total power trip. An unconscious woman can't point and laugh, criticize your poor performance, or compare you to a real man."

"I won't let you provoke me," Malek said smugly. "I already called Dad's secretary, Sonya somebody, told her I had business with the man, and got his current mailing address. Fleur has twenty-four hours to come up with the cash. No bills bigger than fifties. If not, Daddy Dearest gets the tape in forty-eight hours. Forty-eight after that, based on what he offers, it may or may not be available for download on the Internet." He smiled. "Say hello to Fleur for me.

"Thanks for coming and don't let the door hit you on the way out, buddy."

CHAPTER 30

"Of course!" The chief medical examiner's face lit up with sudden recall. "We had two cases that summer, when Miami converted from coal gas to natural gas. Before the natural gas lines were brought in, Dade County used coal gas, which burns differently. So the gas company had to change the burners and nipples in all gas-operated appliances as part of the conversion.

"I remember the first case. The police called our office to report a dead baby in an apartment. The parents were drunk and drugged, they said, and had somehow killed their child.

"When I got there, the windows were closed and a small air conditioner was operating. The parents looked and acted drunk. They staggered and their speech was slurred. She had put her dress on backwards. He kept trying to light a cigarette but couldn't quite manage it.

"Their baby boy lay dead in his crib. The police were about to arrest the parents. When I tried to interview them they could barely respond. That's when I started opening windows.

"They had a Servel gas-operated refrigerator that had been generating carbon monoxide into the apartment since the gas company crew had converted it the day before."

"How could that happen?" Nazario asked.

"There was a little brass fitting with a hole in it where the gas pipe feeds into the appliance. That fitting, that little nipple, had to be precisely the right size with a properly adjusted air intake. But the ones the crew used were not properly adjusted for the airflow. As a result, colorless, odorless, deadly carbon monoxide began to be discharged into the room from behind the refrigerator.

"Within hours, before we could get word out to the public, we had the second case. A woman found sitting dead in her chair, her husband dead in bed, and their dog dead on the floor."

"This may be a third case, never reported," Burch said.

"That will be a challenge to confirm in the lab," said the chief, a man who thrived on challenges.

"When you test for carbon monoxide poisoning," he explained, "you test the victim's blood. But in this case we have no blood. All we have is hard, dry, mummified flesh. There is no lab set up to handle solid, dried material. We'll have to be creative enough to devise a whole new procedure, a way to reconstruct a liquid medium we can analyze from that hard, dried material."

The detectives could almost feel the energy of his mind at work.

"We'll have to invent a whole new method of analysis." He sounded enthusiastic. "Let me hit the books, read some literature, look up some articles, and contact a few colleagues. But first, let me check those dates." He tapped into his computerized statistics dating back to 1956. "Bingo! Here we have it."

The two cases he remembered had occurred three days before the savage murder of Elizabeth Wentworth.

"It all fits," Burch said.

"The tragedy," the chief said, "is that prior to that time there had been several deaths in New York City due to the same-model refrigerators. When the health department outlawed their use in New York, a great many of those gas-operated refrigerators were shipped down to Florida."

•   •   •

Lorraine Plummer couldn't speak to them at her daughter's home, she said, and arranged to meet the detectives at the Children's Museum on Watson Island.

She arrived with her three grandchildren in tow, a boy about ten and two little girls, four and seven. The year-old waterfront museum was alive with the babble and excited cries of children.

The detectives and Lorraine Plummer, now a sweet-faced, plumpish matron, and her youngest granddaughter, Courtney, climbed the spiral staircase inside the Castle of Dreams, a colorful two-story tower covered with mosaic-tile images of mermaids, leaping fish, and seashells.

From benches inside the castle's upper level they were able to see the other two children below. Brandon cast for fish in a huge water tank. He had the edge. His magnetized fishing pole lured darting plastic fish with magnets in their noses.

Steffi, age seven, pushed a miniature shopping cart

through a child-sized replica of a Publix supermarket, selecting fish, cabbages, and carrots.

A curving slide at the top of the castle spilled a constant stream of children down into the lobby. Moments later they'd scramble back up the stairs to do it again.

Lorraine Plummer encouraged the little one to join them. "Go for it, Courtney. You can do it, sweetheart."

The child scampered toward the slide, then hesitated and hung back at the top. "I can't," she said.

Lorraine got to her feet.

"Pete, go help the little girl so I can talk to her grandmother," Burch said.

"Sure."

They watched the detective engage Courtney in conversation, then take her hand.

"I couldn't talk to you at my daughter's home," Lorraine Plummer said, clearly nervous. "My children are very loyal to their dad. They tell him everything.

"I don't know why I went back to him after giving up the baby." She turned to Burch, eyes sad. "Do you really think one of those dead infants is our son?"

"Your ex-husband has agreed to a DNA test. We should know soon."

"I always believed he was growing up somewhere safe and secure with parents who loved him. I prayed his father would never find him. He searched, you know. For years."

Burch nodded. "Are you afraid of him?"

"R.J. has a bad temper, a very bad temper. He always has. The man's obsessive. Do you know that every day since I've known him he's eaten the same breakfast, lunch, and dinner?"

"You're kidding me."

"I wish." She smiled ruefully. "Every morning it's six strawberries, a slice of cantaloupe, a half cup of oatmeal, half a banana, two slices of whole-wheat toast, and two cups of Lipton tea.

"For lunch, it's three slices of roast beef, a quarter-pound of sliced turkey, three slices of American cheese, an apple, six walnuts, a handful of grapes, and a cup of Folgers coffee."

"I don't think I want to hear about dinner."

"His meals must never vary, never change. God forbid if we ran out of bananas, or strawberries weren't available, or that the coffee wasn't his brand. And he counts." She shivered. "He's always counting. If what he wants doesn't happen before he reaches ten, twenty, one hundred, or whatever, he explodes."

"In other words, you're saying he isn't flexible."

"To put it mildly. For example, the first sheet of bathroom tissue on the roll must always be folded into a little V, the way you see it in hotel rooms. He flies into a rage if he finds it any other way. Living with him was like living with a ticking time bomb. I was afraid of him. I still am."

"How afraid?"

"I had to leave because I thought he was going to kill me. Then I had to take out restraining orders against him. He'd follow me, accost me on the street, at my job. I lost several jobs because of him. He broke three of my ribs once. I had long hair when I was young. He used to drag me by the hair, down the stairs, out of bed, or out of the car. It was painful, mentally and physically. Had it not been for the children, I would have run, moved to a place far away where he could never find me."

"If he abused you, Lorraine, why are your children loyal to him?"

She smiled sadly. "R.J. can be a very persuasive man. He would always say things about me. When they were little he kept telling them how I gave away their brother. He always warned them to be careful, or I'd give them away. But the main reason they're close to him, I guess, is that he has the money and he's generous with them. I have nothing. When I had him arrested they were so furious with me that I dropped the charges. I'm lucky I even get to see my grandchildren," she whispered. "I come down to stay overnight at my daughter's once a month. I'm driving back to Boca tomorrow."

"You know that we're investigating the murders of Dr. Wentworth and Pierce Nolan."

She looked at the floor. "Yes," she whispered.

The happy cries of children echoed all around them. Nazario still encouraged Courtney at the top of the slide. Despite his pep talk, she was still reluctant.

"Come on, honey," he coaxed, "I'll go with you." He picked her up, settled into place, and they both vanished, down the slide.

Moments later, they started back up the stairs. "Hold on to the railing, honey."

"Are you my grandma's friend?"

"Yes."

"What's your name?"

"Pete."

"What do you do?"

"I make sure that little girls like you stay safe."

She smiled shyly. "How?"

"By putting bad people in jail."

"Who's he?" she asked, pointing at Burch.

"He's my sergeant, my boss. He does the same thing."

Courtney ran to the top of the slide alone this time. She sat down, shouted, "Look at me!" and disappeared.

Nazario rejoined Burch and Lorraine Plummer.

"Looks like she's got the hang of it now. Wish I was a kid again. It's fun," Nazario said.

"We were just discussing Dr. Wentworth and Pierce Nolan," Burch told him.

"What I can tell you," Lorraine Plummer said cautiously, "is that whenever R.J. got angry, he'd say he'd done things. Throw it in my face. In the beginning he'd say, 'You don't know what I did because of you.' Later it became, 'You know what you made me do. People died because of you. It's all your fault, I hope you're happy.' Through the years, whenever something appeared in the press about the Nolan murder, he'd say, 'Did you see the news? I hope you're proud of yourself. I hope you can sleep at night.' He'd drive me past what used to be her clinic and ask if I wanted to go inside, to see where it happened. He never went into specifics, and I was afraid to ask. But I always believed he was responsible. He's capable of anything.

"Another driver cut us off on the road once. R.J. went into a frenzy, drove like a madman, ran the man off the road. Smashed his windshield with a wrench. I thought he would kill him."

"He had an alibi for the Wentworth murder," Burch

said. "His parents told the detectives he was at home when the doctor was killed."

"They'd say anything, do anything, to protect him," Lorraine said. "His mother always catered to him. She was afraid of his temper until the day she died. She used to tell me how, when he was just a little boy, he'd fly into a rage if any part of the lettuce leaf she put on his sandwich was white and not green. He'd become so violent that she used to tie him up and roll him under the bed until he calmed down.

"Don't tell him I told you anything," she pleaded. "He can't know we ever talked."

"Why? You think he'd hurt you?" Nazario asked.

"I know he would."

• • •

On the way back to headquarters, Burch called Plummer to arrange his appointment to give a DNA sample at ten A.M. the following day, at the station. He asked him to stop by the homicide office afterward.

"Something wrong?" Plummer asked.

"Just a few routine questions," Burch said.

"You already know all I know."

"We still need to tie up a few loose ends."

"You can ask me now."

"We're too busy with other witnesses at the moment."

"Witnesses? Sounds like you're making progress."

"That we are."

"All right," R.J. Plummer said reluctantly. "I'll be there."

CHAPTER 31

"I didn't break the bad news to you last night," Nazario said. "I wanted you to get some rest." He hung his jacket in the closet, took off his gun, and placed it on the dresser, along with his car keys. "I'm sorry."

She sat in bed, arms wrapped around her knees, her eyes red and questioning.

"I went to see your friend Malek. That greedy little bastard wouldn't listen to reason. I did everything I could. The tape goes to your father if you don't deliver the cash tonight."

She whimpered aloud.

"I told him you don't have the money and have no way to get it by tonight, next week, or next month. The son of a bitch has got the upper hand. There's nothing we can do but sit tight and see what happens. How your dad reacts."

"No!"

"It's not the end of the world, *mi amor.* Your dad will get over it. So will you. Chin up."

"Don't say that, Pete! We have to stop him."

He shrugged. "You want to file a police report? You want to see that tape played in court, in front of a jury?

And the press? If you'll agree to go that route, I'll take you downtown right now. We'll go to the Sex Crimes Unit. It won't be easy, but I'll be right there to support you every step of the way."

"No, no! You know I can't do that."

He shrugged. "Then there's nothing to talk about. I've had a rough day. I'm gonna take a shower and turn in early. We may have a major development in our case tomorrow and I need to be sharp."

"But you promised . . ."

"I know. I said I would do what I could. And I did. As much as I'd like to, I can't go put a gun to the guy's head. I could lose my badge."

He turned his back on her, hating himself, and stepped into the bathroom. He peeled off his shirt, stared at himself in the mirror, then turned the hot water in the shower on full blast.

He emerged from the steamy bathroom fifteen minutes later. The apartment was empty.

"Fleur? Fleur!"

She was gone. His gun wasn't on the dresser. Neither were his car keys.

He ran to the window. The driveway below was empty, his Mustang gone.

•   •   •

The cab screeched to a stop in front of the apartment house on West Avenue. He tossed money at the driver and jumped out, praying he was in time. He saw his Mustang illegally parked at the curb.

Nazario ran up the stairs. The door to Malek's apartment stood ajar.

He breathed a sigh of relief when he heard voices.

"Are you crazy?" Malek was pleading. "Don't do it!"

Nazario pushed open the door. Malek cowered in a far corner, his face pale. Fleur stood in the center of the room, the gun in both hands. She was crying.

"You son of a bitch! You thought you'd play that for my father?" Her voice sounded high-pitched and shrill. Her hands shook.

Nazario winced. Her finger was on the trigger.

"Fleur," he said gently, trying not to startle her. "Fleur, it's me, Pete. I'm sorry. Don't do this."

"Thank God!" Malek reacted as though the cavalry had arrived. "You're a cop! Stop her!"

Fleur glanced over her shoulder at him for a moment, then quickly refocused on Malek.

"I won't let him do it, Pete," she cried hysterically. "I'll see him dead first!"

"Good, the little prick deserves it," Nazario said. He closed the door. "I don't care if you shoot 'im."

Larry Malek wet his pants. "No, no," he whined. "You're a cop."

"Wait, just don't pull the trigger yet, Fleur. Not yet." Nazario pulled down a window shade. "You have my gun. Be careful. It has a hair trigger."

She wobbled on her high heels. Her hands shook more.

"Listen to me for a minute, *mi amor*. You kill this piece of dirt with my on-duty weapon and my life turns to shit. *Me vas a joder la vida.* I lose my job, my certification, my pension. I thought we were friends. You can't do that to me.

"I'll show you where to get another gun. I'll give it to you myself."

"Take the tapes!" Malek pleaded. "Let's forget the whole thing."

"Too late for that, pal. Didn't I tell you you can only push people so far?"

Fleur's hair hung in her face. Her cheeks were wet, her knees shook.

"I wanna shoot him, Pete. He's so disgusting."

"You're right, he deserves it."

"Please!" Malek cried.

"Just give me enough time to get you another gun— I've got one down in the car."

"Take the tapes!" Malek howled. "I'm sorry!"

"Where are they?" Nazario said.

"One's in the VCR. The other's in the bedroom, in the briefcase."

"Where are the rest?"

"That's all there is. I swear."

Fleur's outstretched arms wavered. Shoulders hunched, she closed one eye and trained the gun on his chest.

"I swear. I swear. One more! Under the mattress. Take 'em all. Take 'em all. I don't care. Just take 'em and go."

"Don't squeeze that trigger yet, *mi amor*. Let me see if he's telling the truth."

Nazario found the tapes. The one in the briefcase was inside a FedEx envelope addressed to Adair at a Rome hotel.

"Don't move," he warned Malek. "She hasn't slept. She's strung out, wired. Don't make her nervous. That gun has a hair trigger."

He ripped the pillows off the sofa and the bed, checked the kitchen cabinets and bedroom drawers, and tossed the rest of the apartment.

"I think I've got them all," he told Fleur.

He stared at Malek. "You want to kill him now, *mi amor?*"

Malek closed his eyes.

"You sure you got 'em all, Pete?"

"Yeah. You can always kill him later, with the other gun I'll give you. It's got no serial numbers on it."

"Promise?"

"Sure. Let's go now. The other weapon is a .45 caliber, so powerful that if you just hit him in the arm, the concussion will kill him. He'll go into shock and you can watch him bleed to death."

"Okay." She smiled at the thought, lowered the gun, and he gently took it from her hands.

"Let's go, *mi amor.*"

She cocked her head at him for a moment, then took his arm, as though they were about to stroll into church.

"You're a lucky man," Nazario said over his shoulder. "Don't make her come back here. Because I won't even try to stop her next time."

Nazario closed the door behind them.

Holding hands, they ran down the stairs together.

"You're not really gonna give me another gun, are you?" she asked in the car.

"No. I don't want you to hurt anybody. That's why I unloaded my gun on the way home, before I left it out on the dresser tonight."

"I knew that." She snuggled up and rested her head on his shoulder.

"You did not."

"Did too."

"How?" he demanded.

"'Member the first time I picked it up and you snatched it away from me? It was heavier then, a lot heavier. Tonight it felt light. I knew there were no bullets."

"Damn! You know what it cost me to have that cab waiting?"

"You sure we got all the tapes?"

"I think so, *mi amor.*" He patted her knee.

"Thanks, Pete," she said, yawning. She was asleep by the time he pulled into the driveway at the Casa de Luna.

CHAPTER 32

"Plummer probably won't talk to us again after today," Riley said, "so this is our one shot at a confession. God knows we need one. We have no physical evidence. Come down as hard as you have to."

Energy burned at a high flame among members of the Cold Case Squad. R.J. Plummer's fingerprints had been identified among others at the Wentworth murder scene but couldn't be considered incriminating since he'd admitted being at the clinic prior to the crime.

The meticulous killer had left no bloody shoe or hand prints—surprising, given the savagery and apparent spontaneity of the attack.

"I wonder how hard they tried," Riley said. "Given her relationship with certain police personnel, Wentworth's case might have been destined for a back burner even before Pierce Nolan's stole the spotlight and all the manpower."

"R.J.'s already sweating," Burch said. "When I told him we were getting somewhere, I could almost hear the gears grinding in that obsessive mind of his."

At ten A.M. Burch began to watch the elevator door. The DNA sample shouldn't take more than five minutes. At 10:45 Burch called the lab to question the delay.

"Bad news," he reported to Riley. "Plummer's a no-show."

"Maybe he's tied up on business," she said.

"Or lawyering up."

Burch checked the dealership.

"The British broad said he didn't show today and hasn't called. Not like him, she said."

Ping went the elevator and all eyes turned to it as the door yawned open.

"Hey!" Corso emerged. He huffed and puffed toward them. "What's the name a your suspect again?"

"Plummer, Ralph. R.J. Plummer. Due here an hour ago," Burch said.

"He ain't coming," Corso said. "Count on it."

"What you talking about?"

"Just heard some patrol transmissions on my radio coming in. He's involved in some kinda hostage situation in the north end. As the taker, not the victim."

Burch's phone was ringing, a North District patrol lieutenant on the line.

"Guy shows up at a relative's here 'bout an hour ago. Drags his ex-wife outta the house by her hair. Neighbors see him throw her into the trunk of his car and hear him threaten to kill her. Found your business card in the female victim's purse, which was left behind. Thought I'd give you a call. I think the subject is a car dealer in the north end, Plummer."

"I know who he is," Burch said. "Is she okay? Where are they?"

"Anybody's guess. He took off with her in a big Grand Marquis, black, with smoke-tinted windows, a landeau top, and fancy rims. We have the tag number."

"Listen to me," Burch said urgently. "This is a hell of a lot more serious than you know. The man is extremely violent, a suspect in at least two homicides."

"We've got a county-wide BOLO out for him and the car. And somebody watching his house."

"We'll be right out there. Son of a bitch!" Burch slammed down the phone. "How'd he know Lorraine talked to us?"

The entire team, including Riley, went to the abduction scene.

"Get this," said the weathered patrol lieutenant at the house. "The victim, Lorraine Plummer, has been divorced from the subject for more than twenty-five years. Some guys never quit."

"Yeah. First love never dies, or some shit like that," Burch said.

"He bursts in this morning, marches up to her room, and drags her downstairs by 'er hair," the patrol lieutenant told them. "She's in her bathrobe, screaming all the way, right in front of the grandkids and her daughter, who doesn't bother to call the police. Ain't that something?

"Hadn't been for witnesses, it wouldn't even have been reported. Two different neighbors heard screams, saw him throw 'er into the trunk, and dialed nine-one-one. No sign of 'em yet, even though the witnesses say he peeled outta here like a bat outta hell. You can see the rubber his tires burned on the road.

"We've got people at his dealership and with their two grown sons, who say they haven't heard from 'im."

•   •   •

Ralph Plummer's daughter favored her father in more ways than one. Immaculately dressed in tailored linen, her eyes, like his, were dark brown and piercing. And only now, with several police cars, lights spinning, outside her well-manicured, upscale home, was she beginning to show signs of agitation, or was it annoyance?

She checked her gold Cartier wristwatch. "It's been an hour and thirty-seven minutes and I haven't heard from my dad. I've called his house and his cell phone and he doesn't answer."

She frowned at the small clusters of concerned neighbors watching solemnly from the safety of their own yards, tapped her well-shod foot three times, and would have wrinkled her Botoxed brow had that been possible.

"I suppose all this will be my fault." She sighed and pursed her lips.

"Why do you say that?" Burch said.

Her children stopped crying and lit up when they recognized Burch and Nazario, reminders of happier times just a day earlier.

"Hi, Pete," Courtney sang out, waving shyly to Nazario.

The detectives exchanged stricken glances. "Little pitchers . . ." Burch said. "Crap!"

"One of my children mentioned that Mother had

spoken at length to two policemen yesterday. I called to tell my father last night."

She reacted defensively to their expressions. "Why shouldn't my own father have a heads-up? Mother's had him arrested in the past."

"For good reason, obviously," Burch said. "Does he own a gun?"

"Yes," she said reluctantly. "His father was somewhat of a collector."

"Figures. His father ever own a shotgun?"

"I wouldn't know." Her stare frosty, she turned to go back into the house.

"Wait a minute," Burch said. "Where do you think he took her?"

"I wouldn't know."

"Does he have a weekend place, on the beach or in the Keys?"

She shook her head, eyes beginning to show alarm. "He always goes to the same place in North Carolina on vacation."

The Highway Patrol and the airport were alerted, although, as Riley said, not much chance that even R.J. Plummer could succeed in forcing a screaming woman in a bathrobe through airport security. What she feared most was that Plummer might board an outbound jet alone, leaving Lorraine still missing or worse.

"What did he say as he was taking her out of here?" Riley asked.

The daughter shrugged off the question. "Just a lot of shouting and screaming."

"Think about it," Burch warned her. "Think hard.

Nobody's gonna count out his strawberries for him every morning at the Graybar motel, which will be his permanent address if he hurts her."

She licked her lips. "Something about how dare she talk to the police about him after ruining his life. 'I'll show you what you made me do!' The usual sort of thing, lots of cursing."

"What did she say?"

She shrugged again. "Begged him to let her go. Pleaded with me and the children to call the police . . . to call you." Her expression changed as though she suddenly realized the possible enormity of what she had not done, but she shed no tears, just rounded up her children and herded them inside.

SWAT stood by, on alert, should they be needed.

"The more time that passes, the worse it looks for her," Riley told Burch. "Get recent photos of them both from the daughter and transmit them to cars in the field. He might have switched vehicles and/or plates already. The guy has access to an unlimited number of cars. Have Patrol stop every black Marquis that fits the description even if the plate number isn't right."

"Where would he go?" Nazario agonized.

"Wait a minute," Burch said. "She told me yesterday that R.J. used to taunt her by driving her by the clinic after the doctor's murder. That building is long gone; there's a parking garage there now, but Pierce Nolan's murder scene still exists."

"The Shadows," Riley said.

•   •   •

The yellow crime scene tape lay limp on the ground across the overgrown driveway.

"We better check it out on foot," Riley said. They donned their Kevlar vests, left the car, and with silent caution hiked up the driveway, the only sounds their own footsteps, the wind in the trees, and the raucous birds overhead.

"Dead giveaways," Stone whispered, scanning the sky as the feathered alarmists swooped and screamed.

They paused at the driveway's big curve. Burch left the drive, almost disappearing as he edged through the thick foliage. As he did so, through a sticky summer haze and the drone of insects, it flashed through his mind that long ago a killer may have taken the same stealthy steps along that path.

Ahead, through dozens of shades of green leaves and vines, gleamed a shiny black Grand Marquis, its windows smoke-tinted, its trunk lid ajar.

Listening intently, he sensed more than heard a woman's sobs. Echoes from the past? A cry for help from the present? Sweat snaked down the small of his back as he stared at the house, dwarfed by the forces of nature overwhelming it, yet mute and defiant in its own historic presence.

He slipped back to rejoin the others. "They're here," he whispered. "I think she's alive."

Stone and Corso worked their way around to the back of the house, facing the water. The silver bay was still and mirrorlike, with a silky pink sheen across the horizon.

As they watched, a sinuous water spout descended

from a single thunderhead, twisting ominously as it raced across the bright water.

Burch and Nazario stayed out front to cover the car and the front porch, radioed for backup, and prepared to wait.

The birds had settled down, but a flock surged into the air as a woman's hysterical high-pitched shriek came from inside the Shadows.

"We can't wait," Riley said urgently. "He doesn't know me. Let me try."

She took the stairs, light on her feet, angling her body away from the front door and windows. She stood to the right of the door and rapped sharply, her gun down at her side.

"Mr. Plummer! R.J. Plummer! We need to talk to you. We need you to come to the door."

"Who's out there?"

"K. C. Riley, Miami Police Department."

She heard the woman squeal in protest, as though being dragged or pushed.

"R.J.! Send Lorraine out, please. We want to make sure she's all right. We're concerned about your safety."

"No! Go away! Leave us alone!"

"I can't do that, R.J. Your daughter and your grand-children are worried about you both. They need you to come out of there."

He muttered something she couldn't hear.

"R.J., I can't hear you. Come to the door so we can talk."

"You come in, alone," he demanded.

"I can't do that. We need you to come out, or close to the door so we can talk."

"Then it's a Mexican standoff," he said.

"No, it isn't. Because my squad is out here and we have patience. We like to settle these things before they become bigger than they need to be. But the SWAT team is on the way, and you know what that means, R.J. Tear gas, shock grenades, dogs, and snipers. They are not patient people. We can settle this now, just between us, before they show up. Let's cheat them out of all their fun."

"No!" the woman screamed, and there were sounds of a scuffle.

"Okay, R.J. I'm coming in there."

"No!" Burch shouted from behind her.

But Riley pushed open the door and slipped inside.

Nazario and Burch advanced behind her, moving up onto the porch, guns drawn.

"Is she crazy?" Burch mouthed as they waited on opposite sides of the door.

Riley scuttled to the right, crouched against the wall, her eyes adjusting to the shadows.

Lorraine lay on the floor near the stairs, her blue bathrobe askew, one breast partially exposed. Her forehead was bleeding.

"Look what she made me do," R.J. Plummer said, exasperated. "It's her fault."

He stood over her, a gun in his hand.

"Has she been shot?" Riley asked.

"No," Lorraine groaned. "I'm all right."

"She hit her head," Plummer said.

"She needs medical attention. Let's get her out of here," Riley said.

"No," he said stubbornly.

"She can go," Riley said. "I'll stay, we'll talk. Let's not make this a bigger deal than it has to be."

"The police are throwing ancient history at me, old allegations," he protested.

"Whatever you might have done back then," Riley agreed, "is ancient history. Statutes of limitations must have run out a long time ago. You were probably too young to be prosecuted, anyway."

"They want to arrest me."

"Things are different today, R.J. They could never take your baby away now like they did then. Everything that doctor did was absolutely illegal. You have standing in this community. You've never been in serious trouble since then. You're a prominent businessman, a success. You lead an unblemished life. Everybody knows R.J. Plummer, your dealership, and your car commercials on TV.

"You were the victim. So young then. I can't see how any judge or jury could blame you. It wouldn't even get that far. They took your child, for God's sake!"

"That's right." He took a step toward her. "I tried to save him. Just now I was trying to show Lorraine where he was, all these years, in a box," he said bitterly, "in a cellar."

"You don't want to go down there," Riley said quickly. "It's nasty. There are spiders, snakes, and rats."

"Hear that, Lorraine?" He turned and kicked at the fallen woman, who bleated in pain. "That's where my son has been all these years, thanks to you!"

"Hold on, R.J.!" Riley shouted. "Don't touch her

again. That does you no good. You may never be charged with any old case, but hurt her and you'll wind up doing twenty years for aggravated assault or attempted murder. Don't let her do that to you. Let's talk, but first, put the gun down."

"No."

"Why? You're a big guy. You don't need it."

"I might, for myself."

"You don't want to do that. This is nothing to lose your life over. You've lost enough. You lost a child years ago, but you have other children who love you and grandkids that you want to see grow up."

Plummer's eyes roved the shadowy interior of the house and up the stairs. Sounds rustled all around them, and from below, a faint whispering.

"Interesting place, isn't it?" Riley said. "Pierce Nolan lived here. Have you seen it before?"

"Not the inside," he said.

"I know you tried to save your son," Riley said gently. "You did everything you could, but you were so young and people wouldn't listen. Your parents, Lorraine's parents. You even went to the police."

Lorraine began to sob. Riley wished she would shut up.

"What happened, R.J.?"

"All I wanted was my son," he acknowledged. "They were both evil."

"Who?"

"That doctor and Pierce Nolan."

"I never figured out their connection myself," Riley said. "How the infants reached here."

"I saw it." His voice echoed eerily through the empty rooms. "I didn't know what it was at the time, but now I do."

"What did you see?"

Lorraine began to crawl toward the door, her bathrobe dragging through the dust and dried leaves on the floor.

R.J. stepped on it. "Don't move!"

She moaned and sniffled.

"You should have seen her when she was a teenager," R.J. said. "She was beautiful."

"Right," Riley said. "What did you see? The connection between Pierce Nolan and the adoption doctor?"

"They wouldn't let me talk to Lorraine. They were giving away my son. I was desperate, going to pieces. After the doctor called the police on me, I watched the clinic, hoping to see Lorraine. I kept driving by to see if she was there and to stop anybody who tried to take my son.

"I saw Pierce Nolan come out. I thought I recognized him. His picture was always in the newspapers. Everybody knew him. My father had worked in the campaign to elect him mayor. I'd seen his daughters at the skating rink and the Venetian Pool.

"The doctor was with him, she looked upset. They put something, a box, in the trunk of his big Buick.

"He left and I followed. I only wanted to talk to him. I was desperate. He stopped at a White Castle, the one that used to be up on the Boulevard, and I followed him inside. He was using the pay phone. When he got off, I asked to talk to him. Said it was important personal business.

"He said, 'Sure, son,' and bought me a cup of coffee. Seemed to be a nice guy, at first.

"I said I needed his help, I needed him to talk to Dr. Wentworth, to persuade her not to put my son up for adoption. The man had clout. He could have done it.

"But the son of a bitch wouldn't listen. He said I was too young to be a husband and father. Started to give me a lecture, said I had to finish school and my obligation to the military first. Said I couldn't support a family, that I'd have other children someday. He wouldn't listen, either. Said he had to go. I followed him out into the parking lot. In essence, he wanted to pat me on the head and tell me to go home and be a good boy. I resented being patronized. He kept saying I was too young. We argued. I'm a man, I told him. I ain't no kid. I'm a man. I'm a father. I got her pregnant, didn't I?

"The bastard laughed and said that proved I still had a lot of growing up to do. He laughed!

"He talked down to me, then drove off in his big car! I went home. I couldn't eat. I couldn't sleep. I hated them both. A friend called to tell me Lorraine was back home, had been for a few days. When I tried to call her, her father hung up on me.

"I stayed up all night. I couldn't take it anymore. The next day I decided to go to the clinic and take my kid out of there. I didn't care if they put me in jail. I didn't care if Wentworth called the police.

"Funny thing was, she didn't. Not even after I pushed

the door open and shoved her out of my way. I couldn't find the baby. There was nothing but empty cribs. The girl who usually worked there was gone. The doctor was all alone. I wanted to know where my kid was. She said it was too late, he'd been adopted. I wanted the name and address of the family who took him. I went to her office to find the records. She followed me, said there weren't any, and tried to push me out the door.

"She slapped me and I hit her. Once it started, nothing could stop it. I tried to clean up a little afterwards, looked for her records, then left. I called Lorraine that night to tell her the baby was gone. Her fucking father wouldn't let me talk to her. I had nothing left to lose. I'd already lost it all.

"I kept remembering the way Nolan laughed at me, kept hearing it in my head. A detective came to ask where I was when the doctor was killed. My mother lied for me, but I knew the cops would be back. I had nothing left to lose, so I went after him, too, to make him pay. I brought my father's old shotgun to the Shadows the next night. His car wasn't here, so I waited for Pierce Nolan. It was like a dream. It almost didn't happen. I waited so long I couldn't stand it and decided to kill myself instead, but at the last minute, I heard it, I heard his car."

"You see anybody else here that night?" Riley asked.

"How did you know?" His head jerked up and he stared at her oddly from across the dimly lit room. "There was something, somebody else, out there. Scared the hell out of me."

"You scared him, too. It was another kid, a Peeping Tom, watching Summer, one of Nolan's daughters."

There was no hint of humor in his staccato laugh. "Sex," he said, "it makes the world go round."

"You and I wouldn't be standing here without it," Riley said.

"Damn straight. What did you say your name was again?"

"Kathleen."

"You really don't think I'll go to prison if I get it all off my chest, Kathleen?"

"I think everything will be taken into consideration—your age, the times back then, the circumstances, the loss of your son."

He sighed. "All right," he said. "But first I have to show Lorraine where our baby spent all these years." He looked behind him. "The newspapers said that the basement door was beneath the stairwell."

Lorraine gasped as he wrenched her to her feet by her hair. The pine floor groaned and creaked in protest.

Riley winced. "R.J., I really wish you'd stop doing that. It's no way to treat the mother of your children. And you sure don't want to go down there in the dark. There are no lights. You can't see a damn thing."

"We just want to see where it was, then I promise we'll come right back up."

"Then you'll come to the station and make a complete statement? Get it all off your chest? I bet we can even persuade Lorraine not to prosecute you for anything that happened today."

"I won't, I promise," she babbled. "I promise, I promise."

"Deal," R.J. said. "Let's go."

SWAT had assembled outside. Officers in flak jackets, with long guns, were positioned in the dense foliage and undergrowth around the Shadows.

"Riley," Burch called, from just outside the door. "Everything okay in there?"

"Yes," she answered, "keep everybody back. We'll be out shortly. We're just going downstairs for a minute first."

"Downstairs?"

Burch and Nazario exchanged alarmed glances.

"I don't think that's a good idea," Burch said.

"Stay put," Riley said firmly. "For just a few more minutes."

"Ask them for a flashlight," R.J. said.

Riley sighed. "Guys, get us a flashlight from one of the cars."

Reluctantly, Burch brought it up on the porch and pushed it inside the door.

"FYI," he said, "Billy Clayton strenuously objects and says you have five minutes to come out."

"Billy Clayton is an asshole," Riley said.

"Who the hell is he?" R.J. said.

"Our SWAT captain," she said. "An impatient man. You don't want to meet him. He doesn't like waiting."

"I know the feeling," R.J. said.

She rolled the flashlight to his side of the room and he picked it up.

"Come on, Lorraine." He pushed her ahead of him, holding her by the wrist as he pulled back the dusty carpet and groped for the rusted iron ring on the trapdoor.

He jerked it open. The old hinges screeched in

protest and Lorraine joined in. "I don't want to. I don't want to go down there," she whimpered. He nearly kicked her down the stairs, shining the light after her.

"You next," he told Riley.

"No thanks, I'll follow you."

He shrugged and descended.

She secured her gun in the holster at the small of her back, took a deep breath, and followed.

No one in their right mind would do this, she told herself. But she hadn't been afraid of anything, including death, for a long time. The sighs and whispers grew louder as she descended.

"Where was it?" R.J. played the light beam off the limestone walls, the sloping floor, and the hatchlike door to the tunnel.

"The newspaper stories said it was on the west wall, but I've lost my bearings down here. Which way is west?"

"Forgot your compass, huh? It's over there, R.J. That shelf on the far wall behind you."

"Come on, Lorraine." He held her by the scruff of the neck.

"No! No!" She shrieked, and suddenly struggled wildly, catching him off guard.

Her flailing knocked the flashlight from his hand. He grabbed her robe as the light clattered to the floor and went out.

"Hold it!" Riley shouted into the utter darkness.

She heard Lorraine's bare feet slapping the stone stairs.

Plummer scrambled for the flashlight and accidentally kicked it. Riley heard it hit the wall.

"Lorraine!"

"Let her go," Riley said.

"No!"

She heard him cock the gun as he tried to sense Lorraine's movements. Riley lunged toward him in the dark as the gun spit fire with a deafening roar. Ears ringing, inhaling the gunpowder, she heard the bullet ping off the walls as the trapdoor above them slammed shut.

R.J. turned and ran. Riley hoped he'd forgotten the tunnel but then heard him fumble with the hatch in the dark. She tried to go after him but stumbled over something and hit the floor. It was Lorraine's bathrobe.

"Oh, crap," she said, glancing up toward the trapdoor.

She groped frantically for the flashlight and found it, but the batteries had spilled out. No time to try to find them.

She smelled the dank air and decaying greenery of the tunnel, found the door in the dark, closed and secured it.

Then she went upstairs and burst out onto the porch.

"Are Stone and Corso in position?"

"That's affirmative," Burch said.

"Good. Plummer's in the tunnel, he's armed. He's all yours," she told Captain Clayton.

At the bay end of the tunnel, R.J. heard Stone and Corso shout for him to go back the way he came and surrender. There was no way he could slip through the overgrown mangroves and downed trees that blocked his exit to the water, and if he did, they were waiting, guns drawn.

At the other end of the tunnel, SWAT waited with tear-gas grenades.

Two were enough to flush him out, coughing, choking, and weeping.

•   •   •

"I couldn't believe it when that naked woman came flying out the front door," Burch said. "Shoulda seen the look on Pete's face."

"Where is she?" Riley said.

"Gave her the blanket from the trunk a the car. Rescue is checking 'er out. She's got a few bumps and bruises, a nasty cut on her head, but she'll be okay."

"Plummer spilled the whole thing," Riley said. "Go take him away from SWAT, wash out his eyes, and make nice. Count his goddamned strawberries if you have to. He said he'd give us a full statement."

"How'd you pull that off?"

"I lied."

CHAPTER 33

As R.J. Plummer was led out of court in handcuffs after being denied bond, a reporter asked him if he planned a funeral for the infant son he'd sought for so long.

"No," he said. "Why should I?"

DNA confirmed Plummer was the father. The other six infants, two boys and four girls, remained unidentified.

Moved by the news stories, Miamians adopted the unclaimed infants, collecting funds to pay for decent burials. Donations poured in to save them from a mass, unmarked grave dug by jail prisoners in potter's field. Instead there were seven small satin-lined white caskets, an overflow crowd at the church, and seven small white crosses beneath a live oak tree in a local cemetery.

"Did you see all the flowers and teddy bears?" Burch said as they met in Riley's office after the funeral. "Have to tell you, I shed a tear or two myself. The public really came through."

"They always do," Nazario said. "Miami is good that way."

"It was nice," Riley said, "really moving, that after all these years total strangers came to pay their respects. There wasn't a dry eye in the place."

The chief medical examiner had left a message confirming that the infants' deaths were due to carbon monoxide poisoning. The death toll during that gas company conversion that summer of 1961 was not three—but ten.

"What's the matter, Pete?" Riley frowned at his expression. "What's wrong?"

"Nothing, Lieutenant," he said.

As the others left her office, he stepped back inside.

"Lieutenant, are you aware . . . I hate to say anything. But look behind you. . . ."

She turned and stared. "Oh my God! I've been watering it."

The crime scene unit conducted a station-wide search. They found one each in the shift commander's office, the records bureau, in the lobby, in the PIO office, and on the chief's desk—a total of six.

"Six. *Dios mío,*" Nazario confided to Burch. "Remember that pervert Stokoe, the Peeping Tom? I went out there with Corso to pick him up. We confiscated his little garden. There were six. . . ."

Riley summoned them all to her office later.

"Every time I've ever asked you to tell me the truth, you always did. That's why this job is aging me fast." She looked furious. "Who," she demanded, "planted marijuana in my office and all over the station?"

No one replied.

"Did you, Sergeant?"

"No."

"Did you have any knowledge of it?"

"Not until Nazario spotted it in your planter today."

"Everybody kept saying they wanted more green things in the station," Corso protested.

"What if a reporter had seen it?" Riley demanded. "There was one in the PIO office, for God's sake! This department gets enough bad press as it is. I don't want to believe that anyone on my squad is stupid enough to play such a juvenile prank. That's not something I want to hear."

"Then don't ask me," Corso said.

• • •

Fleur was waiting for Nazario at Casa de Luna. "I've got something to tell you."

He held his breath.

"It's good-bye."

"You've got a place?"

"Yes." Her eyes sparkled and she was smiling. "I'm going back to Seattle. My mom called. She needs me. She was crying. Ricardo left her—for another client, a younger woman with more money. She sent me a ticket, one-way."

She literally danced with excitement. "I'll miss you, Pete. But I can't wait to see her!"

"Great news, *mi amor.*" Nazario opened his arms. *"Buena suerte"*—good luck—"and stay in touch. You know how I worry about you."

"I know." She hugged him tight.

He drove her to the airport and went with her all

the way to security. Being needed by someone had truly lifted her spirits, he thought. He hoped her mother would not disappoint her.

He called Kiki later from his empty room.

"Saw you at the funeral today," he said. *"Lucias muy bonita.* Sorry it was so crowded we had no chance to talk."

He invited her to dinner.

"No."

He frowned. "What is this? It's still my turn."

She sighed. "Pete, you are such a neat guy, but I think you suffer from self-esteem issues."

"¿Qué?" What?

"You don't think you deserve the better things in life. You should really get some help."

"How can you make such a diagnosis," he protested, pacing the floor as he talked, "when we hardly know each other?"

She didn't answer.

"What about Fergie and Di? Does this mean I'll never see them again? How can you do that to me?"

"Well. . . . Maybe we could arrange visitation. I'm taking them to the Dog Brunch on Lincoln Road Sunday. They serve a special dog menu. And the humans who accompany them get a free drink. Fergie and Di love to socialize."

"Dog Brunch?" He rolled his eyes. *"Cuenta conmigo."* Count me in! "We can drive over with the top down."

"Okay," she said. He heard the smile in her voice. "See you then."

• • •

A federal magistrate set bond at two million dollars each for Ron John Cooper, Ernest Lee Evans, and his son, Wesley Evans.

Sam Stone was spending more time than ever at his grandmother's house. Ashton Banks was occupying his old room, being fussed over by Gran as she recuperated from her injuries.

Stone held Ash's hand after the bond hearing and explained that he was driving across the state to take another woman out to dinner.

"You're welcome to come along," he said. "You'll like her. Her name is Katie. Just don't let her kid sneak up behind you with a baseball bat."

• • •

"It looks smaller than I remember." Sky Nolan had arrived in Miami the night before, his first trip back since age nine. Burch and Riley accompanied him to the Shadows.

"Childhood homes always do when you go back," Riley said.

"I used to dream about this place," he said. "A shame it's so neglected and overgrown. You should have seen it in all its glory. My mother would give garden parties out here with chamber music and tables set out all over the lawn. It was spectacular.

"I went to San Francisco for Brooke's funeral," he told them. "It was interesting to see them all. I've even talked to Summer a few times since. We're so grateful to know at last what happened to my father."

Burch and Riley wandered out back to look at the water, leaving Sky alone to reminisce.

"This case is a perfect example of how life could be so simple if people just told the truth in the first place," she said.

"Look how peaceful it is here." Burch took a deep breath and drank in the view.

As they watched, a sudden squall blew toward them, materializing like a gray ghost across the bay.

"Let's go before it hits," Burch said.

"No. It's just liquid sunshine," Riley said, her hair whipping like a banner in the wind. "Rain always makes me appreciate the sun."

ACKNOWLEDGMENTS

I am indebted as always to Gradwohl Laureate Dr. Joseph H. Davis, recent recipient of the American Academy of Forensic Sciences' highest honor, the Gradwohl Medallion. He contributed greatly to this book.

So did Dr. Stephen H. Nelson, William and Karen Sampson, the brave and brilliant former Metro-Dade Homicide investigators William Venturi, Raul J. Diaz and Lloyd Hough. My deep thanks go to Sgt. Joy Gellatly of the Savannah Police Department, and to ace attorneys Lisa Kreeger and Joel Hirschhorn. I'm grateful to my kind and generous friends: Renee Turolla, attorney and journalist Siobhan Morrissey, Dale Kitchell, Ann Hughes, Ed Gadinsky, the Rev. Garth Thompson, Pam Stone Blackwell, Shane Willens, and my good, old, new friend Jesse Webb. They work overtime trying to keep me out of trouble.

The usual suspects were there when I needed them: Patricia Keen, Bill Dobson, Howard Kleinberg, Al Alschuler, Pauline Winnick, George Keen, and Dr. Howard Gordon, along with the other stouthearted Sesquipedelians.

My getaway driver, coconspirator, friend, and long-time accomplice Marilyn Lane helped me pull off another caper.

I am ever grateful to my agent, Michael Congdon, to Cristina Concepcion, Mara Lurie, and to the stalwart Josh Martino, who rescued me again, right at the brink. Friends are the family we choose. How cool is that?